MAYHEM
IN THE
ARCHIPELAGO

About the Author

Nick Griffiths is a retired British Ambassador and first time author. His diplomatic career included postings in West Africa, France, Russia and Sweden. In Stockholm, he enjoyed exploring the nearby archipelago in a somewhat unreliable motorboat, eating Swedish food and trying to learn the language. In Moscow, he learnt the language and a lot of other things.

MAYHEM
IN THE
ARCHIPELAGO

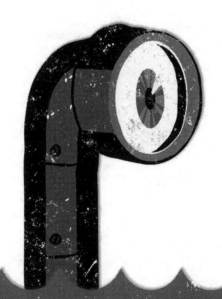

NICK GRIFFITHS

Matador
9 Priory Business Park,
Wistow Road, Kibworth Beauchamp,
Leicestershire. LE8 0RX
Tel: 0116 279 2299
Email: books@troubador.co.uk
Web: www.troubador.co.uk/matador
Twitter: @matadorbooks

ISBN 978 1789018 301

British Library Cataloguing in Publication Data.
A catalogue record for this book is available from the British Library.

Printed and bound in Great Britain by 4edge Limited
Typeset in 11pt Minion Pro by Troubador Publishing Ltd, Leicester, UK

Matador is an imprint of Troubador Publishing Ltd

For my mother and father

ONE

RIGA

In a dimly lit cellar below a nondescript office block in a Riga backstreet, a small group of people were talking in low monotones. The atmosphere was redolent of tension and long-gone gherkins. The low monotones were unnecessary, but they suited the conspiratorial nature of the gathering and had become a tradition. It didn't suit the more demagogic and excitable participants, but they did their best to be apocalyptic in fierce murmurs. All of them had been long accustomed to the demands of living in a world full of cyber spies and hostile surveillance.

One of them, a young woman with steely grey eyes, held the cold stone floor. "We are ready now. Everything is in place. We must commit now. As we all know, the future of our country is at stake. Most of our people might be asleep, but we are awake. Let's act."

There was a murmur of agreement and an almost inaudible round of applause. Fresh coffee was poured and a large mound of local pastries suffered the fate that was awaiting all enemies of Latvia.

MOSCOW

Five hundred miles away, two men sat across from each other at a large teak desk in an airy room burdened by an overcomplicated chandelier and very dull paintings of fir trees. One of them leant forward in his Giorgio Armani suit and drummed plump, hairy fingers on the desk.

"The Master is pleased with how matters are advancing in the Baltic. Every country in the region is scared, especially the smaller ones. The Americans are divided and don't know how to respond. They can't decide whether we are their partners or their enemies. They make a lot of noise, but are inconsistent. That means they have become pussies. And that means NATO is equally uncertain. The noises it has made over deploying a few ships and running around in the Baltic woods all conceal the truth: NATO doesn't know what we intend to do and has no idea of how to stop us."

He stopped drumming his fingers and looked intently across the desk at the gold-braided figure opposite him. "You know how the Master likes to deceive. He thinks it is time to put a decoy into the water. Just to observe for now, but also to trick and unnerve our enemies. That will be your job, Sergei Ivanovich. I will need your proposals by the end of the week." He leant back, easing his overstuffed body further into the chair with a slight sigh.

"By the way, how are your property investments these days, Sergei?" he asked. "The Master thinks we should consider investing in the liberated Crimea as a patriotic act. A contribution to the nation."

The man in the gold braid sitting opposite him thought quickly. His wife had no interest in buying in the Crimea, patriotic or not. She was more interested in Cyprus. But the message that had just been given to him would be hard to ignore.

"My only wish is to serve my country, Vitaly Alexandrovich," he replied.

"Good. We will return to this subject later, Sergei."

The admiral nodded. As he marched across the thick crimson carpet towards the heavy doors he wondered what position the man with the plump fingers now held in the hierarchy. It was always difficult for an outsider to tell, and often dangerous to enquire too closely. His wife might know. The shopping habits of the inner-circle wives and mistresses were usually a good indicator.

Washington

Far away across the Atlantic, a middle-aged woman opened her bedroom curtains with a muted sigh and stared into the stillness of a suburban street. *What are they up to?* she thought, as she gazed across to her neighbour's neat flower beds. She had posed that question to her team at the Defence Department the previous day. It had elicited the usual range of mostly paranoid responses, followed by increasingly improbable contingency plans. Her younger colleagues had energy, but were impatient. They lacked her knowledge of how to build allies before a skirmish with the State Department, and how to choose the right battleground.

Her eyes wandered down the silent street. Politics in Washington had become as complicated as trying to play chess and ice hockey simultaneously, the Undersecretary thought. She would need all her guile to survive. And with that in mind, she would have to make a decision soon. A recent tweet had lauded the presidential purchase of a mansion in Pennsylvania as a contribution to the rust belt's economy. A second tweet had suggested that all patriotic Americans, especially senior government employees, should follow this example. Social media pressure had followed. She would have to buy something, however modest.

STOCKHOLM

Back across the restless ocean, much closer to the gherkin-flavoured cellar, two men and a woman were sitting in a noisy bar in the centre of Stockholm. They were in a corner, huddled unobtrusively against the aural aggression of a band playing covers of past Swedish hits. As members of SÄPO, the Swedish Secret Service, they were not in the habit of drawing attention to themselves. A small mountain range of energetically dancing Swedes stood between them and the bar.

"Look at them!" commented one of the men, pointing with his schnapps glass. "They don't have any idea, do they? Not one of them."

"It's not their job to understand," the other man replied. "That's why they pay us."

"Well then, it's lucky for them that we take our work seriously," added the woman. "Or else when they are our age, either they won't be allowed to dance to this sort of music, or they won't be around to dance at all."

"So we are agreed, then? We're ready to go ahead?"

"Do we have a choice?"

There was a pause as the band approached the final, swelling chorus of *The Look*. They looked each other in the eyes. "*Skol*," they said simultaneously and downed their schnapps.

"Time for me to go," muttered one of the conspirators reluctantly. "Otherwise, the wife will give me hell."

"Same for me," the woman confessed. "See you both at the office tomorrow. Gunilla is bringing in a cloudberry tart. That can't be missed."

The three made their separate ways out of the bar. The band hadn't played *Waterloo* yet, but desperate times called for serious sacrifices.

Two Months Later

It was a gold-and-blue early summer's morning. Matt strolled in a leisurely way along Strandvägen, Stockholm's grandest street. He passed the usual array of designer-clad Swedish men pushing their designer prams, and then ambled through a glade of trees along the Baltic. It was an astoundingly pleasant way to get to work. The Embassy, most unfortunately, had been built during that blessedly short-lived period of architecture known as 'brutalist modern'. It lived up to its name. It had, naturally, won awards at the time, and the Foreign Office was now stuck with it. The only minor compensation was that the much-larger US Embassy nearby was even uglier.

Matt used his key card to open the main door, nodded to Lotta, the perennially lovesick receptionist, and climbed the stairs to the top floor, home of the Chancery. This was where the political work of the Embassy was done. Just a few years ago, Matt thought, it would have been done by white, male British diplomats, wearing suits and writing long reports by hand. Now it was largely done by Swedish women wearing jeans and standing up at their Scandi-style worktops. In truth, their emailed reports were probably of as little real consequence as those of their predecessors. Although there were routine requests from London about whether the Swedes would support UK negotiating positions, Matt was never sure whether their answers were more than cursorily read; Sweden was too reliable an ally. Their similarity of views meant that London usually took them for granted.

He opened the secure door to the Chancery and wandered in. A blonde vision was gliding towards him. It was Helena, the Ambassador's PA.

"*Hej*, Matt," she said with her habitual cool smile. "The boss wants to talk to you. Now." She nodded towards the Ambassador's office. "She is in a tough mood today, but don't worry. I am sure she won't take it out on her favourite." She laughed and strolled elegantly towards the kitchen, intent on making the obligatory strong coffee that was an essential precursor to any Swedish working day.

Matt walked cautiously into the Ambassador's office. He found her peering indignantly at her computer screen. Too many diplomatic receptions and the passing years had given Catherine Watkins a rather matronly appearance, but Matt had quickly learnt that this was largely misleading. She was in her last posting before retirement but her combative instincts hadn't dimmed. Matt himself was in the second year of his first diplomatic posting, and had found himself working unexpectedly closely with her ever since the Deputy Ambassador had disappeared on long-term sick leave. That meant Catherine and Matt were the only diplomats among the fifty-strong Embassy staff. Her regular requests to London for more support had disappeared into a personnel desert. Despite growing concerns over Russian aggression, the combination of austerity and a demand to expand outside Europe had left the Foreign and Commonwealth Office cupboard as bare as a meat counter on a Swedish summer holiday weekend.

"To hell with all things electronic," she cursed. "You can call me a Luddite if you want, but diplomatic life was much easier when I started. We could ignore London for days at a time. Now we have to leap around like a salmon in a Swedish hot tub every time some spotty new entrant wants a reply to some footling question."

She cursed again, and then looked up at Matt with a slight smile. "I exempt you, Matt. You look young enough to have spots, but the Swedish climate seems to suit you. Or do you have a nice Swedish girlfriend now to keep you in good shape?"

Since he wasn't sure what the truthful answer to that question was, Matt smiled back in a non-committal way.

"Anyhow, I didn't ask you in to ask you questions about your love life, nor for you to listen to one of my rants about technology, but because Philip says he has something important to tell me, and I want you here to listen to it."

There was a discreet cough at the door.

"Come in, Philip."

Philip Marshall, the Defence Attaché, strode firmly into the room. He had been in Stockholm for a year, and in common with all defence attachés had an almost messianic view of the importance of his job. He seemed to have an inexhaustible range of military costumes to wear, and had chosen today to wear a dark blue uniform suitable for his naval background.

"Good morning. I wanted to tell you both that there has been another sighting. Very close to Stockholm. Spoke to the Defence Ministry. Nothing confirmed, but they think it could be a Piranha."

Catherine and Matt looked equally blank. Philip stood even straighter to attention; not an easy task.

"A Piranha. Russian mini submarine. A new model. Almost impossible to trace. Very worrying if it is. Could change the whole military balance in the area. All sorts of emergency meetings going on among my colleagues in London."

For some weeks now, there had been a flurry of reports of mysterious objects seen in the archipelago just outside Stockholm. As usual, the media had decided that stories about Russian submarines would give them the best copy, and provide some much-needed excitement in Sweden. Ever since a Soviet submarine had been discovered near Stockholm in 1981, Swedish suspicions about their large, historic adversary had surfaced at regular intervals. Platoons of pensioners with time on their hands had been patrolling the shores of the Baltic Sea with imperfect eyesight and binoculars, providing the media with a constant stream of sightings. The gaseous corpse of a decomposing whale had produced some intriguingly ambiguous photographs. The Swedish military seemed to be convinced that there was something out there. Philip had visited the Defence

Ministry almost every day, spent many happy hours with his US and other NATO counterparts, and sent a stream of reports in unintelligible military-speak back to London.

Matt had been to the archipelago several times during the previous summer. It had been a wholly delightful discovery. There were thousands of islands scattered in a Baltic Sea that had transformed itself in the summer into a benign blue pond. He had relished eating in the many red-painted wooden restaurants and bars, which provided both fresh fish and sunbathing blondes. He felt himself ill qualified to speculate as to whether there really was a Russian submarine lurking in those tranquil waters, but could well understand it if there was. It was a very agreeable place to be.

"Sit down, please, Philip," said Catherine. "You will give me a crick in the neck if this is going to be a long conversation. I am not a military expert, as you know, but are you sure about this? I know from my Whitehall experience how the military likes to exaggerate. Particularly if it might lead to more kit."

Philip sat down with an injured look on his closely shaven face. "We believe Piranhas exist, although we think there are only a few of them so far, and they are a threat to us. If the Swedes are worried, then we should be too. The MOD are taking this very seriously."

"And could we get any sales out of this?" Catherine asked with sudden interest.

"It's possible. We do have some submarine tracking technology that the Swedes might be interested in."

Philip continued talking about the technical merits of the new Piranha, oblivious to the incomprehension of his audience. "I have asked the MOD to send out an expert. Would know much more than me. Expect you would like to meet him if they do, Ambassador."

Expect she wouldn't, thought Matt.

"Americans already have five experts here. Have to keep an eye on each other, of course, as well as everyone else."

"I would be happy to do so," said Catherine, who had been sitting back in her chair with her eyes closed while Philip had been speaking. This habit had greatly disconcerted Matt when he had started working with her, but he now understood that it was a sign of concentration rather than boredom. "Speak to Helena if you need to fix a meeting in my diary."

"Already done. She also seems to know much more than me. Amazing woman, your PA."

Although happily married, Philip had the same tongue-tied awe of Swedish blondeness as his fourteen-year-old son. His wife, being the typically sensible type of woman that defence attachés seemed to marry, was unconcerned.

Catherine sat up and pursed her lips. "I can see why London are getting jittery," she said reflectively. "The last thing they will want at the moment is a clash with Russia in the Baltic, especially given everything that's been happening back home. And the situation around here is tense enough as it is. If the Swedes find a Russian submarine so close to Stockholm, all hell will break lose. NATO will get even more involved, and who knows what might happen then? Who can tell how the US might react? Even Nostradamus couldn't tell us that. Wars have been started over less. More importantly for us, the world's media will descend on Stockholm, and we will have British ministers traipsing through the Embassy every five minutes.

"So, let's do something to show London that we are awake. I'll give the Foreign Minister a call, and I'm playing bridge with Charles and Sara this evening. I'll ask them if they know anything." Charles was the US Ambassador, a keen and competent bridge player. Sara was the leader of one of the parties in the governing Swedish coalition. She was also a keen and even more competent player. Catherine and her husband James weren't in their class, but were very charming losers. "Matt, you should talk to your contacts. Perhaps the other Nordic Embassies might know something. Let's send a report to London tomorrow."

Back in his small office, Matt thought about Catherine's words and wondered, not for the first time, whether he had chosen the right career. When he was growing up, the thought of being a diplomat had never crossed his mind. He came from a small town in Dorset. His childhood had been unremarkable, which meant he enjoyed it without being aware of his good fortune. He had done well at his local school, which had a solid academic record, and his parents, a teacher and a pharmacist, had encouraged him to study. He had always been able to express himself well, which helped him. There was never any discussion in his house about whether he would go to university. Everyone in his school with some academic ability was expected to apply. Given his talent with words, he decided to study English. There wasn't much in the way of career advice at the school; that task fell to a former army brigadier, who taught maths and whose suggestion to all pupils was to join the military. Matt didn't have much difficulty in ignoring that idea, but it did make him think about working abroad. He realised that whatever he ended up doing probably wouldn't give him much opportunity to live somewhere exotic, but a part of him still nursed a hope of leading a dashing life on the north-west frontier.

He had had a very agreeable, but unexceptional, three years at university. He learnt to drink, fell in and out of love, and finished with a surprisingly good degree. On a whim he applied for a job in the Foreign and Commonwealth Office and, to his great surprise, was accepted. From his very first day, at an introductory meeting in one of the grand reception rooms, he had felt like an imposter, the result of a mix-up in recruitment. Although fainter, that feeling still hadn't entirely disappeared.

His time in Sweden had been pleasant so far, but hardly dramatic. He was still haunted by the words of his personnel officer shortly after he had learnt about his posting: "It's unusual for a new entrant like you to be sent to a place like Stockholm. Normally the Office likes to test them out in more demanding places. Your performance in your first posting often sets the tone for your whole career. I am afraid you may not have much chance to shine in Sweden, so you should take every chance you have to make an impression."

That lukewarm support didn't help. But as he prepared for his posting he became increasingly determined to follow the advice he had been given. He didn't think of himself as a pushy person by nature, but this was going to be his chance, and he was going to take it.

A daydream in which he calmly brokered a regional peace deal was interrupted by the arrival of an email from his maybe/maybe not girlfriend, Annika. Matt was in the maybe – in fact, wannabe – camp. Annika seemed less sure. She worked for one of the almost innumerable Swedish non-governmental organisations that campaigned on development issues, and in her limited free time was appealingly fun-loving. She had invited him for a drink at one of their favourite bars that evening. Matt replied far quicker than he had to any of the other messages he had received that day. He remained optimistic that the right setting, coupled with large quantities of wine, might tilt things in his favour.

Since he was the last to leave the Chancery floor, he carried out a security check and locked the double doors. At the bottom of the stairs he heard a polite cough from the shadows.

"Everything all right up there?"

It was Tom, the Embassy's security officer. He was a retired policeman from Dundee, who had apparently come to live in Sweden on a whim, and had been recruited by the Embassy. When Matt first arrived in Stockholm, Tom had been overweight, inefficient and discontented. Embassy security could hardly have been in flabbier hands. A few months ago he had met a younger Swedish policewoman and a dramatic transformation had taken place. He had lost weight and now took an almost obsessive interest in his work. His new woman, whom Matt had met, worked enthusiastically on security issues and Tom now seemed intent on turning the Embassy into a Swedish Fort Knox. It was only their lack of money to spend on security, thought Matt, that prevented the Embassy from being surrounded by an electrified fence, guard dogs and watchtowers. Instead, Tom had to satisfy himself with his own patrols and a mobile phone.

"Everything is fine, Tom. No Russian spies or terrorists in sight."

"You may joke, Matt, but my police contacts tell me that Stockholm is one of the most dangerous places in Europe."

"Yes, but only for anyone found guilty of not buying their furniture from IKEA. Goodnight, Tom."

Strandvägen was bathed in early-evening light as Matt strolled toward the bar where he was due to meet Annika. The East Bar was in the middle of Stureplan, the small square that was the centre of social life for wealthy young Swedes. Despite her hostility towards the wealthy of the developing world, Annika seemed to like being surrounded by the spoilt, rich kids of the developed world. That was probably because she had gone to school with some of them. Coming from a middle-class background himself, Matt had never felt comfortable amongst the Stureplan crowd. They were too well dressed, too confident and much too loud. Most of the tables were already taken, but he managed to find one in a corner. Two glasses of rosé (one for Annika) cost the usual astronomical price. Matt couldn't help thinking of his parents, who would have probably preferred to take their own lives rather than spend so much on a glass of wine.

He spotted Annika walking towards his table. As usual she looked enticing in tight jeans and knee-length boots; the classic Swedish look.

"*Hej, hej.* I am dying for that drink. What a day! Three hours talking about the new monthly targets. I love my job, but sometimes I wish I could be doing something more exciting like you."

When people glamorised his job, Matt was always torn between enjoying their assumption of endless intrigue, and telling them the bureaucratic truth.

"But aren't you saving the world, while I am just saving the UK?" he replied.

"I am happy for you to save the UK. What would we Swedes do without *Midsomer Murders* or *Sherlock*? And our weekend shopping trips to London? Anyhow, my NGO could do more to save the world if it spent less time having meetings, and more time doing things."

"You still want to go abroad and work in the field?"

"Yes. Like you. Somewhere I can make a difference."

"So, how about a luxurious dinner this evening while you still can?"

"Oh, I am not going abroad any time soon. No such luck." Annika drained her glass and gave him an apologetic smile. "And I am sorry, but I can't do dinner this evening. I have so much work to do. But let's have another drink here first."

Not for the first time, Matt sighed inwardly and cursed her job and her very inconvenient work ethic.

When they finally left the bar, a large man bumped into him quite hard on the edge of the square. There was a second moment of contact as both of them tried to move away. "Sorry," said the surprised Matt, being reliably British. The man muttered something and walked away.

"He put something in your pocket," Annika said quickly. "I saw him do it. Do you know him?"

"I don't think so." Matt put his hand in his pocket, and to his surprise found a small piece of paper. "It's some kind of note. It says, *If you want to know what is really out in the archipelago, meet me at Kaknästornet tomorrow at 6pm.*" He stared at the note intently, but it had already revealed all its secrets.

Annika was wide-eyed, her habitual cool temporarily forgotten. "You see. Your life *is* more exciting than mine."

"But what does it mean?"

Annika giggled. "Do you think he was a spy?"

Matt was silent. He was still not sure what he could and could not say to people about MI6, an organisation which still remained opaque to him despite briefings back in London. His first thought was that this note was either a case of mistaken identity, or a joke played by one of his diplomatic colleagues.

"It's probably just a joke."

"That guy didn't look much like a joker to me. Did you actually see him? He looked like an ice hockey enforcer! So what are you going to do?"

Matt hesitated. He wasn't sure whether to treat the incident seriously and report it back to the Ambassador. It seemed too far-fetched to be real. Perhaps it would be better just to check it out first. Then if it was a joke, he would avoid looking too stupid in front of Catherine. "I think it's nothing, but I might go along tomorrow. Just to see."

Annika tossed her blonde ponytail. "Great! I will come with you."

"You can't. What if this guy is some kind of lunatic?"

"No problem. I bet I can run faster than you. Cycle faster, too. It will be you that he catches. Anyhow, I am coming. I just have to know what it is about."

They stared at each other. Her eyes seemed somehow bluer. Matt could almost feel her blood racing. Her perfume was suddenly stronger.

"OK." He surrendered. "And I suppose we probably will cycle. It's the easiest way to get there."

"Excellent. I can't wait!"

She strode away, ponytail flying.

The next morning, Matt dutifully reported to Catherine his exchanges during the previous afternoon with his colleagues in the Nordic Embassies. They didn't seem to know any more than him, but said their capitals were also getting jumpy.

"I didn't learn much either," she said. "But I will cobble something together for London. Let's hope that this Piranha turns out to be a false alarm. I know that both you and Philip are hoping that Stockholm will become the centre of the world's attention, and I can understand that. You both have your careers to think of. But I was looking forward to a peaceful summer."

Mid afternoon, Anke, one of his Chancery colleagues, put her head around the door. "*Fika*," she said, and disappeared.

Fika was a Swedish custom of which Matt wholly approved. Once a week, regardless of work pressures, all the Chancery staff met for thirty minutes to chat, eat cake and drink coffee together. Talking about work was forbidden. It was often the only time in the week when people had a chance to talk to each other casually for more than a few minutes. Everyone took turns to provide the food. Matt had noticed that despite the emphasis on gender equality in Sweden, a few traditions remained unchanged. Swedish women seemed to regard baking as an essential part of their heritage, so often tried to impress with a home-made offering. The men simply went to a bakery. It was the turn of Tina, the science and technology officer, this week, and she duly produced some professional-looking cinnamon rolls, or *kanelbullar*, while giving the modest impression that she could have baked something worthy of a royal wedding if required.

The conversation ranged over the usual topics: movies, TV shows and weekend plans.

"Anyone going to look for submarines in the archipelago this weekend?" asked Anke. "I guess that you might be, Philip?"

"Yes, when are you going to take us out for a ride in your floating palace?" asked Tina.

Philip had recently bought an elderly and slow, but stylish motor boat, and ever since had suffered a succession of the usual maintenance problems that beset boat owners. To become a fully fledged Stockholm resident, it now only remained for him to rent a summer house in the archipelago and be stranded there several times a year due to boat breakdowns. Philip began to lament the state of his engine, which led to a sharing of stories about past boating disasters, which led to the end of *fika*. Everyone returned to work.

Matt stopped Philip in the corridor. "Do you really think there is a submarine out there?"

Philip paused. "There is something out there. I just wish I knew what it was. It would make this posting even more exciting if it was a Russian sub, wouldn't it? The boys back home would be so jealous if we could catch them in the act. Wouldn't mind either if it turned out to be a Chinese sub. Only thing I wouldn't want would be for it to be American. Or French."

"Could it be?"

"Could certainly be American. They don't tell us everything they get up to. Could be the devious Frogs, too. They tell us less. Don't think any Jihadis have a sub. Don't have a naval base. But then submariners do like having beards."

Matt couldn't tell if Philip was joking or not. The military mind was a mystery to him.

Just before 6pm, Matt left the Embassy on his bike for the short ride to Kaknästornet, a tower on the edge of the Baltic which was used for TV and radio broadcasting. At the bottom of Valhallavägen, he met Annika as agreed. After a gap of several years, Matt had taken up cycling again, after recognising that Stockholm was a cyclist's paradise, at least in the warmer months, and that it was by far the best way to get around the city.

"What do you think will happen?" asked Annika excitedly.

"Probably nothing," said Matt, who by now was becoming convinced that the whole thing was too ludicrous to be taken seriously. "I don't expect anyone will turn up. But I suppose we'd better go just in case."

The grey concrete tower of Kaknästornet loomed before them. It too had been built in the brutalist modern era. It had a revolving restaurant on the top floor, presumably on the basis that at some points in its rotation, it was blessedly possible to avoid catching sight of the nearby British and US Embassies. Matt and Annika paused near the entrance. At 6pm, all good Swedes were already at home, eating their evening meal. The place looked deserted.

"I told you," said Matt. "No one here."

But he spoke too soon, since just then the large man who had bumped into him in Stureplan cycled around the corner.

"He came by bike, too!" said Matt. "What sort of spy turns up on a bike?"

"A Swedish one," Annika replied.

The man gestured at them to follow him, and set off at a fast pace towards the small forest at the back of the tower. Annika immediately followed. As usual, Matt was in the rear. As a casual cyclist at university in the UK, he had been amazed at the competitive nature of Swedish cycling. Everyone cycled as though the world was due to end in five minutes, and only they could save it. Matt had got used to being passed by all other cyclists. Even octogenarians sped past him, leaving him in their dust. So he wasn't surprised to find himself being quickly left behind by the other two.

"Come on!" Annika yelled back at him. "This is no time to dawdle."

"I'm going as fast as I can," croaked Matt, pedalling furiously.

Annika just threw him an exasperated glance over her shoulder. No Swede seemed to believe it was possible to cycle at less than forty miles per hour. Panting, he followed her into the forest.

He pursued them along a narrow dirt track winding through the trees. He had cycled here once before and knew that it led down to the sea and then along the water's edge. It was a secluded and quiet area, perfect for a very private meeting. *Yes, or for some sort of threat*, thought Matt. There would be no one around to help if there was. This small forest was usually so little visited that deer lived there, and wolves had been seen during hard winters.

The procession of cyclists continued until finally the man came to a halt. He spoke quickly. "I want to talk to you, alone," he said to the breathless Matt. "Who is this?" he added, looking suspiciously at Annika.

"I'm with him," Annika replied. "You can talk to me too."

"I don't know who you are," the man said. "But I know that Mr Simmonds here works for the British Embassy, and I will only talk to him."

Matt didn't know how the man knew his name and that he worked for the Embassy, but guessed it would have been easy to find out in Sweden, a country where everyone's tax records were freely available.

"Come with me," the man said impatiently. "It won't take long. You can wait here," he added, looking at Annika.

She began to protest, but Matt intervened. The man looked more nervous than they did. He wasn't going to be a threat.

"It's OK. I'll go with you. I'll be back in a minute," he said, turning to Annika. With bad grace she sat down on the side of the track and muttered something in Swedish. Nothing complimentary, Matt imagined.

He followed the burly figure for a short distance into the silent forest until they were alone. Close to, the man looked older and less intimidating.

"I am sorry to bring you out here like this," he said. "I wouldn't normally take these sorts of precautions, but what is happening is something new to me, and to tell the truth I am a little scared."

"So who are you and why do you want to talk to me?" Matt asked.

"I am just a concerned Swede. I used to work for SÄPO. You know, the Swedish Security Service. I came across some British diplomats then. Maybe I am naive, but I thought that you have a conscience. At least, you would think twice before doing something you thought was wrong. So when I realised that I had to tell someone what I knew, I decided to choose a British diplomat. It seems you are the only one at the Embassy, except for the Ambassador herself. And she is too senior."

"So what do you want to tell me?"

"I don't have anything detailed to tell you. But I still have a couple of friends in SÄPO and they are worried. There is a lot of secrecy about a submarine in the archipelago. Some people in SÄPO are talking to some unusual contacts. Dangerous contacts. And they are not talking to the people in government that they are supposed to. Things are being concealed. So my friends are worried that there is a conspiracy. It wouldn't be the first time, of course. You remember all that nonsense in the 1980s?"

"Yes, sort of," said Matt, unwilling to reveal his ignorance.

"My friends are worried that it could be happening again. They won't give me anything concrete, as you might understand. But if you want to find out whether there really is a submarine, and, if so, who it belongs to, you need to find out all you can about *Upptäckt*."

"*Upptäckt*?" said Matt. "What's that?"

"I am going to leave that to you. It's not difficult to work out, if you try. Now I will leave you."

"But… at least tell me your name."

It was too late. He had already set off through the forest with the usual Swedish alacrity. Within seconds he had disappeared.

When Matt got back to their bikes, Annika looked relieved.

"So what happened? He took his bike and left without a word."

"It's OK," Matt told her. "Let's go. I will tell you when we get out of here."

He followed in Annika's rapid wake until they got back to the road. Over coffee in a nearby cafe, he told her what the man had said.

"So, what is *Upptäckt*?" he asked.

Annika thought for a moment, biting her lip in concentration. "*Upptäckt* used to be a TV programme. One of those investigative ones. You know, scandals, cover-ups and so on. *Upptäckt* means 'discovery' in Swedish. But it hasn't been on the air for a few years."

"That doesn't help much."

"No, but maybe they did a piece on that Soviet submarine in 1981. Some people made a whole career out of writing about it. I will ask around to see if *Upptäckt* did anything on it."

"So tell me, what did he mean about SÄPO cover-ups in the 1980s?"

"I know there was a big scandal," said Annika, "but I can't remember much about it."

"I'll ask Catherine. She will know."

"So we both have some work to do," said Annika. "Better get to it."

Matt sighed. She was always rushing away. Not a good sign, he thought.

TWO

The next morning, after a few minutes at reception consoling a teary Lotta, who had discovered that her most recent boyfriend had a wife and four children, Matt went to see Catherine. He told her about the meeting and the ambiguous message. She looked pensive.

"It does seem to hark back to the Cold War era here. And I would say that, given Russia's current activities, we are very close to repeating that era."

"What happened with SÄPO in the 1980s?" asked Matt.

"It's a complicated story, and much of it remains unclear. Some of the leading protagonists are dead, some have always stayed silent, and only a few have been willing to say anything. As a result, the conspiracy theorists have had a field day. Their main claims are that some members of the then-Security Service – SÄK – believed that Sweden was at risk of attack from the Soviet Union, and that Prime Minister Olof Palme was unable, or unwilling, to defend his country. They thought he was at best too weak, at worst a closet communist.

"Those men – allegedly – tried to destabilise the socialist government by all sorts of means and were covertly supported by the US. The Americans needed

Sweden to be battle ready so as to provide a counter to any Soviet invasion of Western Europe via the Baltic. One of the tactics supposedly used by the US was to send submarines to the Swedish coast to provoke anti-Soviet scare stories. The Security Service and their allies in the Swedish military would then fan the flames in the Swedish media."

"Was there any truth in this?" asked Matt.

"It was all very murky. Of course, the US denied it. There were lots of reports of submarines off the coast. The one concrete fact was that a Soviet submarine was discovered in 1981 near a Swedish naval base, after it got stuck on a rock. There was a lot of military excitement and at one point things got very tense. There were bellicose bellows from both sides. But in the end, common sense prevailed and the Swedes allowed the sub to be towed away.

"Of course, there was even more pressure from the military on Palme after that. Relations between the government and the Security Service were difficult for some years. Part of the problem, according to some involved at the time, was that SÄK was reluctant to pass on information to ministers whom it suspected were unreliable. There wasn't much trust, and the assassination of Palme in 1986 didn't help. That's why SÄK was replaced by SÄPO in 1989. But there are plenty of people around who think that it hasn't changed under the skin."

"So what should we do with the message I heard yesterday?"

"Do you think this man seemed genuine?" asked Catherine. "Is he worth taking seriously? Or is he just a crackpot?"

Matt thought back to the meeting in the forest. "I think he meant what he said."

"I'll think about it," Catherine said. "I might have a word with the spooks in London. See if they know anything. I could ask them to speak to SÄPO liaison."

"But what if SÄPO is involved in some sort of conspiracy again?" asked Matt.

"Then we are all in trouble. But it will probably turn out to be a false alarm."

"Should I say anything to Philip?"

"You had better not; he is excited enough already. No need to throw more petrol on the flames." Catherine gave him a wry smile. "One thing you will have to learn in your FCO career is to keep the soldiers in their wooden box as much as you can. Only let them out when it is safe for them to play and they can't do any harm. I remember my first Ambassador telling me that, and it is just as true today. The other thing is to take anything the spooks tell you with plenty of salt. They always have their own agendas."

"So we should only really trust our own," said Matt.

"That depends," Catherine replied, with a slight smile. "You will have to find that out for yourself."

Back in his office, Matt wondered whether Annika had had any luck in finding out anything interesting about *Upptäckt*.

Knowing her, she won't rest until she has discovered something, he thought. Whether there would be any truth in it was another matter. Matt was beginning to suspect that the way Sweden was run was more complicated than the open, democratic image the rest of the world saw.

RIGA

The aroma of gherkins had finally driven the core group of plotters out of the cellar and onto a bench in a peaceful park near the city centre. In the distance, the remnants of a stag party collapsed inelegantly into a flower bed.

"Has it entered the Baltic, Vanda?" one of them asked the woman with the steely grey eyes.

"Yes. It is close to the archipelago."

"Has it been spotted?"

"There has been no indication from NATO that they have noticed it yet. And if they haven't seen it, then the Swedes certainly won't have."

"So what happens next?"

"We have already agreed that we need someone to help us. Someone not connected to us, who has no knowledge of what we are doing, but could be persuaded to help. Someone who is well intentioned, but also naive."

"Have you found such a person?"

"I have someone in mind," said Vanda, flexing herself on the bench. "But I have yet to approach him. I have to find the right moment. But it will happen soon."

MOSCOW

"So, Sergei. What can I report to the Master? I understand that you have some good news?" The plump, hairy fingers were drumming on the desk again.

"Good progress, yes."

The admiral felt confident that his rather unusual plan was working. In truth, it had been his wife that had suggested it to him. At first he had dismissed it as a piece of civilian fantasy, but she had persuaded him. She had explained to him once again the cobweb between the wives. He knew now that the man with the plump fingers was riding high this year: he had recently bought a very extensive property in Surrey. But the admiral's wife suspected that he had overreached himself in doing so, and that his position could quickly become vulnerable if he fell out of favour.

She had told him about that creep Osipov, who had recently bought an experimental type of mini submarine to accompany his very large yacht. The submarine had been designed for the military, but a sizeable contribution to a Kremlin fixer's pension fund had allowed Osipov to buy it for 'research purposes'. Osipov's wife had been boasting incessantly about it during the wives' skiing break in Zermatt. The admiral's wife had suggested to him that Osipov could be persuaded to lend his submarine to the state, as a gesture of loyalty to the Master. That would be popular among the other wives, who were fed up with the boasting. It wouldn't be worth having a submarine if you couldn't use it.

He had engineered a meeting with Osipov and put the idea to him, with the strong hint that it came directly from the Master. Osipov, of course, then had no real choice in the matter, but had made an unexpected request to go with the submarine, even if he would have no control over its destination and operations. It seemed that he was quite keen to escape from his wife.

The admiral said nothing of this to Plump-Fingers. He gave a military response. "We have a Piranha in position just outside Stockholm, Vitaly. For now, it is only tracking the movements of other submarines in the area. We are awaiting the Master's orders."

"Excellent, Sergei. Do nothing further until you are instructed."

The admiral rose to leave. The fingers drummed.

Washington

The Undersecretary was having another sleepless night. She stared at the curtains. She hadn't agreed, of course, with the Defence Secretary when he had ordered the deployment of a US submarine to the Swedish archipelago. It made no operational sense to do it now, especially without telling either the Swedes, or NATO allies. The Secretary, while flicking through *Deer Hunter Monthly*, had argued in his shouty style that the US needed the freedom to respond flexibly to the Russian threat. But the Undersecretary knew that was only part of the picture. Like everyone else, her boss was trying to stay on the high wire in the Washington circus. These days there was no career safety net. One week the Russians were toxic, the next they were partners. She guessed that the decision to deploy the submarine had been a two-way bet. If there was an aggressive tweet in the night, the Secretary could claim to be ahead of the game. And if there was the opposite sort of tweet, the submarine could be quietly withdrawn.

The Undersecretary also knew there was another, more personal reason. During a recent visit to Washington, the Swedish Defence Minister had not only comfortably outscored his US host during a day spent hunting deer, but had undiplomatically boasted about it afterwards. Her boss felt that the Swede had got one over on him and he wanted revenge. If it were to be revealed that the US had casually deployed a submarine to Swedish waters without the Swedes suspecting anything, their minister would look both weak and incompetent.

She sighed and turned over.

STOCKHOLM

In a quiet corner of a Stockholm restaurant once popular among businessmen for its fish lunches, two men and a woman were huddled together.

"Have you heard any more from our friends?" asked the woman, toying with a rather limp piece of trout.

"They have put the first stage of their plan into operation. In the meantime, I am helping them with the logistics. They are not very good at it, and need a lot of assistance. I am not impressed."

"Well, they are still our best chance," said the woman. "We are all agreed we need to do something quickly. An election may not be far away."

"Agreed," said the other man. "The situation is getting more dangerous every week. The Russians are almost at our throats. By the time our government wakes up they will have us."

There was a long pause.

"This fish isn't very good today. I am still starving. Whose turn is it to do *fika*?"

"Sven's."

"Good. He always buys those big Danish pastries. Let's go!"

On his way back home, Matt had a text from Annika. She had found out some information about *Upptäckt* and suggested a meeting the following evening. Matt sent an enthusiastic response.

The next day was again a beauty. The Swedish summer was short-lived, but often glorious in a temperate, Scandinavian way. It didn't really compensate for the long, gloomy winter months, but at least it gave the Swedes a brief burst of happiness – without having to fly to Thailand. There were several bars along Strandvägen, filled with healthy-looking locals eating seafood and drinking wine. Motor boats lined the quay, and the bars. The latest Swedish hits played against the background of the stately museums on the opposite bank. Matt's favourite bar was on a small jetty, so people could drink while dangling their feet over the water.

Annika was already there, perched on a large cushion by the waterside. "*Hej, hej*, Matt. Come and share these crab cakes."

"So, what did you find out?" asked Matt, after a few happy mouthfuls.

"I looked on the internet, and asked some of my older colleagues who used to watch *Upptäckt* in its heyday. It did do some programmes about the submarine saga; not just the Soviet sub in 1981, but all the other rumoured sightings at that time. They caused a stir because they came up with some evidence that the Swedish military and Security Service were hiding the truth from the government. It was assumed that this was because they didn't want to admit that they were unable to stop the Soviet Union from doing what they liked in our waters. Of course, they denied it, and the story seemed to fade away, or at least *Upptäckt* stopped making programmes about it. I found out the name of the guy who produced those programmes, though. He's called Lars Eriksson. He is retired, but he still lives in Stockholm. I thought we might go and see him. It could be interesting, even if he might not be able to tell us much about this latest submarine story."

Matt agreed. He told Annika that he had also done some research and gave her an edited version of what Catherine had told him. "We are going to ask people back in London if they have anything more," he added, without mentioning anything about MI6.

Having been at one point an avid reader of spy thrillers, Matt had been surprised by the rather casual approach his colleagues sometimes seemed to take towards protecting information. One of his older teammates back in London had put this down to a number of factors. They included the end of the Cold War, budget cuts, and the increasing use of local staff in Embassies. These meant that the incentive to protect secrets had reduced, as had the ability to do so. In an Embassy in a friendly place like Stockholm, Matt was aware that there were few 'secrets', except for transient operational details, that he knew but the local staff didn't. Nonetheless, he still felt that he had to make an effort to follow the rules. He felt reluctant as yet to share everything with Annika, however helpful she might be.

"Right," said Annika, "I will try to arrange a meeting with Eriksson. But I can't stay long now, sorry – I have a meeting with colleagues visiting from Paris."

"Of course," Matt replied, filled with a sudden hatred of those colleagues and a hope that something very unpleasant would happen to them in the near future.

After Annika left, he looked mournfully at the surrounding drinkers, who seemed suddenly to have metamorphosed from small groups into couples. *Unless she loses her job*, he thought, *maybe it's always going to be like this. I will always be second priority. If only she were less Swedish and less conscientious.*

The next morning, Matt had to go to a briefing for diplomats at the Foreign Affairs Ministry. These took place every month and were almost invariably dull. The Swedes would talk about forthcoming international events and explain what their minister might say and what Swedish priorities were. There would then be an opportunity to ask questions. Very few of the other diplomats bothered to do so. Swedish views were largely predictable. Usually the Danes or Finns would ask something, just to show a little Nordic solidarity.

Overcome by boredom, this time Matt felt impelled to say something to break the torpor. "Would the Ministry comment on the recent reports that foreign submarines have been seen inside the archipelago?" he asked.

His question was met with a firm gaze from the usual sombre spokeswoman. "There is no evidence that there are foreign submarines in Swedish waters." That was clearly as much as she was prepared to say. She moved on to the safer subject of international terrorism.

After the meeting, Henrik Svenson, the ultra-urbane Director of Political Affairs, took Matt to one side. "Are you British really that worried about the submarine reports?" he asked.

Not for the first time, Matt cursed himself. As an inexperienced diplomat, he sometimes forgot that words were important in his work, and that most diplomats weighed them very carefully before saying anything.

"No," he replied, trying to backtrack, "that isn't a view from London. Just my curiosity about what is happening out there."

Svenson looked at him for a long moment before replying. "Good," he said finally. "We don't want anything to get out of proportion. No need for our friends to get worried. There are plenty of real problems to solve. Everything that's happening in the Middle East, for example."

Matt agreed, feeling slightly rebuked and warned off the subject. When he later wrote his short and dull report of the meeting to send back to London, omitting any reference to his question, he wondered why Svenson had been quite so keen to steer him away from talking about submarines. *The Swedish newspapers are full of it*, he thought, *so why not discuss it?* He knew that Philip talked about it regularly with his military counterparts, so why were the Foreign Ministry reluctant?

On his way out of the building, Matt felt a tap on his shoulder. He turned to face a full-on smile from a curvaceous brunette.

"Well, hello to my favourite diplomat. What are you doing here?" Marcella was the Deputy Ambassador of Panama. Due to Sweden's generous aid programme to Central American countries, started out of sympathy for the Sandinistas, they all had Embassies in Stockholm. They were also staffed almost entirely by women, though whether by accident or design Matt had yet to find out. They provided a colourful and lively element to the diplomatic community and were among its most assiduous partygoers. Marcella, who was an avid anglophile, had taken a fancy to Matt, and he had begun to feel somewhat haunted by her.

"You are probably doing something very important. I bet you know how to get the better of these Swedes," she said, fluttering her eyelashes. "Everyone says British diplomats are the best."

Matt didn't know what to say, so made an indeterminate noise in reply.

"What are you doing this weekend? Some of us are going to the archipelago. Do you want to come?"

Matt made an excuse. He liked Marcella, but she couldn't compete with Annika in his eyes. He had always felt more attracted to women who were hard to get, or even unobtainable. He didn't feel comfortable being pursued.

"Well, I will get you out there sometime. You won't escape!" With that, she waved and left, hips swaying. Matt wondered whether he would escape. She was very persistent.

As he cycled back to the Embassy, he wondered, not for the first time, whether he had chosen the right career. His exchange with Svenson, although of little consequence, had reminded him of how careful and focused diplomats had to be; often, he felt, at the expense of creativity and self-expression. He wasn't yet sure if the frustration that caused him was simply part of a learning experience, or something more fundamentally at odds with his nature. As yet, he had no answer.

THREE

A couple of days later, Matt called Annika. She sounded stressed. It was her day to provide *fika* in her office. She had, however, managed to get in touch with Lars Eriksson. "He wasn't keen at first, but I managed to persuade him to meet us. Tomorrow at 7pm. Let's talk later. My colleagues are waiting and they are tough judges of baking. Wish me luck!" She rang off before Matt had a chance to offer his services as a cake taster. He always seemed to be a second too late.

The next evening Matt met Annika at the Södermalm Tunnelbana Station, the Tunnelbana being the Swedish underground train system. Södermalm had been a working-class area that had followed the inevitable progression from being poor, to bohemian, to chic, to overhyped and then over-expensive. Annika was curious as to why Lars Eriksson lived there.

"He must have moved here when it was still working class. It would have been a natural choice for a left-wing journalist then. He probably feels completely out of place now among all these designer boutiques."

She had arranged to meet Eriksson in a coffee shop. On entering, Annika spotted an elderly man in a corner, engrossed in that day's *Aftonbladet*, a Swedish counterpart of the British *Mirror*. In Matt's experience, *Aftonbladet* usually contained reports about the small but endlessly swirling pool of Swedish politics, money scandals, and the Swedish football deity known as Zlatan Ibrahimović. No edition of a Swedish paper was complete without a Zlatan story, even in the twilight of his career. Matt was pleased to see that Eriksson was reading an article about the internal warfare in the left-wing Social Democratic Party. *Yet more similarities between Sweden and the UK*, he thought.

The man looked up at them curiously. "*Hej*. I am Eriksson. You want to talk to me about submarines?" Matt had learnt quickly that the Swedes had a low tolerance for small talk. His meetings with Swedish diplomats over lunch tended to be disappointingly brief and very focused. He had listened with envy to the descriptions by a fellow first-poster in Paris about liquid, four-hour, four-course sessions.

"I'm interested in these reports of sightings," he replied. "I understand that you investigated them a lot some years ago and that you might know what's going on now."

"That was a long time ago. You British weren't interested in talking to me then. You were too busy being friendly with our Defence Ministry." Eriksson laughed quietly. "Our government didn't like *Upptäckt* much. Probably because we got too close to the truth. Anyhow, you are wrong to think that I knew a lot about submarines. We never found out what they were doing, or where they came from, apart from that Soviet one that got stuck on a rock. We were interested in what SÄK were doing. They were subverting the state. They thought they were the government. Controlling information about the submarines was just one of the things they were up to." He stopped. "But you must know all that. What are you after now?"

"We don't exactly know," Annika admitted. "But we think that some of what happened then might be happening again now. We are a bit in the dark, to be honest. We think maybe you can give us some ideas about how to find out more."

Eriksson thought for a while. "It's been a long time since I was in that game," he muttered.

"Yes, but this is Sweden," Annika replied. "Things don't change quickly here."

Eriksson looked at Matt. "Until recently, I wouldn't have had much incentive to help you. But now I read that good things are happening in your politics. You have a proper socialist party there again. So maybe there is something I can do. I still have some contacts within SÄPO. They had to let some lefties in after the big scandal. I can arrange a meeting for you with someone who might know if something is being covered up."

Being still a little uncertain about diplomatic proprieties, Matt felt nervous about relying on this expression of support for Her Majesty's Loyal Opposition, but was too intrigued to back out now. "That would be very helpful."

"To tell the truth, it makes me nostalgic," Eriksson replied. "It seems we are going back to the 1970s. You will understand that was my favourite decade. A real difference between left and right. Mysterious submarines. Protest marches in Stockholm. I don't even mind a little flavour of the Cold War. Although, I have to say something really treasonable. I never liked ABBA."

Matt and Annika left him to his newspaper and walked back up the hill to the Tunnelbana. "Well, that was a surprise," Annika said. "I didn't think he would be so helpful. I guess he is still intrigued after all these years. Let's hope he gives us that name. I have never met anyone from SÄPO. Could be exciting!"

"Don't get your hopes up," said Matt. "You shouldn't imagine that all spies are glamorous. He is probably a very dull guy in a suit."

"Spoilsport!" said Annika. "Anyhow, I have to go—"

"Don't tell me. Another meeting."

"Yes, but this one is with an old boyfriend who is in town this week. We are having dinner together."

"An old boyfriend?" questioned Matt, feeling both nervous and jealous.

"Yes, my first love. *Hej, hej.*" With that she disappeared into the depths of the station, leaving Matt once again at a loss for both words and movement.

The next day at the Embassy, Matt told Catherine about the meeting. The Ambassador looked thoughtful. "We are getting into MI6 territory here. They like to handle all contacts with SÄPO themselves." She paused. "I'll have to tell them about this and they can decide whether to take it forward or not."

Matt felt he had no choice but to accept this, although he was disappointed. His curiosity had been piqued. He had started to think that this submarine saga might help him learn more about the hidden Sweden. It had also given him a good reason to spend more time with Annika.

"This Eriksson sounds quite an interesting chap," said Catherine. "Not many like him around now, but I do run across them sometimes. A sort of living history. Maybe we should invite him to something one day. Perhaps when we have some Labour MPs in town. Ah! Talking of events, we have another meeting on the Queen's birthday party now."

They both sighed. Hosting the annual – or, in recent cash-strapped days, often biannual – QBP was a regular task for most Embassies. Some Ambassadors relished them. Others viewed them as an unnecessary evil. Neither Catherine nor Matt were enthusiasts; Catherine due to over-familiarity, and Matt due to a lurking fear of a spectacular cock-up on his part. But he understood that the resident British community seemed to enjoy them, and there was usually the compensation of a drunken staff party afterwards.

There came a knock on the door, and Helena glided in, notebook at the ready. She was followed by John, head of the Consular Section; Bjorn, head of the Commercial Section; and Philip, representing the military. They, together with Catherine and Matt, were the QBP team. They had already met several times and had been wrestling with the usual problem of trying to present a decent event on a low budget. It had been John, an unconventional, locally engaged Brit who had moved to Sweden some years before, who had come up with a potential solution. Having overt sponsorship of the QBP was frowned upon in

London, implying as it did more than a hint of desperation, but John had cunningly suggested a third way.

"IKEA is almost as famous in the UK for its meatballs as it is for its furniture. Why don't we follow their example and invite a British company to provide the food for the QBP under the guise of a culinary exhibition? Then they can pay for the whole thing."

Catherine had taken to this idea, Bjorn had cast around for a sponsor, and so it was that Northern Powerhouse Engineering, a company never before associated with food, had unexpectedly found themselves invited to Stockholm as champions of traditional British fish and chips. The QBP was now just two weeks away. Invitations to the British community, the great and good in Swedish society, various Ambassadors, and potential Swedish buyers of engineering products, had been issued. A Swedish celebrity TV chef was due to cook the fish and chips. It only remained to sort out who would look after each of the VIP guests.

As usual, Philip was first into the breach. "Some Swedish top brass coming, and the usual defence attachés. My team will look after them. I'm hoping that a senior man from Swedish Missile Systems will come. If he does, I would be grateful, Catherine, if you could give him some time."

The MOD had been trying for some time to help British Aerospace sell some missile guidance kit to the Swedes, who had become increasingly nervous about the Russian military presence in the Baltic. Swedish Missile Systems were, of course, enjoying the attentions of several suitors. Catherine was privately convinced that there would be a last-minute, cunning and legally questionable offer from the French that would swing the deal their way. She shared this thought only with Matt, being unwilling to discourage her still-bright-eyed DA.

"My team will look after cycle parking and run the crèche," John offered. Bjorn explained how his team would handle Northern Powerhouse Engineering and the other commercial guests.

"Chancery will do the meeting and greeting and keep the VIPs circulating," said Matt. His team had not initially been enthusiastic about coming to the QBP, but the promised presence of the TV chef had changed that. In addition to their passion for baking, they all avidly followed Swedish cookery shows and wanted to see one of their heroes in action. Matt guessed that the VIPs would quickly be neglected once the fat started spitting.

Catherine wound up the meeting with a reminder that some of the leading Swedish newspaper editors would be attending. "Best to avoid any embarrassing incidents," she suggested.

Matt recalled a story he had been told when he first arrived in Stockholm. One of his predecessors had held a party in his flat which a visiting British boy band had unexpectedly gate-crashed after their concert. A journalist trailing in their wake had surprised one of the band and a groupie in an act of very close Anglo-Swedish union. The resultant story, with photos, had appeared on the front page of *Aftonbladet* with the inevitable title of *Orgy at British Diplomat's Flat*. Embassy credibility had been hard to regain after that.

✦

The next few days passed slowly for Matt. A cold front had moved in and Annika seemed to have disappeared. He spent his time replying to a range of tedious requests for information from London.

Finally, Annika called. She launched straight into business in Swedish style. "*Hej, hej.* I just heard from Lars Eriksson. He has given me the name of someone in SÄPO who is willing to talk to us. It sounds very exciting. She can meet us this evening. Can you come?"

Matt cursed as he recalled Catherine's decision to hand things over to MI6. "Let me get back to you," he eventually replied. *Better tell her*, he thought.

He found the Ambassador also cursing over the latest instruction from London. "Can you believe it?" she said, waving her hand towards her computer. "The government are compiling their National Happiness Index, and some idiot wants every Embassy to write its own. I have to guess in advance how happy each member of staff is and then check by asking them. Every Ambassador will be judged on how accurate their guesses are. I suppose it's a test on how well I know my staff. Ridiculous."

Matt had by now become accustomed to the constant flow of random orders from London, but this one seemed stranger than most. "It could be worse," he replied. "At least Swedes don't hide their feelings. You will score better than Ambassadors in most of Asia."

"That's true." Catherine looked more cheerful. "I'll organise a little competition on our private Ambassadors' network. Maybe a sweepstake. The loser gets to run the Human Resources Directorate."

"There is a private Ambassadors' network?" Matt was surprised.

"Yes, but you are not supposed to know about it, so keep it to yourself. How do you think we keep ourselves sane with all these idiocies from London? Of course, only the right sort gets invited to join. No ultra-ambitious types, or time-servers. We exchange ideas on how to beat the system, that sort of thing. They will be foaming at the mouth with this latest nonsense."

Matt thought this might be a good moment to report Annika's news. "I remember, of course, what you said about contacting MI6. Have you heard from them?"

"No, I bloody well haven't. Not a word. Not even the decency of an acknowledgement." Catherine paused. "Well, on their heads be it. I gave them a chance to take this on. They are clearly not interested. So, go ahead. Meet this woman and let me know what she says. Don't promise anything and keep away from any conversation about MI6. I'll take responsibility for any fallout. In fact, I would welcome it. About time the spooks remembered that we exist." In her last year before retirement, Catherine was beginning to enjoy a few rebellious moments.

This time Matt met Annika at the entrance to Humlegården in central Stockholm. The park was a small green island amongst some of Stockholm's older and most stately buildings. On sunny summer evenings it was a popular place for students to hang out and for pensioners to sit and watch the world go by.

"Who are we meeting?" asked Matt.

"I don't know her name," Annika replied. "Eriksson said that she would approach us. I offered to wear something distinctive, but he just laughed. I suppose she is an expert at this sort of thing. Do you think she is here already?"

Matt looked around. Most of the park benches were occupied, but he couldn't see any obvious candidates. He felt slightly foolish just looking. He had started telling Annika about a new bar he had discovered when a middle-aged woman silently approached them. She gave them a stern stare.

Matt had frequently wondered about the mysterious change that came over Swedish women when they reached a certain age. Young women strode around in jeans and boots, with blonde ponytails – admittedly often dyed – and seemed ready for all sorts of fun. They were usually prompt to ignore social conventions and to pour scorn on the establishment. They had spiky relations with their mothers. In middle age, in accordance with some internal signal, they cut their hair short, began to wear scary red-rimmed glasses and sensible skirts, and became ferocious guardians of the social order. Matt's immediate reaction was that he and Annika were sitting on a bench reserved for pensioners and they were about to be unceremoniously evicted. But the stare was replaced by a slight smile.

"*Hej, hej*, move up please," she said. "We are going to have a little chat. Lars has told me about you, and I have done some research myself. So I'm not going to waste time asking about you and why you have such an interest in submarines. Nor am I going to tell you much about myself, except that my name is Gunilla. Lars and I have known each other for many years and have helped each other more than once, even though I work for the oppressive Security Service and he is a left-wing freedom fighter."

She smiled in a rather fond way, clearly thinking about Lars. "We may not agree on everything, but we do agree that in a democracy governments should not mislead the people, at least not deliberately. And we are both worried that there is a group here trying to do just that. It was done before, as I am sure you know, and it looks as though it is now happening again."

She stopped for a moment to watch a procession of toddlers being marched past. "You know, of course, that there are many in Sweden – and, by the way, many in SÄPO – who are very worried about what Russia is up to in our region. They believe that Russia intends to do in one or more of the Baltic States something similar to what they are doing in the Ukraine. They think an invasion is not only possible, but likely, and that NATO is not taking this threat seriously. By NATO, of course, they mean the Americans. Having some German ships and Polish troops on manoeuvres in the Baltic doesn't count."

She paused and looked at Annika. "As you know, Sweden is in many ways a very conservative country. If we get into trouble, we often look back to our past to try to find solutions. So it's natural, I guess, that some in SÄPO are remembering the submarine crises of the Cold War. The US were very ready to help us then and these people think they may do again, if we put some pressure on them.

"In the 1980s there were Soviet submarines in our waters, very close to Stockholm. It is easy to believe that

Russian submarines might be out there now. It is also easy to create some evidence that they are there. There is always an audience in Sweden for stories about submarines. Plenty of people claim they have seen them. And it's not so difficult to play with technical information, even in these days of satellite surveillance."

She turned to Matt. "I expect you have heard about this untraceable submarine – the Piranha. There is a lot of talk now between Swedish and American experts about this. Some of their experts want to believe that there is at least one out in the archipelago. Perhaps there is. But it might also be a game being played by some in SÄPO and in our military to attract US attention; to get them to have a bigger military presence here." She hesitated. "It's not the game that I object to. We all have to play games sometimes. But it's not right to deceive our government and our public, and it's too dangerous. These people think they have the right to make decisions on behalf of the rest of us."

"So why don't you stop them?" asked Annika.

"It's not that simple. They conceal what they are doing, and are the people that talk the loudest about being open. SÄPO is very divided. To stop them I would have to have real evidence. Otherwise, it would be easy for them to discredit any accusations. There are so many stories in the media already, people would not know what to believe." She looked at Matt. "I am telling you this because you are an outsider and you have contacts and information that I don't. I am not going to ask you to do anything, but if you do, maybe we can work together. Discreetly, of course. And if this comes back to me, I will deny everything."

"So what could I do?" asked Matt, intrigued, but also increasingly nervous.

"Just find out the truth," she replied. "After that, you will be able to work out what to do. Good luck." With that, she got up and marched away without looking back.

Annika was immediately full of questions, and for once Matt was grateful that she had to rush off to a meeting. He needed time to think about what he had just heard, and indeed about the whole of this increasingly murky saga. Everyone seemed to have a conspiracy theory, but there was a distinct lack of actual evidence.

"Lots of smoke, but no herring," agreed Catherine later.

"Maybe a few red herrings," Matt added.

"So what are you planning to do now, Agent Simmonds?" she asked.

"Nothing. I can't see there is anything to do. I feel that I am just being used by people who are probably a bit deluded. I don't know why they want to involve me. If they want me to believe in their submarines, they can take me for a ride in one. In the meantime, I am just going to be a diplomat again."

"Good idea," said Catherine. "I need one of those to help me with the QBP."

FOUR

MOSCOW

The admiral looked again at the photos his wife had sent him. He had been nervous ever since that slimy Vitaly Alexandrovich had mentioned 'patriotic duty'. So he had asked her to go house-hunting near the Sevastopol naval base. Just in case.

His mobile rang. He listened for a few moments. "No, I don't want to speak to him. I don't care if he is bored. He is doing his patriotic duty. That should be enough for him."

He put down the phone with a smile. Not only was the Piranha project going well, but that creep Osipov was being made to suffer into the bargain. He sighed and looked again at the images of the twelve-bedroom 'rustic dacha' his wife had found.

RIGA

The three of them were panting very rapidly now; it would be all over very soon. "Ooh," gasped the grey-eyed girl, rolling over onto the carpet of pine needles. "That was the best yet!"

"Yes, fifteen kilometres today," replied one of the others.

They lay, still breathing heavily, under the blue Latvian sky.

"When will you make contact, Vanda?"

"Soon. When I am back in Stockholm. The man I have in mind is already asking the Swedes about submarines. He is going to be easy to convince. The British always like to support the underdog. That's how I will hook him."

"Perfect. Fifteen back to town. Shall we go?"

Washington

There was a light in the house opposite. Perhaps her neighbours couldn't sleep either. She thought again about what her contact in Stockholm, Mason Hunter, had told her. The Defence Secretary had gone ahead with the submarine deployment. The damned thing was already in Swedish waters and it was only a matter of time before it was discovered. They no longer thought it likely that the Russians had deployed a Piranha there, but believed they had sent an older submarine. Although Russian intentions were unclear, it seemed likely it was going to be used for some kind of provocation.

Luckily, Mason Hunter, although working in the State Department and thus theoretically in the enemy camp, was an old friend, and had been equally appalled by the deployment. He was working on a plan to get the submarine removed; something to do with the British. There was a young British diplomat whom Hunter thought he could use, in some as yet unspecified way.

She had at least solved one problem. There had been an intensification of tweets attacking those who had not done their patriotic duty, so she had bought a small house next to a disused steel factory. The view was a little rusty, but at least her job was a bit safer.

STOCKHOLM

"You still have some sugar granules on your lower lip," the woman said.

The offender amongst the two men licked his lips. "That was a top *fika*. Maybe the best this year."

"Agreed," said his colleague. He looked surreptitiously along the empty corridor. "So, do we have any news?"

"It appears to be spending most of its time at the bottom of the Baltic," the other man replied. "They are telling us that they are waiting for some sort of contact to be made to move things along. They want to use a young British diplomat. They say he knows nothing and will be easily led."

"Well, they can't leave it too long. Once the summer holidays begin here there won't be anyone left to react."

"I will send them a hurry-up," said the woman. "I don't want to miss my annual month in my summer cottage either."

"*The Great British Bake Off* is on TV this evening."

"Excellent!"

During the next few days Matt did indeed have to concentrate on preparations for the Queen's birthday party. As far as he could tell, they seemed to be going well. The only problem was with Tom, the head of security.

As John explained, "The trouble with Tom is that he doesn't like anyone visiting either the Embassy or the Residence. He is only happy when the gates are locked. He wanted to have a complicated pass system for all the guests, involving a photo ID check, and no space for parking bikes. I told him that doesn't happen here in Sweden. The Americans do that sort of thing, but the Swedes expect them to. They don't expect anyone else to do the same. So I insisted that he'll just have to ask guests for their invitation cards, as usual. He has agreed, but he is very unhappy. We will have to keep an eye on him."

For his part, Matt felt confident that his team would take care of the political VIPs; they could all be very charming when they wanted to be. As he walked the short distance from the Embassy to the Ambassador's Residence with them, he even began to enjoy himself. He had been to a number of national day receptions at other Embassies and felt ready to play his part as a host. He liked going to the Residence, which was a substantial and agreeably proportioned town house backing onto the Baltic Sea. Catherine used it often for meetings and dinners for visiting British VIPs. Control of this pleasant little realm was divided between two monarchs: Catherine's husband, James, and their cook, Birgitta.

Matt had arrived in Stockholm full of lurid stories told to him by veteran colleagues about Ambassadors' spouses and the powerful and erratic influence they could have on Embassy life.

"Lunatics, some of them," seemed to be a common view.

"Be polite, but keep away from them."

"Don't let any Ambassador persuade you to work with them."

"And never get caught in the middle of an argument between Ambassador and spouse or partner."

"You'll be back home on the next flight with your balls following you in the diplomatic bag."

After such a build-up, James came as a pleasant surprise. Not only was he perfectly normal and pleasant company, but he kept a discreet distance from Embassy life, being fully occupied with his own online business. He did, however, get involved with events at the Residence when he wanted to support his wife. It was only on these occasions when Matt found himself remembering those lurid stories.

Birgitta was a large and imposing woman with very clear views on her role as not only a cook, but also a combination of maître d' and society expert. She had worked for a leading Stockholm restaurant before leaving to spend more time with her daughters, and had briefly written a society column for a Swedish magazine. She knew many of the Swedish VIPs invited to events at the Residence and they would often come into her kitchen for a chat.

For his part, as a veteran diplomatic husband who enjoyed entertaining and believed himself to have a flair for it, James also had good reason to think of himself as an experienced host with a role to play. Early on in their diplomatic life together, there had been conflicts between him and Catherine about that role. She also had plenty of ideas about entertaining guests. They had eventually decided that it would make more sense for James, who had more time on his hands, to take sole responsibility. Ever since then she had restrained herself, left things to him, and bitten her tongue on a regular basis. In their previous posting in Colombo, James had ruled the roost whenever he wanted to do so. Birgitta had other ideas. James, who liked to look on life with amused indulgence, suddenly found himself caught up in increasingly tough territorial disputes. He felt it was ridiculous, but he couldn't give in.

Catherine, who wanted to remain out of the fray, had fatally begun to compromise with both of them. Birgitta insisted on coming to her to discuss menus, seating plans and all other minute details, and she found herself agreeing with all her proposals. In subsequent bedroom scenes she equally found herself in full retreat. The Residence staff were now in two camps, and the other Embassy staff, who were well aware of what was happening, tended to view it as live entertainment.

As Matt entered the Residence he could hear Catherine attempting to mollify her husband. "Yes, I know that's what we agreed. But I gather Birgitta couldn't buy any today, and herring is always very popular here. I'm sure the Swedes will approve… Yes, well, I'm a bit tired of herring myself, but we are in Stockholm. We are expected to eat it… OK, darling, well, you don't have to eat it… Yes, well, we can't prove that, can we? We just have to believe her… Yes, I will talk to her later… Yes, and we can talk too."

Matt coughed and walked into the room. "*Hej, hej,*" he said. "Just practising. I really am getting quite Swedish now."

"Well, then I wish you a life spent eating nothing but bloody herring," snapped James as he strode out.

Matt and Catherine exchanged glances.

"Explain to me why you haven't got married?" she said wearily. "OK. Let's get ready for our beloved guests. I expect they will all arrive together."

A jingling of bells indicated that the first guests were indeed wheeling their bicycles into the front courtyard. In true Swedish style, they were exactly on time. To the minute. Stockholm must be one of the few places on earth, Matt reflected, where the biggest risk to a social function was a bicycle pile-up almost before it had begun.

A queue was already forming by the gate where Tom and two assistants from the Management Section were slowly scrutinising the visitors' invitation cards. Matt went over to see what was happening. He took Tom to one side.

"Tom, you don't have to ask every guest to give you their life history. Just tick off their names on the guest list so we can see afterwards who came and who didn't."

Tom was unhappy, but the queue began to move forward.

Matt positioned himself by the door, and kept an eye out for senior Swedish diplomats and Ambassadors from other Embassies. He knew most of the Ambassadors from similar events. They tended to be very status-conscious. They normally didn't want to spend any time talking to junior diplomats, unless they had a favour to ask, usually involving last-minute visas for relatives wanting to visit the UK. These requests were quite frequent, and were always difficult to deal with. Diplomats coming from countries where government officials had a lot of clout found it impossible to believe that Matt had no power to overrule UK immigration officials. They assumed that he was being deliberately unhelpful, and often took his polite explanations as either the opening of a negotiation, or a sign of a secret conspiracy against either them, or their country. After such requests, Matt would later be publicly snubbed, or briefly thanked in a lordly manner, depending on whether a visa was eventually issued.

During his first months in the FCO in London, Matt had been entertained by stories of diplomatic life abroad from some of his veteran colleagues. They had started their careers in days before annual performance reviews, management targets and the like. A sort of golden age if you didn't mind being subject to the whims of the more tyrannical Ambassadors, and the vagaries of the roulette-style posting system. It certainly produced better stories. His colleague Francis had an almost unlimited store of them. Sipping Chablis in one of the Whitehall bars after work, clad in his usual bow tie, Francis always did his best to brush away the dingy surroundings.

"My first posting was in Laos just before the communists swept away the nationalist government," he'd once said dreamily. "The red horde were getting ever closer to the capital, Vientiane. We expats, a small and undistinguished community, did our best to ignore the inevitable by partying every night. The gloomier the situation became, the more champagne was drunk. Supplies quickly ran dry, even at the French Embassy.

"As you have probably noticed, numeracy is not one of my strong points. A few months before the end, I had mistakenly ordered forty cases of champagne instead of four. Easily done after a long lunch. So I quickly became the most desirable bachelor in town. There I was, previously lurking unnoticed at the bottom of the diplomatic pond, and then suddenly and briefly feted by Ambassadors and wealthy Laotians, and pursued by their newly affectionate daughters."

He sighed and twirled his Chablis. "Everyone wanted to come to parties in my little house. Even my Ambassador, who until then had preferred to ignore my existence, was calling me 'Francis'. He didn't have to hold a QBP that year; I had generated enough goodwill singlehanded.

"Couldn't last, of course. Once the last bottle had been drunk, I quickly sunk back to the bottom of the pond. We all had to make a run for it soon after, all the diplomatic community. It was back to the bedsit in Tooting for me. But, glory days. Glory days! More Chablis anyone?"

Matt still didn't recognise all the Swedish guests, but his female Chancery colleagues did, expertly picking them up at the door, flirting briefly and efficiently with the men, and leading them all to the large dining room. The Residence staff circulated with plates of canapés, most of which seemed to involve fish.

"Hello, my favourite diplomat," said a familiar voice.

How did she get here? Matt thought.

"My Ambassador couldn't come at the last moment," Marcella said, with a large Panamanian smile. "I knew you wouldn't mind if I came instead. Oh! What a lovely house. Maybe you will live here one day. When you are Ambassador." She paused for effect. "With your wife, of course. You will need a wife. Someone who knows about this strange life we diplomats lead."

"You are welcome here, of course, Marcella," Matt replied, ignoring her comment. He looked around for help, but could find none. "I have to stay here to meet our guests, but I will catch up with you later. There is food in the dining room."

"You bet, *mi amor*," she replied, with a flirtatious look. "I will keep something warm for you."

"Actually, it's mostly cold fish."

"Yes," she said, "I have heard that about you British. But let's find out, shall we?" With that, she swished into the dining room, with plenty of movement off the seam, leaving Matt busily thinking about escape strategies.

A sudden commotion refocused his attention. A tall man with a blond ponytail, a goatee and a T-shirt depicting a fleeing elk strode through the gates, followed by an entourage of blonde women and a man labouring under a large camera. It was the celebrity chef. Before Matt had a chance to say anything, he was shoved aside. Anke and Tina arrived at the door, hot and in a dead heat, closely followed by Lotta. There were plenty of *hej, hej*s, except from the dumbstruck Lotta, and some polite but serious jostling for position.

As usual, Helena made a perfectly timed entry and whisked the chef away towards the kitchen. "I'll be looking after you here today," Matt heard her say. "Leave everything to me." The others crowded close behind. Helena's victory was by no means assured.

As he looked on with some jealousy, he heard a cough. "Yes, makes you want to be a chef for a day." It was the southern drawl of Mason Hunter, the US Deputy Ambassador.

Matt had met Hunter several times and never felt quite at ease in his company. The man was friendly enough, but always gave the impression that he knew a lot more about the undercurrents of diplomatic and political life than he would ever share. He had disarmingly told Matt at their first meeting that he was in Stockholm on sufferance. As an unabashed Democrat and a career diplomat, he would normally have been sent to a more obscure post, but had somehow ended up in Stockholm, working for an Ambassador who was one of the Republican Party's more generous campaign donors.

Both Matt and Catherine were intrigued by the complicated relationship between the two Americans, which seemed to involve high levels of mistrust, coupled with an uneasy mutual dependence. The boisterous bridge and tennis-playing Ambassador, a businessman from Seattle, made no pretence about knowing much about foreign affairs and diplomatic protocol. He arrived in Stockholm promoting one 'big idea', which was centred on a new bilateral mining partnership. He was energetic in doing so, but he had to rely on Hunter to steer him through the thickets of EU life, Baltic security and Swedish politics. Hunter had his own set of contacts within Sweden and often surprised Matt both with the quality of his information, and the blunt judgements that often accompanied them. Matt suspected a nostalgia for the more exciting periods of the Cold War. Hunter treated him with a degree of condescension, which Matt found understandable, but irksome.

"So I hear that you are now an expert on submarines," said Hunter.

Matt laughed. "Hardly. I have never seen one in my life. But it's true that they are a popular subject of discussion just now."

"Well, my sources tell me that you are the person everyone wants to talk to about that subject."

"Which sources?" asked Matt, trying to conceal some nervousness.

"Ah, you know we can never reveal sources. Right? Still, I can tell you something you might find interesting. Just between ourselves. Not to be repeated."

"Of course."

"There is at least one Russian submarine in the archipelago. We are not sure what they are up to, but it's nothing good. It's very unhelpful just now. Makes everyone jumpy. That's why we are not saying anything in public. Not yet, anyhow."

"Our Defence Attaché has been talking about it quite a lot," said Matt.

"Well, those military guys may not know everything," Hunter replied coolly. "They don't always get the full picture. You understand me?"

"So why are you telling me?" Matt asked.

"This is your first posting. You want to make an impression. But it's quiet here. So if I were you, I'd put myself about a bit. Pull up some trees. Get out of Stockholm sometimes." He paused. "You like going out to the archipelago, I guess. So go out there. You might have a little adventure. Take a picnic. You Brits like picnics, don't you?" With that, Hunter patted Matt on the shoulder in a mock-avuncular way, and wandered off into the Residence, leaving Matt motionless.

Catherine appeared, looking reassuringly calm. "I think all the VIPs have arrived now, so I suggest that you go and chat up the guests. I think your team have abandoned everyone except that chef. They are like piranhas around a… well, whatever piranhas eat."

"Did I hear 'Piranha'?" said Philip, approaching from leeward. "Anything new? I have just been having a chat about it with the Russian Chargé d'Affaires. He's not giving much away, but I am sure he knows something."

"Not that sort of piranha, I'm afraid," Catherine replied. "Anyhow, always worth a chat with the Russians. Just to keep them on their toes. Right, let's return to the battle, shall we? And please encourage the guests to eat up. Otherwise, we'll all be out selling fish for the next week."

Matt began to circulate, greeting those he knew, mostly fellow diplomats, and chatting to a few he didn't. On the large balcony overlooking the Baltic, he began talking to a small group of what turned out to be editors of some of the larger Swedish newspapers. They were Catherine's contacts and were busy discussing their holiday plans. Matt was always surprised by the extraordinary length of the holidays that senior Swedes were able to take in the summer months. He understood and sympathised with the desire to make the most of the brief period of warmth, but still couldn't quite work out how they were able to take several weeks off to go to their summer houses, in addition to two or three weeks in Thailand in the depth of winter, plus time off for skiing and skating. But the Swedes didn't think it unusual and their productivity didn't seem to suffer. *Must be a lesson for the rest of us in there*, Matt often thought.

Feeling unable to compete, Matt wandered back inside. Mikhail Rogozhin, the Russian Chargé d'Affaires, came over, looking as urbane as usual. "Hello, Matt, thank you for inviting me to your very agreeable Residence. Tell me, how have you managed to hold on to it? I understand that London are anxious for you to make saving cuts." Like Hunter, Rogozhin always seemed well informed.

"I don't know," Matt confessed. "Maybe someone back home likes us."

"Or maybe they think that it's important to have a good Embassy here," said Rogozhin. "Perhaps they think interesting things will start happening."

"What sort of things?" asked Matt, taking a bite of a herring canapé, and feeling a bit like a fish on a line himself.

"You tell me. Perhaps something to do with submarines?"

"Why does everyone here want to talk to me about submarines?" Matt replied.

"Yes, that's an interesting question," said Rogozhin. "It could be because of the company you have been keeping recently. What do I know? But one thing I can tell you is that there is a submarine in the archipelago. It's not Russian, as your friend Hunter would probably have you believe. And if you want to find out the truth, go out there yourself and see." Chuckling, he left Matt, half-eaten canapé in hand.

Matt was mystified by this sudden collective desire for him to go to the archipelago. He had no objections. He liked it. But the most memorable thing he had seen so far had been a very shapely blonde losing her top while diving in.

No submarines. He went in search of his team. They were clustered around the chef, who was producing elegantly presented fish-and-chip snacks in mock ice-cream cones. Anke had persuaded him to show her his technique, which seemed to involve an unnecessary amount of close contact. The others were impatiently waiting for their turn.

Matt was about to try to tear them away when he heard some high-pitched cries coming from the balcony overlooking the sea. For a moment he thought that James and Birgitta had finally come to blows. But nothing prepared him for what he did see.

The balcony was full of young women shrieking, giggling and busily taking off their clothes. John from the Consular Department was standing in front of him, beer in hand.

"What…?" gurgled Matt.

"Quite a sight, isn't it?!" said John. "Only in Sweden! Except they are not actually Swedish. I met them in a bar last night. They are a women's rugby team from Somerset. They are here for the Stockholm Tens tournament. I just had to invite them. They are Brits after all."

"But what are they doing?"

"Well, I guess they are probably still a bit pissed. They certainly were last night. Thought they would have sobered up by now. Apparently, there's a bet going on. A Swedish guy bet them they wouldn't go skinny-dipping. I think he might lose."

Looking around, Matt saw one of the Swedish editors, camera in hand, who gave him a big wink. "Front page, tomorrow," he laughed.

There was an even louder shriek as a large brunette

dropped her thong and climbed down into the chilly water below. "Come on, you pussies!" she yelled. Her teammates followed, climbing over the balcony and adding to the pile of thongs.

"John, we have to do something," said Matt desperately. "This will be all over the press tomorrow."

"And what do you suggest I do?" John replied, not unreasonably.

"Well, you invited them; get them to come back."

"If you are worried about photos, I would keep them in the water, if I were you."

Matt looked around and saw that Catherine, together with a handful of Swedish ministers, had joined them on the balcony, attracted by the noise. "Are they British or Swedish?" asked the Environment Minister.

"British," John replied.

"Excellent!" said the Justice Minister, a youngish man who still wore a ponytail. "Skinny-dipping in the Baltic is an old Swedish tradition. I am happy to see that you follow it too."

"I couldn't stop them," Matt blurted out, feeling irrationally responsible for the mermaids now splashing about in front of them.

"Well, as the ministers say, it's a Swedish tradition," said Catherine, making a quick damage limitation assessment and deciding that her guests were amused rather than shocked. "And it is a warm day."

"Are they some sort of sports team?" asked the Deputy Finance Minister, herself a noted skier.

"Rugby team," John explained, now feeling he might even take some credit for inviting them.

"I thought rugby players were meant to be very large," said the Justice Minister, taking a very close interest in the mermaids. "But some of these girls look slim. Even petite. Surprising."

As John began to explain the requirement for different sizes in a rugby team, the girls began to swim towards the far shore of the inlet, about a hundred yards away. One of them, possibly drunker than the rest, stopped swimming and began to flail around.

"She's in trouble," said the Deputy Finance Minister. "She needs help." Everyone looked at each other.

"Matt," said Catherine, "better go to the rescue. Quickly."

Matt froze for a moment. Why him? He was wearing his best suit. He couldn't even swim that well.

"Quickly!"

"OK, OK," Matt muttered, taking off his jacket, shirt, shoes and trousers. The girl began to flail more wildly. He clumsily climbed over the balcony and, still in underpants and socks, waded in.

He had swum in the Baltic several times before and knew that after the first shock, it was quite pleasant on a hot summer day. Stifling his initial gasp, he began to swim slowly towards the girl, with the encouraging cries of the by now large crowd on the balcony behind him. It seemed interminable, but it was probably only a couple of minutes before he reached her. As he did so, she threw both arms into the air and sank completely. Matt panicked even more. He knew nothing about life-saving. There was a splash as she suddenly surfaced, right into his arms. He could smell a mixture of vodka and seawater; the former winning hands down.

"What are you doing?" the girl asked indignantly.

"I came to save you," Matt spluttered.

"I don't need saving, you idiot," she replied. "I do synchronised swimming. I'm practising. We're in the South-West England Cup next month." She slid out of his arms, pirouetted in the water, and began laughing. "Oh! That's funny," she said. "Saved by someone who can hardly swim. Still, I'm going to count it as my first pull of the trip. Excellent!" With that she spun around again and swam off powerfully towards the other girls.

Matt slowly returned to the shore. It took even longer this time. Most of the crowd had left the balcony by the time he waded ashore. There was a small round of applause and a lot of laughter. "Didn't know you had it in you," said John, between giggles.

"I have some good photos," said one of the editors. "But I don't know if the headline would be 'hero' or 'zero.'"

"Hero! Hero, of course," said an indignant Marcella, who had gathered up Matt's clothes. "He was so brave. Come on, you must get out of those wet clothes. Where can we go?" She took his hand and pulled him inside, where he was rescued by Catherine.

"Come on, Sir Galahad," she said, disentangling him from Marcella. "You can go upstairs and change. Actually, I thought you were rather brave," she added, as she led him past a row of smiling faces and up the stairs. "I hope she was grateful, that girl."

"She thought it was very funny," said Matt ruefully. "Story of my life!"

By the time Matt had dried off and changed, with the loan of one of James's shirts, most of the guests had left. National day parties tended to be brief events. Most of the Embassy staff were still there and gave Matt an ironic cheer. As he looked out to the balcony he could see the now-shivering mermaids putting on their clothes. The Swedish chef had left in a cloud of blondes, having promised tickets to future shows and, apparently, an invitation to Helena for a private cooking lesson in his summer house. The jealousy was still evident in Chancery body language.

Catherine seemed pleased by the party. The performance of the mermaids had certainly made it memorable, and although the more staid Ambassadors had been shocked, the Swedes had appreciated it. The editor had promised not to print any photos as a goodwill gesture.

"You can plan as much as you want," said Catherine, "but sometimes the unexpected can ruin or make a party. Luckily, this made it. But I don't think we will repeat it in a hurry. I guess you will be going to the bar now?"

Matt correctly interpreted this as a hint, and duly rounded up the remaining staff and headed back to the Embassy. To John's great disappointment, the mermaids decided to head into town to find new diversions, so it was a fairly small group that ended up back in the bar. Matt, who was by now the subject of a new superhero naming competition, was content just to have a couple of beers and reflect on the day. It hadn't exactly been his finest hour. There still seemed to be some seaweed in his boxers and he doubted that many of his diplomatic colleagues would quickly let him forget his swim. But at least he wouldn't be on the front page of *Aftonbladet*, and it would be a good story to tell junior colleagues back in London in a few decades' time. So perhaps it was best just to have another beer and become the only superhero to wear Union Jack boxers.

FiVE

The next week passed quietly. At a wash-up session with Catherine and Philip, the Defence Attaché, Matt passed on what Hunter and Rogozhin had told him. Philip stiffened when he heard Hunter's remarks about the military.

"It's not for me to comment on what one of you diplomats might say. But I am sure that my US military contacts are fully in the picture. And they believe there is at least one Piranha in the archipelago."

Catherine was sceptical about both sets of remarks. "They're playing games. I don't think we need to take any of this too seriously. I am not proposing to pass it back to London unless there is something more concrete to report. So keep me informed, and let's talk again in the next few days."

As Matt was about to leave, Catherine asked him to stay behind. "I don't want to alarm the staff, but I have had a long email from London about cost-cutting. A new government budget settlement is imminent and the axe will fall heavily on the FCO. They are going to take a hard look at all their properties. I hear on the grapevine that they are going to ask all Embassies to explain why they should keep their buildings. The presumption will be that we should sell them. So we need to get our arguments ready. Don't do anything for now, but we may have to act quickly."

Matt walked slowly back to his room. Scares over cost-cutting were not new, but Catherine had seemed more than usually worried about this one.

Annika was bemused rather than sceptical about the conflicting submarine claims when Matt met her a couple of days later. He realised that he had begun to tell her everything, including things he wouldn't normally share outside the Embassy, but he told himself that none of it was actually classified information. And he trusted her. They met in the garden of a small café on one of Stockholm's smaller islands. It was a delightful spot which reminded Matt of a classic English country garden. Once a week a jazz band played summer standards and Matt often came to sit among the roses, listen to the music and eat smorgasbord. The Swedes wore floppy sun hats, some sat in deckchairs, and the scene always reminded Annika of *Midsomer Murders*, one of the favourite British imports.

"So, who is telling the truth, if anyone?" she asked.

Matt had to confess he didn't know. "I don't really believe any of them. If it wasn't for Lars Eriksson and his SÄPO friends I wouldn't take any of it seriously. But I still don't understand why everyone wants to involve me?"

"Maybe they think you know all about fast-moving, dangerous objects in the Baltic," said Annika, giggling.

"Oh! So you heard about my heroic swim. Who told you about that?"

"Word gets around," she said. "Stockholm is a small city, remember. I'm just disappointed that I haven't been able to find any photos. But I will! And who is this English rose that you tried to rescue? Was she pretty?"

"Pretty drunk. And more like an eel than a rose. If eels drink vodka."

"What a shame for you," said Annika, with what to Matt seemed a disappointing lack of jealousy. "But let me know next time you want to save someone. I'm sure some of my colleagues would volunteer on a hot day. The ones that have time on their hands for a very slow rescue. Just joking," she added as she saw Matt's crestfallen expression. "I am really rather proud of you. More wine?"

There was a noticeable increase in excitement during the next few days as Midsummer Day approached. Despite being Protestant, the Swedes had still preserved their major pagan festival. Midsummer Day remained one of the highlights of the year; *the* highlight for many Swedes. During the centuries of strict Puritanism, it had been one of the few times when they could enjoy themselves. Although religious restraint was now a distant memory, they still celebrated with abandon. There were plenty of parties and the consumption of spectacular quantities of schnapps and herring. It was also a family event and many Swedes went out to the countryside to spend time with their relatives.

To Matt's regret, Annika was going to a small town in the west of the country to see her parents. He felt at a loose end, especially since almost all the other Embassy staff were also busy with friends and family. So it was a relief, as well as a surprise, when he received an invitation from Lars Eriksson to join him on his boat for a Midsummer trip to the archipelago.

"I go every year and invite some friends to join me. I have a cottage there. We can all stay the night and celebrate Midsummer in the traditional way. I thought maybe, as a foreigner, you might not have had a chance to do this."

Matt accepted with pleasure. He had liked the laconic journalist and guessed that he would have some good stories to share once the schnapps started flowing.

Lars's boat was moored at a jetty on Strandvägen, a very exclusive spot as it was the home of the Royal Swedish Motor Boat Club. Matt had only a short walk to get there, and wondered how Lars had managed to get a berth in such a place. He walked along the wooden jetty, down a line of elegant speedboats and spotless cruising boats. In the distance he recognised Lars, dressed in a faded shirt and shorts and with a pipe between his lips. Lars gave him a wave and continued uncoiling a rope. His boat was like him, Matt thought: no longer young, a bit scruffy, but solid-looking. There were two other men of similar vintage on board, who gave Matt a nod as he arrived. Lars introduced them as Bo and Sven: one also a former journalist, the other a former teacher.

"So, you are the submarine guy," said Bo.

Lars gave Matt a grin. "Sorry, they wanted to know how we met. So I told them. At least some of it. Don't worry. They are discreet."

As he spoke, there was a sudden cry. "My favourite diplomat!" It was Marcella, swaying down the jetty, followed by two dark-haired women. "This is amazing! How come you keep following me around? That can give a girl ideas, you know. Is this your boat?"

Matt resignedly introduced her to Lars. "Lars is kindly taking me out for Midsummer," he explained.

"Oh, Lars," she said, "maybe you could help us. We are all from the Embassy of Panama. We have been trying to find a boat to take us out to the archipelago. Someone told us we could hire one here, but we can't find anything." She fluttered her eyelids, and her two colleagues smiled warmly.

"Well," said Lars, evidently impressed, "we are just a group of old bachelors, but you would be welcome to join us."

"That would be lovely," said Marcella, stepping aboard, overbalancing, and almost taking Lars into the water. Her colleagues followed with trepidation. Marcella introduced them as Luisa and Maria, both new to Sweden.

Matt sighed, but said nothing. It was clearly his destiny to be haunted by Marcella. *Fine*, he thought. *If there are some Russians out there with evil intent, they can have her. Serve them right!*

Lars steered the boat out into the canal that led into the archipelago. They passed the Ambassador's Residence and Marcella gave Matt a wink. "I know I shall be safe if we have an accident," she said. "There is at least one hero here amongst us."

This naturally intrigued Bo and Sven, and so Matt reluctantly had to tell them the story of his rescue swim, which they found very amusing.

"But what happens if we fall in the water?" asked Bo. "I think you only save women, yes?"

"Sorry," said Marcella. "Latinas first, Swedes second."

Bo and Sven both agreed this merited a toast, and so the evening's drinking began. Lars drove out of the canal and into the Baltic proper. The first of several thousand islands came into sight. Many had at least one house on them, often several, and often very imposing. The women began to play a game of deciding which they would want to live in. There were boats everywhere, mostly moored, but some scooting off in different directions around them.

Lars explained that they were aiming for Utö, one of the outlying islands in the southern part of the archipelago. Their route would take them through another canal, past the summer resort town of Saltsjöbaden, and then weave through a maze of islands. As they neared Saltsjöbaden, they passed a wooden hut perched on a small raft. Naked men were sunbathing on it. Swedish music was playing. The three Panamanians rushed to get their cameras, and the male sirens happily posed for them, beckoning the women to join them. Lars had to drive the boat around the raft four times before he was allowed to continue.

"Wow!" said an excited Luisa. "That is better than anything I have seen on our canal."

"It's a floating sauna," Sven explained. "Very popular at Midsummer. Do you want to join them?"

Luisa was clearly tempted, but Marcella asserted her authority. "While you are here, you are representing Panama. Not the Horny Latinas Club."

The rest of journey took about three hours. The beauty of the scenery increased with the first slight hints of twilight. Everyone fell silent. At this time of year, there was very little real darkness, about two hours at most. On some of the larger islands Matt could see the distinctive outline of the Midsummer poles, a bit like British maypoles, but with extra flourishes. People splashed about in the shallower bays. The small seaside restaurants were full. It wouldn't be a good day to be a teetotaller. Or a herring.

As they neared Utö, Lars took Matt on one side. "There is another reason I brought you here. The light in the archipelago can play tricks. It might help you understand how people can imagine they have seen a submarine. You might even find your Loch Ness monster here, on holiday in Sweden."

He took the boat past the small cluster of red-painted buildings that was Utö's village, and around the far side of the island. He drove further out and finally reached a very small island on the edge of the gently lapping sea. He pulled alongside a small jetty next to a one-storey wooden house.

"Welcome to my summer home," said Lars, as he helped Maria onto the jetty. "It's not your English country house, Matt, but the fish will taste better here."

Matt was the last to disembark, and Lars tossed him a rope. "Tie up her, please." Matt stared at the rope, the boat and the jetty and said a quick, silent prayer. He had always had a difficult relationship with knots. *But how hard can it be?* he thought, suddenly full of Swedish courage.

When he had finished, he followed the others to the house. Inside, there were only two rooms, one of which was furnished with some mattresses and a bunk bed. The women looked at each other.

"Don't worry, ladies," said Bo. "We are not going to waste Midsummer by sleeping. We will be outside, with the schnapps."

"You can stay here and protect us, Matt," said Marcella.

Yes, but who is going to protect me? thought Matt.

The men had brought some fish and prawns with them and quickly lit a barbecue outside the house. There was, of course, herring in various dips, cold meats, and crispbread. The women had brought chicken and salad. Matt contributed the meatballs and wine. The party was soon underway. The Swedes tried to teach the women some traditional drinking songs. They responded by demonstrating some salsa-dancing steps. It was hard to say who performed worse. Toasts were made and everyone was rapidly getting into the compulsory state of Midsummer drunkenness.

Matt had just finished downing yet another schnapps when he was struck by a sudden feeling of anxiety about the boat. Had he tied it up properly? He left the others and walked unsteadily back past the house to the jetty. In the deepening twilight the sea was still and silent. He could hear the raucous sounds of a Swedish toast, he could see the dim shape of the jetty, but he couldn't see the boat.

He cursed quietly, but thoroughly. Where was it? He peered anxiously into the half-light, wondering already what he was going to say to Lars. Then, outside the small cove, he saw a shape resting against a rock. It had to be the boat. He looked around, and quickly decided he could remedy the situation himself without the others ever knowing about it. It wasn't cold. He stripped and waded into the water. He could hear a mangled version of *Guantanamera* behind him as he slowly swam towards the shape. As he got closer, he could see it was the boat, apparently undamaged, with a rope drifting in the sea. But as Matt reached out for it, his wake caused the boat to move away from the rock into the sea. *Bugger!* He swam after it, but every time he got close, it seemed to have a sudden burst of aquatic energy.

By now, he had swum out into the sea, out of sight of the house. As he continued his frustrating pursuit, he suddenly saw a large, dark object passing the cove. He rubbed his eyes with one hand, and looked again. Whatever it was had disappeared. But it had looked remarkably like a submarine. *Can't be*, he thought. *It must be the schnapps. Or Nessie.* He giggled to himself. He made some further efforts to reach the boat, which continued drifting out to sea. Just as he finally grabbed the trailing rope he heard a splashing noise behind him. A hand grabbed him around the neck and powerful arms pulled him backwards out of the water. Then everything went as black as a Swedish winter night.

Matt woke from a confused dream of having a bath in his childhood home to find himself with a throbbing head and an unfamiliar towel wrapped around him. He was in a tiny but opulently furnished room, decorated with paintings of cavorting mermaids, and was lying on a sort of gold divan. It was like a cross between the closet of a Premiership footballer and a French bordello. Whilst this was far from the perfect way to wake up, Matt was relieved that he wasn't back in that bath. He really didn't fancy taking his GCSEs again. He was alone, and could hear only the dull throb of some sort of machinery. But perhaps that was his head?

He got up cautiously and tried the gilded handle to the door, but it was locked. He sat there for a few minutes trying to work out what might have happened. Had he been saved by the Swedish coastguard? But why was he locked in what looked like a boudoir, and who or what had hit him on the head?

The door opened and a man wearing a gold-and-crimson smoking jacket stepped in, ducking his head under the metal lintel. "Have to be careful," he said. "I am always hitting my head here. My next boat will be better designed. Anyhow, let me welcome you aboard. I will introduce myself in a moment, but perhaps you might tell me who you are first, and what you were doing in the sea."

The man was speaking English with an almost perfect accent, but somehow didn't seem Swedish. So probably not the coastguard, Matt thought. But he didn't look threatening, just curious. Some impulse prompted Matt to be straightforward, whoever his host – or was it captor? – might be.

"My name is Matt Simmonds, and I work for the British Embassy in Stockholm. So who are you, and how did I come to be here?"

The man laughed gently. "A British diplomat. How funny. Of all the people to pick up in the archipelago." He thought for a moment. "That complicates things. I am not sure now what to do with you. Actually, you are lucky that we came across you today. Oleg isn't here."

Matt had no idea what he was talking about, but decided to wait for an explanation. The man mumbled something to himself, and walked over to a cabinet decorated with yet more cavorting mermaids in gold leaf. Matt was briefly and painfully reminded of the Queen's birthday party.

"Would you like a vodka? You look as though you might need one. I certainly do." The man handed Matt a full glass, made a quick toast to "beautiful mermaids, wherever they may come from" and swallowed his vodka in one well-practised motion. Matt had the impression that it was the latest of many.

He gave Matt a long stare. "How did you come to be floating out here on Midsummer Day? What were you doing when my men rescued you?"

"I don't recall anyone rescuing me," said Matt, with some irritation. "My boat was drifting out to sea and I was trying to stop it. And then I think something, or someone, hit me on the head. So perhaps you could tell me what happened?"

"I didn't see anything, of course; I was in here. But my men tell me they found you floating in the water and they saved you. So perhaps you might even thank us."

Matt hesitated. He remembered that hand around his neck, but decided that perhaps it wasn't the right time or place to press the point. "Well, if your men did save me, then of course I am grateful."

"Mmm. Better," said the man. He walked over to the cabinet and poured both of them another vodka. "According to Russian tradition, I should now make a toast to friendship between the nations. And I do actually believe in such friendship, unlike Oleg, to name but one. So because of that, and because I am extremely bored, I have decided I'm going to be open with you. First you have to promise as an honourable Englishman not to tell anyone else what I am going to tell you. I studied for three years at Marlborough. I know you Englishmen always keep your promises, if you are honourable ones. Are you an honourable one?"

Matt hesitated. Curiosity, fear and a strong desire to get off the boat overcame any reservations. "Yes," he said.

"Good. That makes everything easier. Oleg would say that I am being naive and foolish, but I think we have to trust each other sometimes. And who knows? One day, maybe we might find we can help each other."

"So who are you and what sort of boat is this?" Matt asked.

"My name is Alexander Osipov and this is not a boat. It's a submarine. Although my crew always call it a boat. It's very confusing. But don't worry, I didn't know that either until quite recently. And I am not Swedish, of course; I am Russian. Maybe you have heard of me?"

Matt shook his head, gingerly.

"Disappointing. But I suppose I haven't bought any English football clubs. Not yet, anyway, although I am told that Sunderland would be extremely cheap now. I am what you would probably call an oligarch. Not one of the very richest ones. But I am catching up."

He took a turn around the room. "We are a small group of men, and there is always competition between us. First it was mansions in Russia, then mansions abroad, then football clubs and yachts, then mega yachts. Now it's submarines."

Matt widened his eyes.

"Designer submarines. Stupid, I know, but once my friend Arkady got one, we all had to. My wife insisted. This one is a Piranha. Customised, of course. My wife's cousin has developed a niche market as an interior submarine decorator. That's why I have to live in this," he said, waving his arm around the room. "I had no choice. If you met my wife, you would understand that. But it does have its benefits. It's very discreet. Good for the more delicate business meetings. And my wife can't easily find me if I run on silent. These boats are kind of invisible.

"But you know, everything has a price for us. You are a diplomat, so you will realise already that we have to do favours sometimes for our Master in Moscow. It's really not possible to refuse. When he heard that I had bought my little boat, he asked me to come here. I wanted to go to somewhere tropical, but no; it had to be the Swedish archipelago! To drive around, search for the other submarines here, and be ready for action if needed. Although the only action I am interested in just now is having another vodka." He turned and did just that, offering another glass to Matt as well.

"There are others?"

"Yes, there are at least two others. One of them is American. The other is a bit more mysterious. I have been told to keep my boat off the radar, at least so far. The others are not as good at that as we are. Anyhow, I don't ask too many questions. I do what Oleg tells me to do."

"Who is Oleg?" asked Matt.

"He is my 'political adviser'. He reports to Moscow, tells me what to do, and keeps an eye on me. Just like the old days. That's why you are lucky he is not here. My men had told me that this little bay would be safe, and I wanted to have a swim. But then they saw you in the water and knew that you had seen us. So they brought you here. I apologise for that, by the way. They have standing instructions from Oleg, who is in Stockholm at a meeting in our Embassy."

"So what are you going to do with me?" asked Matt, with a suddenly dry mouth.

"Oleg would not want to let you go. And since I don't like Oleg, I am going to return you to where we found you. He doesn't understand about honour, as we do. And this is my toy, not his. So I will ask you again to forget about what you have seen. And maybe I will drink a cocktail with you at an Embassy reception sometime."

"But I still don't really understand what you are doing here," said Matt.

"I believe it's something to do with keeping the other side guessing. And maybe my Master wants to find out whether the Piranha is truly invisible. What do you know? Do the British think there is a Russian submarine out here?"

Matt didn't know quite how to reply, but Osipov saved him the trouble. "Oleg tells me that you, the Swedes and the Americans all think that there is. We know, of course, that the one they are thinking about is not one of ours. We believe, but can't prove, that the Latvians have hired an old submarine from the Ukrainians. When we liberated the Crimea, one Ukrainian submarine went missing and we haven't been able to reclaim it yet. Those Ukrainians never did know how to maintain their submarines properly, so if the Latvians do have it, it is probably all they can do to keep it from sinking to the bottom of the Baltic. Oleg is not quite sure what they are up to, but keeps telling me that it won't be helpful to us. So he has been looking for it in my Piranha, instead of letting me go to these pleasant little islands around here and meet Swedish girls.

"I would invite you to stay longer and give you a little tour, but we have to keep moving. So my men will take you back to your little boat. It was actually an unexpected pleasure to have a visitor, even an uninvited one. Goodbye, old chap." With that, he bowed slightly and left, leaving Matt speechless.

A few minutes later a couple of burly men escorted him out of the room, along a very low-ceilinged metal corridor. He managed to hit his head twice, and so was once again a bit dazed as he was unceremoniously pushed through a hatch and dropped into the Baltic. *They could have left me the towel*, he thought. As he surfaced, he could see Lars's boat bobbing gently nearby. He swam painfully towards it and pulled himself very inelegantly aboard. Lars had left the key in the ignition, but Matt was filled with a strong desire not to draw any attention to his nocturnal misadventures. He found a couple of oars and laboriously rowed the boat back to the jetty. There he tied it with as many knots as he could and put on his clothes. The sun was already rising and he was shivering as he made his way back to the summer house.

The men were still sitting outside with an impressive pile of bottles beside them. They greeted him with slurred cries. The women had gone to bed. "No stamina, these Latinas," Bo mumbled. Matt decided to follow them. Inside, he could see two of the women asleep in the bunk beds and one gently snoring on a mattress. He quietly lay down on the other mattress and closed his eyes.

Some hours later, Matt woke from another dream. This was a very pleasant one involving Annika. And it seemed to be continuing. There was a warm, perfumed body lying next to him. Still dozy, he put his arms around it. "*Hej*, sweetheart," he murmured. There was a slight grunt in response. *How did Annika get here?* he thought as his still-sore head began to flicker into life.

A disturbing thought jolted him fully awake. He opened his eyes and took a quick look. Dark, not blonde. Latin, not Swedish. *Oh God!* he thought. *How do I get out of this one?* He looked again. At least they were both partly clothed. Marcella seemed to be asleep. Very slowly, he began to withdraw his arm. She rolled even closer. He gently pushed her away. A sort of somnambulistic wrestling match began, which ended with Matt freeing himself with a movement that almost dislocated his collarbone. He got to his feet. The two other women were also still asleep. Outside, the three Swedes were slumbering in almost the same positions in which he had left them. Sven even had a glass of schnapps clutched firmly in one hand.

Matt wandered down to the waterside. To his great relief, the boat was still there. The sea was still calm and the only sign of life was a seabird in the distance. There was no sign of a submarine, and the mere idea of one appearing seemed fantastical. He tried to replay the events of last night, but his mind didn't want to cooperate. After all that schnapps, he felt he couldn't be entirely sure what had happened. But he did have a bump on his head, and the boat seemed to be moored with an excessive amount of knots. So something must have happened. He sat lethargically for a while, looking at the peaceful scene.

When he got back to the house, the others had woken and were sitting bleary-eyed outside. Lars was brewing some coffee and had opened a bag of pastries. "*Hej, hej*," he said. "Did you go for a morning swim? The water is beautiful here."

"I know," Matt replied.

Marcella gave him a coquettish smile. "Guess who I found sleeping next to me when I woke up in the night. In Panama that means marriage, or a shotgun."

I'll take the shotgun, thought Matt, as he smiled manfully. "It's very dark in that house. I must have got lost."

"You can't fool me, Matt. You British. So bashful!"

Matt distracted her by asking Lars when they would return to Stockholm. The answer was after breakfast, so it wasn't long before they were back in the boat. The Swedes had a hearty laugh about Matt's knots. The fresh breeze cleared his head, and he began to wonder what, if anything, he could say to Catherine and Philip about last night. He remembered making a promise to Osipov to say nothing, but it wasn't that which was his biggest concern, but whether his sanity might be called into question. The events just seemed too fantastic. After some wrestling with his judgement, he finally decided to say nothing, either to them or to Lars. But he would tell Annika. He felt that she might believe him.

When they got back to Stockholm, the others decided to carry on with the party. Matt made his excuses and left. He had a lot to think about.

SIX

Back in his apartment, Matt took some aspirin and reflected on the events of the last few weeks. None of them matched his initial ideas about diplomatic life.

Stockholm had not been Matt's first taste of foreign travel as a diplomat. His first had not been an ideal debut. The dream of every new entrant was to go on a work trip abroad. In the sunlit days of old, desk officers were often sent to the country they covered on a familiarisation visit. Austerity had put an end to such pleasures, so most junior FCO staff were firmly grounded in London. Matt's first job had been in the Latin America and Caribbean Department. That department was viewed as something of a backwater, but he didn't mind. It seemed to him to be excitingly exotic. At the end of his first year, he still had a thrill from even entering the FCO building. Then one day, Janet, his immediate boss, summoned him to her office.

"We have a problem that I need you to help me with. You probably know that the Parliamentary Cultural Heritage Committee are going to Cuba next week and the Cuba desk officer was due to go with them. But she has a domestic crisis and can't go. Everyone else is tied up, so you are the only person we can spare."

This was very exciting news.

"I am really sorry to dump this on you. I know it will be bad news." She went on to explain that the committee had been established a few years ago with the ostensible aim of promoting UK expertise in preserving cultural heritage. "Of course, it's really a jolly for MPs who like free travel. This committee has a particularly bad reputation. Some of the MPs are OK, but others can be very difficult to deal with."

Matt now remembered some scathing articles in the press.

"Normally, we would leave it to the Embassy in Havana to deal with this visit, but because of some problem last year with duty-free on their flight out to Bali, the committee are insisting that someone from the FCO accompanies them throughout. Basically, you have to be a sort of travel agent and nursemaid. Usually their parliamentary clerk would do that, but apparently he is a waste of space. So it will be down to you. Keep calm, try to keep them happy, and don't make any promises that involve FCO money. Good luck."

Matt's initial high spirits at the prospect of a week travelling around Cuba began to sink when he saw the sympathetic looks his colleagues were giving him. The advice that everyone offered about visits by parliamentary committees was to book them into good hotels. That seemed to be more important than anything else, including their programme. But it was out of Matt's control, so he just had to hope that the Havana Embassy had done a good job. He and Janet met the committee members once before travelling for an initial briefing session. They were a small group: three Conservative, two Labour, two SNP and a solitary Liberal Democrat.

Their clerk, Horace Sockett, a short man with a self-important air, met Matt and Janet at the House of Commons and took them to a small meeting room. He was accompanied by an attractive, but very bored-looking young woman, whom he introduced as Nicola Roberts.

"Nicola is actually a political adviser, but she has joined us temporarily as part of a scheme to improve understanding in ministerial offices of how Parliament works." Sockett looked at her admiringly. "I am delighted to say that she will join us in Cuba. I am sure she will add something special to our visit."

Sockett was much less impressed by Matt and his lack of experience. "I will be relying on you throughout, so I hope you are a quick learner. The Members can be a bit difficult. I will be busy with keeping the record, and I won't have time to do much else. You had better hope that your colleagues in Havana have lined up some good hotels for them."

The MPs were all men and most had been in Parliament for some years. They gave Matt and Janet a mixed reception. Some were friendly, others indifferent. The SNP MPs seemed disappointed that neither Matt nor Janet was Scottish, although Matt partially retrieved this by referring to his cousins in Dundee, a distant branch of his family whom he had never met. The chairman was George Bowditch, a veteran and patrician Conservative. He was unhappy that a senior FCO official had not come to the briefing, and equally unhappy that Matt was so junior. He had a series of detailed questions about the draft itinerary, which Matt guessed had been put together by Sockett.

"I want you to understand how important this visit is," Bowditch said. "It's not only about cultural heritage, although the Cubans are doing are a lot of restoration and there should be some opportunities to showcase UK expertise. I spoke to the Prime Minister in the lobby the other day and he told me he wants us to give our bilateral relations a boost. He said that our visit will be just the sort of thing the Cubans want. It will be a big event there. So I don't want any cock-ups. The FCO have disappointed us a few times already. I don't want to report another failure to the PM. I am expecting perfection this time."

The other MPs didn't seem quite as convinced as their chairman about the importance of their visit, but nodded at his mention of previous cock-ups.

As Matt and Janet were leaving with this threat still echoing in their ears, Arwel Williams, an MP from the Welsh Valleys, intercepted them. "Cultural heritage can mean many things," he said. "We have a carnival in my constituency every year, so I would like to go to one of the top nightclubs in Havana. The ones with the girls in feathers. It could give me some ideas."

I bet it could, thought Matt.

"And I know that the SNP MPs want to visit one of the older rum distilleries – maybe share some ideas on how to market alcohol."

"Right," said Janet, as they finally left, "you'd better tell Havana to lay on girls and rum. Welcome to the diplomatic world." Matt wasn't entirely sure she was joking.

A few days later, he lay on his bed under an erratically revolving fan in the Grand Hotel Tropicana in Havana. He was exhausted, but sleep was a stranger as he thought about his Cuban experience. He had met the MPs at Heathrow. The trip had got off to a difficult start. The parliamentary clerk, Sockett, had been taken ill the previous night, which meant that Nicola Roberts had to take on his role. Visibly irritated, she took Matt to one side near the check-in desk.

"I am going on this trip to see for myself what a mess socialism can make of a country, and I am not going to be sidetracked by playing nanny to this bunch of deadbeat MPs. So basically, you and the Embassy are going to have to do that." She stalked away.

After a delayed flight, they finally arrived in a hot and dimly lit Havana as night was rapidly falling. As he looked out of the windows of the Embassy minibus at the mysterious and enticing world of an unknown city at dusk, the tensions of the trip were temporarily forgotten. They returned with a vengeance when the convoy arrived at their hotel. They had been met at the airport by the Deputy Ambassador, a jittery woman called Jessica, accompanied by a man about Matt's age. Jessica gave them a nervous welcome and told them they would be staying in the Grand Hotel Tropicana, one of the most historic buildings in Havana. "It's not the most modern hotel, but it reeks of cultural heritage. So we thought you would like it."

Matt heard Arwel Williams give a low groan.

"And this is our Second Secretary, Simon Rawston-Smith, who will be accompanying you throughout." Matt and Simon, who was wearing a very tropical suit, exchanged sympathetic glances. "If you have any problems, turn to him."

The Grand Hotel Tropicana did indeed reek of something, although Matt could never find the source. It also had a very grand reception area, in Spanish colonial style, which looked newly refurbished. The same, unfortunately, could not be said about the rooms, which, although also grand, looked as though they had been untouched by hand of either painter or plumber since their construction. Matt wasn't sure if it was the heat, or the indignation that turned the committee members quite so pink. Very reluctantly, Nicola had to sort out an unseemly scramble for the better rooms. "I don't know what the Embassy were thinking of," she hissed to Jessica, "putting us in here. London had warned you about hotels. You're going to have find a better hotel for tomorrow night, or the Ambassador will be out of a job."

The MPs were still ready for head-to-head conflict when they met the Ambassador and the other senior staff at the Embassy the next morning. They might as well have been issued with burning torches and pitchforks. Their mood had not been improved by a grudgingly served breakfast of soggy fruit and stale bread in the faded elegance of a huge dining room.

Matt had been told back in London that the Ambassador, Henry Mott, had a reputation for being clever, but pedantic and irascible. His talent for concise analysis had impressed his past bosses, which explained his rise, but his inability to suffer lesser intellects antagonised everyone else. His opening welcome was brutally cut short by Bowditch, who told him in cutting tones that the Grand Tropicana might be large and in the tropics, but it was the worst hotel the committee had stayed in during their many travels. "Worse even than the Star Dome Yurt in Tajikistan. And that had open-air bathrooms."

The other MPs grimaced and nodded.

"Just because we are interested in cultural heritage does not mean that we want to live in it. I demand that you move us to an acceptable hotel today."

His words only seemed to arouse the fighting spirits of the Motts, who had a long history of bloodshed in augmentation of the realm. Henry Mott replied that the Embassy had diligently observed the committee's own strict budgetary rules in finding accommodation. Owing to the artificial exchange rate that applied to foreign visitors to Cuba, the Grand Tropicana was one of the few hotels that fell within those rules. "If you are unhappy there," he added, "we can move you to another hotel. But it will probably be worse. I am afraid, gentlemen, that you cannot escape cultural heritage in Cuba, for better or for worse. In the absence of a functioning economy, it is all they have."

After further red-faced expostulations from the MPs, and a final threat by Bowditch to call the Foreign Secretary that morning, there was a temporary halt to hostilities as they discussed the programme. This had changed almost completely while the MPs were in the air; a Cuban speciality. Matt was by now relieved that they were no longer going on any long trips, due to transport difficulties on the Cuban side, and would mainly stay around Havana. The thought of being stuck with the committee members in some remote town was not an appealing one. During this lull in the MPs' revolt, Mott gave a clear and insightful analysis of Cuban politics and their economy, which met with some reluctant appreciation from his audience.

While he was doing so, the Embassy management officer, who looked as though he was a veteran of many MPs' visits, called Nicola and Matt to one side. "There is a way around this," he said. "You can't overspend your budget, but we have some spare in our annual entertainment budget. If we don't spend it soon, we will have a reduced allocation for next year. So I will use that to subsidise you moving to a better hotel. There is one that the Italians always use. Expensive, but it must be good. It's not strictly within the rules, but I know how to do creative accounting. You can tell your lot that you have found a solution, and I will tell the Ambassador the same. We'll keep quiet about the details and everyone will be happy." He turned to Matt. "You will have to stay where you are. We don't spend money on junior desk officers."

The new hotel was characterless, but clean and functional. The move helped to subdue the revolt, as did the protocol-laden meetings and receptions offered by the Cubans during the visit. Bowditch lapped them up, and although some of the other MPs, notably Williams, were a little more cynical, it was clear that they were enjoying the attention. Given everything that divided the two governments, cultural heritage was harmless enough for both sides mutually to enthuse about. The Cuban press gave the visit decent coverage. There were flowery speeches and ambitious proposals for future cooperation. The MPs had little time for any individual exploration, but Williams had reminded Matt several times about visiting a cabaret.

"I know a place," said Rawston-Smith, who seemed to have an extensive knowledge of the Havana nightlife, despite, or perhaps because of, an Embassy ban on intimate relationships with the locals. "It's a little bit risqué, but if your MPs want to see something a little different, they might like it."

Matt mentioned this to Williams, and he and the Liberal MP decided to give the place a try on the third evening of the visit, after yet another banquet.

Rawston-Smith, wearing a shirt festooned with palm trees, and matching socks, picked them up in the Embassy minibus and took them first to a couple of the better-known tourist bars. There weren't many Cuban customers to be seen, but the bars still retained that special atmosphere generated by places whose historic resonance had yet to be ruined by extensive restoration. The two MPs began to mellow after a few rums and started to exchange political gossip. Rawston-Smith chatted to Matt about diplomatic life in Havana. It was one of the few places where Cold War rules still largely applied. This gave a posting there an archaic appeal, although it also had its frustrations.

British diplomats were followed everywhere by the Cuban secret police, their houses were bugged and searched, and sometimes unwelcome calling cards were left. Although the advent of large-scale tourism had increased the number and quality of restaurants, there was little food in the shops and the diplomatic supermarket had a limited selection of goods. "It is a fascinating place," said Rawston-Smith, "and there is plenty to do. You get used to being followed around, and then it becomes a game. It's like being in a spy novel sometimes. The thing that really gets me is that it's difficult to get to know the Cubans, especially the women. They can be gorgeous. But we can only look, we are not allowed to touch. It's like being a small boy in a sweet shop, with no pocket money. And most of the Cubans are nervous about talking to us. They know we are being watched, which means they will be too. Some will be friendly, but we never know if they are being brave, or are working for the government."

After the bars, Rawston-Smith took them to a cabaret. "It's not one of the big, famous ones," he explained, "but it does have a local ambiance. It's mainly music, but there is a short show. Girls with lots of feathers, if you like that."

"We don't have many girls with feathers in the Valleys," said Williams. "The birds aren't large enough. Although, come to think about it, maybe with feathers, the smaller the better."

The Liberal MP, a man no stranger to the gossip columns of his local press, could only agree.

The cabaret was called Cuba y la Noche, and consisted of quite a small room, with a stage and bar. It was about half full, mainly of locals rather than tourists. The party were soon seated at a table, with Cuba libres before them, provided by a scantily clad waitress. A band was playing salsa and a few couples gyrated expertly around them. "All we need is a pint or two of Brains SA and we could be in Pontypool," joked Williams.

"I have been here quite a few times," said Rawston-Smith, to no one's surprise, "and I know the manager. He's OK, but a bit of a chancer. Unpredictable. So if he comes to speak to us, don't say too much about who you are."

After several more rums, a troupe of dancers, wearing the promised feathers and sequins and not much else, took to the stage and began an energetic performance that increased the temperature both inside the room and around their table. "Any chance of a chat with any of them?" Williams asked. Rawston-Smith was too engrossed in the spectacle to reply.

Just as the girls were leaving the stage, a suave middle-aged man carrying a bottle of rum came across to their table. He greeted Rawston-Smith, introduced himself as the manager, helped himself to a seat and poured rum into their empty glasses. His English was serviceable, and within a few minutes he was chatting easily to the MPs. Matt gathered over the music that they were already telling him about their visit. The conversation then moved on and the man beckoned to a couple of the dancers who had re-emerged from a back room. They also joined the by now crowded table. "Now this is what I call cultural heritage," Matt heard Williams say. "Living heritage. Heritage you can touch." Rawston-Smith had to act as interpreter between the girls and the MPs, so Matt was left with the rum for company.

He was beginning to feel a bit light-headed as the dancing couples swirled around them. Suddenly, as one of them finished a dance, the woman, a bit older than Matt, came up to him, took his hand and pulled him, with a big smile, onto the floor. Unsure, he looked at Rawston-Smith, who caught his eye, grinned and nodded. Matt had never danced salsa before, and wasn't sure whether he was now, but it didn't seem to matter as the woman expertly guided him through a few steps. He somehow managed to avoid trampling on her feet more than two or three times, and when the music stopped, he was immediately grabbed by another. He began to realise that they had noticed he was being ignored by his companions and were just being friendly. Everyone around him was smiling at him, but in a supportive sort of way.

While he was still stuttering his stuff on the floor, there was a commotion on the stage. The dance troupe were in action again. The two dancers that had been sitting at their table got up, and with encouragement from the manager, grabbed the hands of the two MPs and led them in wobbly fashion to the stage. The two men, red-faced and grinning, stood in the centre of the stage as the girls flowed around them. As the music reached a crescendo, the girls moved to the side of the stage and struck dramatic poses, accompanied by serious expressions and arms pointing to the heavens. The nearest girls were encouraging the MPs to follow suit, and they did.

As they posed, a large banner was unveiled behind them. It read, *Viva La Revolucion. Muerte a los Americanos*. Cameras flashed and the girls flourished their arms in revolutionary pantomime. The MPs couldn't see what was displayed behind them, but with surprising speed, Rawston-Smith reached the stage, spoke urgently to them, separated them from the girls and led them out of the room. Matt gave a quick farewell to his dancing companion and followed them.

Back in the minibus, Rawston-Smith swore loudly. "It was a set-up. I don't know what that manager was playing at, but those photos could be all over the front pages tomorrow. It will depend on the Cuban government, since they control the press. Maybe something political has happened."

The MPs were by then tired and emotional, and were more annoyed that they had been taken away from the cabaret than about any photos. By the time they reached their hotel they were ready to sleep. "I'll have to wake the Ambassador," said Rawston-Smith grimly. "He hates being woken up. But he will hate what I'm going to tell him even more. This is going to be very bad for me."

The next morning, Matt took his hangover into the Embassy briefing room, where Mott was already in agitated conversation with Bowditch. There was no sign of Rawston-Smith. Williams and his Liberal colleague were looking serious, but otherwise unaffected by their Cuban rum excesses. They all sat as Mott unfolded a copy of *Granma*, the main national daily. The front cover was dominated by a large photo of the two MPs against a background of the banner. The headline read, *Los amigos Britannicos juntos contra el imperialismo Americano*. Mott translated. "It reads, *Our British friends support us against the American imperialists*. That banner behind you said, *Death to the Americans*." He added that there had been a big diplomatic row between the US and Cuba at the UN the previous evening. "The Cubans are portraying it today as US bullying. Our UN Ambassador had no instructions, so said nothing in the debate. I guess the Cubans are trying to embarrass either us or the US with this headline. They acted very quickly. Quicker than us this time, I'm afraid. They obviously decided that a public conflict with the US would suit them more just now than exchanges on cultural heritage."

The next two hours were filled by a mix of red-faced anger and consternation as the MPs swung between rage at the Cuban government, and blame aimed at the Embassy for not preventing the incident. Mott had little choice but to front up to the cannonade. Eventually, as tempers cooled, a plan emerged. The MPs would cut short their visit and return to the UK. The Embassy would issue a statement of damage limitation. Mott would send a full report to the Foreign Secretary, as would Bowditch.

Matt watched all this with growing anxiety as he wondered what reception he might receive back in London. He didn't think that an explanation that he was dancing salsa when the photos were taken would sound very impressive. The Embassy management officer had already told him during a coffee break that Rawston-Smith's days in Havana were coming to a quick end. He was being sent back to London. "Probably to Finance and Resources, the poor devil. A three-year sentence without the option."

The committee spent the afternoon in the Embassy drafting various letters of complaint. Matt thought he had better write his own account. The MPs largely ignored him, although Williams was surprisingly sanguine. "This Labour Party leadership won't like it. But in our party what goes around, comes around. Maybe in a few years' time, that headline will be a godsend to me. And the boys at the miners' clubs will like these." He showed Matt some photos taken on his mobile phone with the two dancers draped over him at their table. "Good trip. Well done!" As he later lay looking at the unwieldy fan in the Grand Tropicana, Matt reflected that he would at least have one supporter when he got back home. It wasn't much consolation.

The committee left the next morning for the airport. There was a small Cuban delegation to see them off, but it was a lacklustre event. Only Nicola Roberts seemed in good spirits.

"This trip has confirmed everything I thought not only about Cuba, but also about most MPs, and your lot at the FCO. A waste of space, the lot of you. Believe me, things are going to change. It's time our country woke up. I don't expect our paths will cross again, but if they do you had better be ready."

When they arrived at Heathrow, the MPs slunk away. Fortunately, the media were distracted by rumours of a royal pregnancy, and by a sex scandal involving a woman jockey, a UKIP councillor, and an American wrestler. The photo in *Granma* was reproduced in the press, but relegated to the inside pages. It provided much scope for entertainment on social media, but didn't provoke much political reaction.

"You have been lucky," said a sympathetic Janet back in the FCO. "If there had been a big scandal, the story would have followed you for the rest of your career. Just keep your head down for a while, and you might get away with it." Nobody blamed Matt for what had happened. Difficult experiences with visiting MPs were not unusual. "It's a question of luck," Janet said. "It's like herding cats most of the time."

Matt duly kept his head down, although he wasn't given much opportunity to raise it. People seemed to forget about his Cuba crisis quickly enough; staff were constantly changing in his department, and new crises surfaced on a regular basis. He occasionally reminisced with Rawston-Smith, who was languishing, as threatened, in Finance and Resources, and who relished the chance to escape to the bars of Central London, of which he seemed to have an encyclopaedic knowledge.

Eighteen months later, it was time for Matt to prepare for his first foreign posting. When the posting roulette wheel stopped, Matt discovered he would be going to Stockholm.

His initial reaction was one of disappointment. He had wanted to go to somewhere hot and exotic. His knowledge of Sweden came mainly from watching Scandi noir, and occasionally reading travel reviews in the Sunday magazines about 'achingly cool' restaurants on the shores of the Baltic. It seemed he would spend his time eating expensive shellfish and avoiding homicidal neighbours. Unusually, it was very difficult to find any FCO colleagues who had been there on a posting and so could tell him what life in Stockholm was actually like. There were plenty of people who could reminisce at length about Lagos or Mumbai, but Sweden was a mystery.

He duly read up as much as he could, talked to the Swedish desk officer, who also covered the Baltic States, which she clearly found much more interesting, and watched some subtitled Swedish movies on DVD. He would normally have been sent to the FCO language centre for thirty or more hours of Swedish, but this was cut short because the Embassy in Stockholm claimed to need him immediately. So it was that he arrived in Stockholm for his posting with an impressive degree of ignorance. In the best FCO, and indeed British, tradition, he would have to muddle through. Given what had happened to him in the last few weeks, he felt that he had moved from muddle to complete confusion.

Back in a hung-over Embassy the next morning, he felt uneasy about not recounting his aquatic adventures to Catherine, but consoled himself with the observation that she was too concerned about the fate of her Embassy to focus on other issues. She had received another message from London, this one threatening a possible visit from an estate inspection team.

"It's getting worse. They are suggesting that we will probably either have to sell the Embassy building, or find some co-tenants."

"But we can't sell, can we?" said Matt. "I thought that this land could only be used for diplomatic purposes."

"True, so we will have to look for a country that wants to share a largish Embassy in Stockholm. Any new countries wanting to open here?"

They both thought for a few minutes.

"No, still can't think of any," said Catherine. "No recent velvet divorces. I have already spoken to the friendly Ambassadors here, but they are happy where they are. However, I have heard the Iranians are looking to expand their Embassy. Maybe we should offer that option to Her Majesty's Treasury?"

"But we don't want to share with Iran, surely?" said Matt.

"Of course not. But if we suggest it, there will be a battle in London between the Treasury, who will want the money, and the FCO, the spooks and the MOD, who will all object. With any luck, they will still be arguing by the time you and I leave here. And who knows, they might have other savings targets by then."

Two days later, Annika returned and Matt arranged to meet her at Stureplan. He was early as usual and once again sat watching the wealthy young Swedes at play. Annika arrived looking rosy and healthy after her trip. She waxed lyrical for a while about the glories of the Swedish countryside. Matt was relieved to note that she never expressed a desire actually to live there. He then told her about his Midsummer adventure, including what he could remember from his conversation with Osipov.

"I am still not sure if it was real," he cautioned.

"I am sure it was, and I am so jealous," she said. "How could you be so cruel as to do all that without me?! I am not sure if I can forgive you." She paused. "I might possibly forgive you if I can go in that submarine too. A Russian submarine with bling. Perfect!" Annika was a big fan of British reality TV, and perhaps because she wore next to no make-up or jewellery herself, was fascinated by gold and glitter.

"Somehow, it didn't seem the right time to ask for his mobile number," replied Matt, "and I had nowhere to put it if he had given it to me. But if I meet him again, I'll ask him to give you a tour. So, what do you think we should do now?"

Annika thought for a while, swirling her glass of rosé. Her eyes looked very blue. "I think we should speak to Gunilla from SÄPO. We did tell her we would keep her informed. Maybe she will know if this Osipov really exists and is telling the truth."

"Good idea," said Matt. "We can ask her about those other submarines as well. Do you really think there can be a Latvian one?"

"I don't know, but they really don't like the Russians, so I wouldn't be surprised if they wanted to get involved. Good for them if they are!"

"OK. Can you contact her via Lars?"

"Yes, I can do that."

"But I suggest we don't tell him anything," said Matt. "He is a journalist, after all."

The next day, Annika called to say that she had fixed a meeting. "Same place. Same time." This time, they had barely arrived when Gunilla appeared.

"*Hej, hej.* So you have found something?" she asked, taking a seat on the bench in her calm way.

Despite considerable reservations and some private agonising, Matt had decided to share most of what he knew with her, including his meeting with Osipov. If she believed him, perhaps Catherine might. She listened intently and then sat silently for a while when he had finished.

"It could make sense," Gunilla said finally. "It could make sense that there are three submarines out there. But it could equally make sense that there is only one. A Russian one. And you found it, or they let you find it. That would mean that my more hawkish colleagues are telling the truth after all." She stopped. "But are you sure it was Russian?"

"No," Matt admitted. "I didn't see any flags or national markings."

"So it could have been an eccentric millionaire, or someone trying to mislead you."

Matt had to agree it was a possibility.

Gunilla paused again. "Well, what I can do is to make some enquiries. Someone in SÄPO might know about this."

"What about the military?" asked Annika.

"Yes, them too. I have a few contacts there."

Matt offered to go fishing among his diplomatic contacts as well. Hunter might know something, he thought. Maybe he could provoke him to reveal it. They agreed to meet again in a few days.

"Be careful," said Gunilla, as she left. "This may look like a game, but there are important issues here. Some people would like to heat things up in the Baltic. Maybe not a war, but something close to one."

As they left the park, Matt looked at Annika. "It's a cliché, I know, but I feel we are getting into deep water."

"Not in the Baltic," she replied. "It's mostly very shallow."

The next afternoon, Matt had to go to the Swedish Foreign Ministry to carry out some standard lobbying. A British candidate was standing for a significant international post, and the UK wanted Swedish support. Matt usually enjoyed going there. It was a friendly place for a British diplomat; the staff tended to be young, sociable and open. Coffee and cakes were often on offer, along with the compulsory fruit. As usual, Matt cycled there, via a pleasant route beside the sea. As he rode along the well-marked cycle path, being passed by furiously pedalling pensioners, he debated whether to invite Annika for a weekend away. He had already suggested this a couple of times, but she had replied that she was too busy. Perhaps now, in the sleepier days after Midsummer, he might have more success.

He was still weighing the pros and cons as he entered the Ministry, having waved his ID in the vague direction of a bored security guard. Despite assassinations and terrorist attacks in Stockholm, the Swedes still couldn't bring themselves to take their security seriously. They were the good guys, after all.

Matt's meeting was with a very efficient thirty-something official whom he had met on a couple of earlier visits. As often happened, the Swedes were willing to do a deal. They were prepared to back the UK candidate if the UK lent its support to a Swedish candidate for a UN post. Matt agreed to pass the offer back to London. He ate a cinnamon-flavoured bun, and the meeting was over.

As he was leaving he heard his name being called. It was the Political Director, Henrik Svenson, who gave him a serious stare. "I hear that you have been talking to SÄPO a lot recently. So what is that about?"

Matt was uncertain how to reply. He had heard that there was considerable rivalry between the different branches of Swedish security, the Foreign Ministry and the military. Information was power and was jealously guarded. He wasn't sure whether Svenson was just fishing, or whether he was annoyed that Matt had been talking to a rival. He wondered how Svenson knew about his meetings with Gunilla. Was he being followed?

"I do know some people in SÄPO," he finally replied. "I meet them sometimes. Nothing serious. I'm just trying to understand better how things work here."

Svenson gave him a cold look. "And how do they work?"

"Well, of course… I think… I mean, you know…"

"We are a small country," said Svenson, "with some difficult near neighbours. It's important for us to be able to trust our friends. We don't want to see them meddling in things they don't understand. It would be better if you talked to us. Leave SÄPO to MI6. Otherwise there might be some confusion."

"Of course not. No. I understand. Yes, point taken," Matt stuttered.

"What does Catherine think about your meetings? Of course, I can ask her myself next time I see her." Svenson gave him a final stare, and then relaxed. He led Matt to the stairs leading to the exit. "Please let us know about that UN post," he said as Matt walked down. "The guy we want in that job is a good friend of mine."

Matt wasn't surprised. In the small world of Swedish politicians and bureaucrats everyone seemed to know each other. The political was always also the personal.

As he cycled back to the Embassy, Matt wondered again about Svenson's agenda, and how he knew about his meetings with Gunilla. He was also increasingly worried about not sharing what he knew with Catherine. He felt he had to give her his version of events before Svenson, or someone else, did. His mind made up, he relaxed a little. He still wasn't sure if Catherine would believe him about the submarine, but at least she would be better prepared to answer Svenson's questions.

He parked his basic bike amongst the sleek machines in the Embassy bike rack and was met in reception by the unexpected sight of a serene Lotta. She smiled beatifically and told him that she had just finished an internet course on how to live without love.

"I am free now," she said. "I know I can live without men. I am going to go on long walks, eat healthy food and read some good books. Maybe do some baking. I can't think why I didn't start doing it ages ago."

Matt wished her luck, and went upstairs to be met by an even more unexpected sight. The fragrant Helena was looking very slightly disconcerted. She told Matt that Catherine's son had been injured in a car accident back in the UK. It wasn't too serious, but she had already gone to Arlanda Airport with James to fly back. She expected to be away for a few days. Matt would be Chargé d'Affaires in her absence. He wasn't sure whether Helena's stress was due to having to reschedule Catherine's diary, or because he was now in charge of the Embassy. He also realised that he wouldn't be able to tell Catherine about Svenson, SÄPO and Osipov. He would be on his own until she returned. He fervently hoped for a few quiet days. No intrigues. No international incidents in Sweden. Nothing.

SEVEN

Unfortunately, Matt's time as an untroubled boss only lasted until the next morning. He was sifting through the morning's emails when Helena glided in and revealed the reason for her earlier micro-stress. It was due to sympathy.

"*Hej, hej*, Matt," she said, shuffling slightly in a most un-Helena-like manner. "How are you today?"

Matt looked up, suddenly wary. Helena didn't usually bother much with formalities.

"Catherine would like you to do something for her. She says it will be a great opportunity for you."

Matt turned away from his computer screen. That didn't sound at all good.

"Have you heard about the Royal Clubs' dinner?" she asked.

Matt looked blank.

Helena quickly continued. "There are three of them: the Royal Yacht Club, the Royal Automobile Club and the Royal Motor Boat Club. They have a dinner once a year and invite the King to attend. The Automobile Club are hosting it this year. It's a big event. Are you sure you haven't heard about it?"

Matt was sure, and was equally uncertain why Helena was telling him about it, although an increasingly nervous sensation was rising from his stomach.

"It's the tradition for an Ambassador to give a short speech and a toast at the dinner. I don't quite know why. It's the turn of the British Ambassador this year. Of course, Catherine was going to do it. I think she was quite looking forward to it, actually. She likes that sort of thing. But now she can't."

"Why can't she?" asked Matt, fearing the answer.

"She was planning to come back to do it, but her son is more badly hurt than she thought, so she has decided to stay in the UK for a few more days."

"But when is this dinner?"

"In two days' time. She did ask me to speak to all the neighbouring British Ambassadors in case one of them could do it. But none of them can. So she would like you to do it."

Matt's spirits sank as fast as the Swedish winter sun. He had little experience of public speaking and his few past efforts had not given him much reason to be confident. But Helena hadn't finished.

"One thing you should know," she said; "you must make the toast in Swedish. It is expected."

Matt looked at her, wide-eyed. With only two hours of lessons per week, he had been making slow progress with his Swedish ever since his arrival. Although Swedish was largely a combination of Old English and German, its guttural pronunciation and idiosyncratic sentence structure made it frustratingly impenetrable.

"You can ask Ann-Britt to help you," added Helena,

sending Matt's spirits descending even further. Ann-Britt was his Swedish teacher, an unremittingly severe woman with a pair of the scariest Swedish glasses Matt had yet seen. He felt sure that in her youth she must have been particularly fun-loving and liberated to make her obligatory middle-aged transformation all the more dramatic. "She can help you to write and learn your toast," Helena explained. "It will be fine, don't worry. No one will expect you to say much."

They will be lucky if I say more than 'Hej, hej', thought Matt. *Even that might pose a problem in the presence of the King and Queen.*

"Who goes to this dinner?" he asked. "And how many people will be there?"

"Oh! Lots of VIPs. Around five hundred guests, I think. And the press, of course."

"The press?!"

"Oh yes, it's a big event. You will get a lot of coverage. Swedish radio covers it live. I will ask Ann-Britt to come here this afternoon, shall I? You don't have much time to prepare."

With that, she glided away. Matt stared out of the window for a while, but the peaceful scene didn't give him any solace.

He spent the rest of the morning reading about the various Royal Clubs online. He saw that the Dutch Ambassador had made a well-received speech at last year's dinner. He did now recall seeing a parade of vintage cars in Stockholm earlier that summer that had been organised by the Royal Automobile Club. The cars had been lovingly preserved, as had most of their owners, who looked as though they had come straight from the set of a 1920s film. It had been a surprising sight, but not as surprising as the regular appearance of ancient American cars in Stockholm. It seemed that many Swedish farmers hankered after a life on the prairie. Driving to the big city in a twin-finned Cadillac, then striding around in a Stetson and cowboy boots was the nearest they could get to it. American country music and dances were also popular in the countryside, although no sophisticated city dweller would admit to something so uncool.

Ann-Britt arrived at 2pm. Matt had earlier gone with Anke and Tina to eat lunch at the cafeteria of the Swedish Development Ministry, which was conveniently located nearby. The food was subsidised by the taxpayer, but the cafeteria was generously open to all. The Swedish aid budget was obviously all-encompassing. Over meatballs and salad, Matt told them about his forthcoming ordeal. They were sympathetic, but initially dismissive of his future audience.

"The people who join these clubs are all rich men," said Tina.

"Middle-aged, or elderly," Anke agreed. "They aren't really representative of modern Swedish society. They don't live in the same world as the rest of us. The only women there will be their wives and mistresses."

"So, these men aren't that important?" asked Matt hopefully.

"Oh, yes. They can be very influential. Some of the most important CEOs," said Tina.

"And media owners," added Anke unhelpfully.

They both looked at him. "Better spend a lot of time with Ann-Britt," they chorused.

At the end of what proved to be a long and arduous afternoon, Matt felt slightly more confident. In her serious, methodical fashion, Ann-Britt had helped him to prepare a short speech and toast which he felt he could pronounce in a more or less comprehensible fashion. She knew enough royal protocol to provide the correct wording. She also gave him some tips on presentation. She was always relentless in setting homework, but this time Matt was happy to do it. He decided to learn his speech by heart and recite it to her the next morning.

He had already told Annika about the dinner, and she was also eager to help him when they met for a drink that evening. She had never had anything to do with any of the Royal Clubs herself, the NGO world being at the opposite end of the Swedish social spectrum, but she had friends whose fathers were members.

"You will be fine," she said. "Those guys love everything old-fashioned and British."

"I'm not that old-fashioned!" Matt protested.

"You are a bit – but in a nice way," she added quickly. "Do you know anything about cars?"

"As a child I had a toy fire engine that I really liked."

"Mmm. OK. You may have to do better than that. How about the cars in James Bond movies? They are often British."

Matt thought this was an excellent idea. He did like Bond movies and would be able to say something intelligent about their cars, after a little research.

"And you went out to the archipelago recently in a motor boat," Annika added. "You could talk about that. Oh! Of course, you can also talk about submarine bling. You are an expert now," she said pointedly. She never failed to remind Matt that she was still waiting for her promised invitation.

Annika also had some advice about addressing the King and Queen. The popularity of the royal couple had waxed and waned in recent years. As with all other royal families in Europe, theirs had not been free from scandal. Nonetheless, most Swedes did feel a loyalty to them and the two princesses were generally popular, as much as anything because many of their contemporaries could identify with their sometimes chaotic love lives.

"I hear that the King likes hunting and fast cars," Annika said. "So if you need to say something, ask him about those things."

Because he had been focused on his speech, up to then Matt hadn't thought about social chit-chat. His stomach tightened again. "Is there anything I shouldn't talk about?"

"Fast women. Especially if the Queen is listening."

Matt made a mental note to speak to Helena the next morning. She would know what he should say, and about the etiquette of speaking to a Swedish monarch.

He had brought the text of his speech and toast with him, and gave it to Annika to read.

"Yes, it's OK. The Swedish is perfect. But it's very dull."

"You said that the audience will be dull. So this should be just right," he joked.

"Yes, but the press will be there. Don't you want to give them something to report? At least a sentence or two that will be good PR for the UK. That is part of your job, isn't it?"

Matt couldn't disagree. He had been thinking of the dinner solely in terms of damage limitation. But perhaps he could turn it into something positive.

"OK. I'll think about it."

"Me too," said Annika. "I am sure I can find a few words that will make an impression here in Sweden."

The next morning, Matt was trying to memorise his speech when Philip marched briskly into his office. "With the Ambassador away, I thought I'd better brief you on some new developments. I will be sending a signal to London too."

Matt found it slightly endearing that the military still liked to refer to 'signals' in the age of emails and smartphones. He had visions of a relay of military staff waving flags across Sweden and the North Sea.

"The Swedes have found conclusive proof that there is a foreign submarine in the archipelago. A signal has been detected close to one of the larger islands."

"But isn't the Piranha untraceable?" asked Matt, remembering his conversation with Osipov.

"We had feared it was. But it's possible the captain might have made a mistake. Done something to give himself away."

"Like in *Star Trek* when the Klingon cloaking device fails?" asked Matt mischievously.

Philip looked blank. He obviously wasn't a sci-fi fan.

"So what happens now?" said Matt.

"The Swedes are going to increase their surveillance and I have asked the navy to send one of their experts over. I am not sure that they will, but if they do, it will show the Swedes that we are on their side. And we might learn something. After all, the Russians send subs to our coast as well. We need to be able to catch the buggers."

After Philip had left, Matt thought again about what Osipov had said. If it was true that there were three submarines off the Swedish coast, the one found by the Swedes might be the Latvian one. Although Matt remained deeply sceptical about that possibility, and had inwardly sworn to avoid anything to do with submarines, he felt a strong temptation to have a word with his Latvian opposite number next time he saw her. Just to see if he could get a reaction.

After a final session with Ann-Britt the next afternoon, he cycled back to his flat to get ready for the dinner. Since Sweden was theoretically an egalitarian society, black tie was not normally worn, not even at a high-profile event such as this. Matt had quickly had his best suit, fortunately undamaged by the Baltic, dry-cleaned again. The dinner was being held at Berns Salonger, a large restaurant and event centre located conveniently close to Strandvägen, so he was able to walk there. It was once again a beautiful evening and he envied the carefree Swedes strolling along the waterside.

He knew that some of his colleagues, especially the older ones, would relish an evening as guest speaker to royalty and a mass of VIPs. He wondered whether it was something he would grow to enjoy, or whether he would always attend such events with reluctance. Not for the first time, he also wondered whether the diplomatic life was the right one for him. But that was a question for another day. He had to relax now and make the most of the experience.

As he neared the venue, he could see a mix of limos and bicycles as the guests arrived, although many were on foot since they had apartments in this exclusive part of the city. He was delighted to see Annika waiting at the entrance.

"*Hej, hej.* I came to wish you luck. And to give you this." She held out a piece of paper. "I just thought of something you could say that the audience would appreciate. You know that we love British cookery programmes – Nigella, Jamie Oliver and so on. So you could say something about this shared passion. Especially as this is a dinner."

"Great. Yes, sounds perfect. Thank you!" Matt gave the paper a quick glance. It contained a few handwritten sentences. "Yes, I can read it. I should be able to work it into the speech. No problem."

"Good luck. But I'm sure you won't need it. The audience will be on your side. Give me a call if you need any help."

Matt thanked her again and went into the building, feeling much better for her support.

Once inside, he looked around hoping to find the master of ceremonies for the evening. Helena had told him that a Swedish Radio channel was hosting the evening on behalf of the three Royal Clubs. Their top presenter would meet Matt and explain when and where he would make his speech. Helena had added that she was a well-known radio personality with a reputation for having a vibrant style, both in front of the microphone and behind it.

"*Hej, hej.* I am Anna. You must be Matt." A woman in a short, glittery black dress approached him with a wide smile and plenty of confidence. "You are very easy to spot. Birgitta told me you would be the youngest person here, and the most nervous."

"You know Birgitta?"

"Yes, we are old friends. Actually, she stole some of my cake recipes. She asked me to look after you this evening. I understand you are a late replacement. And you are going to speak in Swedish. That's very brave of you. Hardly any guest speakers do."

"But I thought they all did."

"No. They might say, 'Good evening' in Swedish, but that's all."

Great, thought Matt. *I could have been saved from all those hours of torture with Ann-Britt.* Still, now that he had taken the trouble to learn his speech and toast in Swedish, he might as well use it.

Anna took him into an enormous dining room full of tables, most of which were already occupied. She showed him the small rostrum from which he would make his speech, and how to adjust the microphone. She explained that she would call him to the rostrum when it was his turn to speak, gave him the programme, and said that she would be standing near him when he spoke in case of any problems. Her ebullient personality gave him some more confidence. Perhaps it wasn't going to be too bad after all.

Anna took him to what Matt guessed was the top table and introduced him to a serious-looking man in a black suit. His name was Fredrik, and he was in charge of royal protocol.

"Welcome, Chargé d'Affaires," he said formally. "We are honoured to have a representative of Her Majesty's Government with us this evening."

The man showed Matt where he would be sitting. "You are here," he said. "You will be sitting between Baron von Torstensson and Baroness von Marburg. His Majesty will sit over there," he gestured to a seat on the opposite side of the table to Matt, "and Her Majesty next to him."

Matt felt relieved that he wouldn't be sitting quite close enough to the royal couple to speak to them. It meant he could focus on his speech rather than what would have undoubtedly been a nerve-racking conversation.

He had been very surprised to discover that there was a Swedish upper class and a hereditary Swedish nobility with barons and counts. There was even an established House of Nobility in Stockholm. Catherine had told him that although the House itself had a largely ceremonial role in modern Sweden, a number of its senior members still had a discreet but significant degree of influence in Swedish society. Some families had in the past used their position and wealth to build up industrial or financial dynasties. They were still at the heart of the informal network of politicians and industrialists that continued to shape the country's long-term economic policy. This influence was not exactly a secret, but was often strangely ignored by the media and in political debate. Matt assumed there was a tacit understanding not to mention it. After all, media owners were also part of society and some probably went to the same schools as the aristocrats.

As Matt was uneasily hovering around his seat, the first top-table guests began to arrive. Since he was the only stranger there, they all took a careful look at his name on the place mat, before giving him a brisk "*Hej, hej.*"

Matt could at least be confident of considerable goodwill. Most of the Swedish guests would be frequent visitors to London, and some would probably have children who were either studying or working there. His two neighbours arrived together. Baron von Torstensson was a cheerful, amiable man, very much at his ease. Baroness von Marburg looked like an alarmingly serious dowager, and gave him a reserved greeting.

The room was completely full by now. Suddenly everyone got to their feet and silence fell as the King and Queen entered. They took their seats and conversation restarted. Matt noticed that the King had taken a quick glance at him as he sat down, then spoken briefly to an aide standing behind him. He then gave Matt a slight nod and turned to talk to his neighbour. Matt relaxed a little, guessing that might be the beginning and end of their interaction for the evening.

A starter of prawns decorated with edible flowers arrived, wine was poured, and Matt was happy enough to sip at it while quietly observing the busy conversations around him.

"What you are seeing is very deceptive."

Matt was startled by the baroness's bony hand on his arm.

"Everything here looks very solid and safe, doesn't it?" she murmured. "All this ceremony and fine clothes. It's like Sweden. The outside world thinks we are a Volvo. We used to be, but now we are a kind of hybrid. And the road we are driving on is starting to shake."

Matt wasn't sure how to reply.

The baroness released his arm briefly to impale a prawn, then gripped it again. "You are a diplomat, so you must report often to London. I hope you are telling them about the threats to our country, and that we need the help of our good friends. My mother came from one of the Baltic States and married here. Our family have done well in Sweden, but we have not forgotten our roots. My relatives who stayed behind suffered terrible things when the Russians took over there. We can't let it happen again. Your colleagues back in London don't want to believe that Russian tanks could roll into Riga or Tallinn again. But trust me, they could."

She clutched Matt's arm even more tightly and looked around the room. "All these military men in their fine uniforms will do nothing to help. They prefer to pretend that the Russians are no threat to Sweden and to our Baltic neighbours. They are wrong, and they are making a calamitous mistake. That is why we need you British to help us. You don't trust the Russians and you won't let them bully you. Will you?"

Matt was beginning to lose circulation in his arm. The baroness was surprisingly strong.

"They are getting so confident now that they are even sending their submarines to our archipelago. They are here as we speak, just outside Stockholm. And yet our navy does nothing. But I know that you can help us, you British." She looked at him intently as a waitress whisked the prawns away. "I can rely on you, can't I?"

Matt wondered if he could make his toast with a paralysed arm. "Yes, of course," he said hurriedly. "Anything to help."

The baroness gave him one final stare, finally released his arm and turned to talk to the guest sitting on her other side. Matt surreptitiously massaged his arm and looked around. If anyone else shared her concerns, they certainly weren't showing it.

More courses arrived, including some tender venison and a delicate cloudberry dessert. Glasses of schnapps appeared and the first *skols* began, like a sort of alcoholic evening chorus. The Swedish toasting ritual of *skol* had been one of the few things that Matt had learnt about the country before he arrived. Guidebooks were unanimous about its importance. Swedes would forgive many things, but incorrect *skol* etiquette was a great sin. There was a lot of advice about when and how to do it, who should *skol* when, and who should respond. It all made Matt slightly nervous and determined to be a perfect *skoler* from the very beginning.

Actually, it turned out to be a very simple and agreeable aid to social drinking. Most of the Swedes he had met didn't seem to be particularly obsessed with the finer points of ritual, although there were a few that were. Most just wanted to get some schnapps down their necks. After the first couple of shots, etiquette tended to be forgotten. Part of the ritual involved looking into the eyes of your fellow drinkers before swallowing. If some of those drinkers were attractive, this became an increasing pleasure. A good way to break down Scandinavian reserve and pass the long winter evenings, Matt had concluded.

As the time for speeches drew near, he started to feel nervous again. He could have sworn that the prawns had been cooked, but it felt as though one of them was still very much alive and trying energetically to escape from his stomach. His neighbours were still engaged in conversation, so he had time to take a look at the piece of paper Annika had given him. It had become quite crumpled in his pocket, but her handwriting was still legible. It seemed to say something about a shared love of cookery and that Swedes and Brits, including royalty, liked eating plenty of good food. Matt recognised most of the words, although he didn't understand all of them. It didn't matter. He trusted Annika.

The last course was cleared away and Anna strode confidently up to the microphone to begin proceedings. After a few formal remarks, she cracked a few jokes which went down well with the audience. The first speaker was the president of the Automobile Club, who made a short, formal speech. He was followed by a speaker from the Yacht Club, who seemed to be the comic turn. There was a lot of laughter. Finally, it was Matt's turn. Anna announced him and he rather clumsily made his way to the rostrum. He felt as though the whole world was looking at him, including everyone he had ever met in his life and had failed to impress. Even his maths teacher. Especially his maths teacher.

Anna gave him an encouraging smile and whispered that everything would be OK. He had memorised his speech, but put his notes on the lectern just in case his mind went blank. He looked around to see plenty of smiling faces and wished everyone good evening in Swedish. To his surprise this provoked a round of applause. His second sentence resulted in even more applause. He realised that two sentences in Swedish had already been more than the audience expected. He began to relax. This was going to be all right. He made some comments about the joys of travelling by boat and car in the Swedish summer, a rather lame joke about James Bond cars, and spoke about the British enthusiasm for Scandi noir. The audience seemed to love it all, even the lame joke. Feeling confident, he decided to finish with Annika's words. Her note had got even more crumpled and some of the words were now unclear. He improvised as best he could.

As he read them out, there was a sudden silence, followed by a few nervous laughs. Everyone turned to look at the King, who in turn was looking at Matt with a startled expression. Matt suddenly felt the creature in his stomach begin to do laps. It appeared to be joined by several friends. What had he said?

The King seemed uncertain how to react. Time had stopped. Finally, after a few interminably slow seconds, the King decided to take whatever Matt had said as a joke. He smiled, said something to his neighbours, and raised his glass. This provoked an immediate and relieved *skol* from the whole room.

Anna walked swiftly across to Matt. "Let's take that as your toast, shall we?" she whispered as she led him away from the rostrum to polite applause.

"What did I say?" he asked, feeling dazed.

"Well, for a moment, I thought we might have a major diplomatic incident on our hands, but I think you got away with it."

Matt made his way back to his seat with his mind in the same state as one of the legendary Baltic whirlpools. He looked across to the King, who was busily talking to a neighbour. The Queen caught his glance and gave him what seemed to be a sympathetic smile. The baroness tapped him on the arm. "I don't know who your Swedish teacher is, but she won't be at all happy with you."

The baron gave a chuckle. "Thanks. You made my evening."

"What did I say?" asked Matt in some desperation.

"You talked about cookery and then said that the British and the Swedes all like being drunk, including their kings. Is that what you meant to say?"

"No, of course not. My friend gave me this to read." He handed the baron Annika's script.

"Ah. I see. You have misread what she wrote. You used the British word 'full'. It means 'drunk' in Swedish, not 'well fed.'"

Matt felt the creature switch from breaststroke to butterfly. He remembered now why the word was familiar. It was one of John's favourite words in the Embassy bar.

The baron was very amused. "Don't worry. You certainly surprised the King at first. But I think he understood that you made a mistake. People will know that. But they will remember your speech for a long time."

Matt's mobile started vibrating. It was a text message from Anke. *Heard you on the radio. Will contact all the media to say you made a mistake. Damage limitation.*

This was followed by a series of further texts. Matt cursed. Everyone seemed to have been listening.

Never mind. You did your best, from Helena.

Ann-Britt will either kill you or go into exile, from Tina.

Congratulations. True socialism is alive again in the UK, from Lars.

Come down to the Black Boar, mate. You need a few stiff ones, from John.

The event had now finished and guests were leaving. Anna came up to him. "I have spoken to my colleagues," she said. "We won't make a big thing about what you said. But thank you. You made it memorable for all of us."

Matt left as quickly and unobtrusively as he could, accompanied by sympathetic smiles. There was one good thing about the evening, he thought miserably, as he walked back along the seafront. He wouldn't be invited to speak publicly in Sweden again. He called Anke, who told him that the media were not intending to report it as a deliberate attack on the Swedish monarchy. But it would get some press coverage the next morning. Matt had become a temporary celebrity.

"Look on the bright side," she said. "You might even be invited to appear on TV with that chef. He likes a drink."

As he got close to his building, he heard footsteps behind him. He turned to see a flushed Annika.

"Oh! I heard what happened. I'm so sorry."

She was clearly upset, even though Matt tried to explain that it had been entirely his fault. He had already drunk plenty that evening, but felt he needed at least another. As did Annika. She followed him into the spectacularly ancient lift, an original fixture in the grand 1880s building. For the first time since he had known her, she looked less than completely self-assured. He wanted very much to kiss her, and he did. And for the first time since he had lived in that building, he was grateful that the lift was both very small and very slow.

EiGHT

When he woke the next morning, it was with an intense mix of emotions and a sore head. There was relief that the dinner was behind him, embarrassment at the recollection of his performance, fear about what he might see in the press, nervousness about what might happen to his career, but joy about what had happened after the lift had struggled up to his flat. Annika had not left until the morning. As he showered, Matt thought that he should make mistakes in Swedish more often. The benefits of linguistic perfection were much exaggerated.

Despite his hangover, he sang loudly during his bike ride to the Embassy, attracting some very disapproving looks from the usual line of silent dog walkers. His mood, however, began to change as he entered the Embassy gates. The creature in his stomach, dormant throughout the night, began to stir again. A miserable-looking Lotta greeted him with a long sigh. Clearly she had abandoned her romance-free diet. He decided not to ask her about her latest overindulgence. They just exchanged sympathetic glances.

Upstairs, in the Chancery, he was met by some amused smiles. He bumped into Philip, who commiserated.

"Heard you made a bit of a Horlicks of your speech last night. Don't worry. Happens to me all the time."

Anke followed him into his office with the morning papers. Matt was officially the Embassy press officer, but it was Anke's job to follow the Swedish media and report anything of note.

"Well, the good news is that you didn't make any front pages," she said. "The serious press have decided not to report what you said. But *Aftonbladet* and *Expressen* couldn't resist having a little joke."

Expressen was the right-wing tabloid version of *Aftonbladet*. The morning edition had a cartoon of a caricature drunken Brit waving a bottle. *Aftonbladet* had done some historical digging on the subject of the British monarchy and alcohol. Matt's slip had a basis in truth, they concluded.

"None of this is likely to be picked up in the British press," Anke reassured him.

That was probably true, Matt thought. The British press were usually singularly uninterested in Sweden.

"What will you say to Catherine?" she asked.

"I'll wait until she gets back. Hopefully the story will have died down a little."

"Yes," said Anke. "There might be something more exciting by then. The Swedish coastguard might actually find a submarine."

"Or Zlatan might have a new tattoo," joked Matt.

Anke was silent. Zlatan, still a football god, was above jokes.

Luckily for Matt, none of the diplomatic corps had been invited to the dinner, so he didn't receive any emails about his speech. He was able to nurse his hangover in peace. After work, he cycled across to Djurgården, one of the many islands around which Stockholm was built. This one had been deliberately maintained as a green space. It contained several historic houses, a zoo, a funfair, and the famous Vasa Museum. It was possible to cycle around its perimeter; one of Matt's favourite routes.

There were some quiet bays where the cycle path almost ran through the water. He sat for a while and watched the small waves, the seabirds and the distant tacking of white sails. The visual peace was temporarily disturbed by one of the enormous Baltic cruise ships, which suddenly and silently appeared, looming like a mobile skyscraper over the trees. He could see a handful of tourists waving to him from ten storeys up. Matt wondered if they were envious of a man sitting by his bike in such apparent tranquillity. It was easy to be seduced by the Baltic in summer. *You can have my diplomatic life with pleasure*, he thought. *Just leave me Annika.*

That evening, Helena called him to say that Catherine would be back in the Embassy the next morning. Helena hadn't told her about the Royal Clubs' dinner, but Matt expected that she would have heard about it by now. The next day he got to the Embassy early to find the Ambassador in her office, cursing as she trawled through her emails.

"Hello, Matt. Or should I call you the new Oliver Cromwell, scourge of monarchy and sinful drinking?"

Matt was relieved to see that she seemed amused, rather than irate. He began to explain what had happened, but stopped when he saw that she was well informed.

"I had several phone calls that evening," she said. "From Fredrik, from the Protocol Office, and Baron von Torstensson, among others. I think there was no real damage done. And I'm not blaming you. You were thrown into the deep end and didn't drown. You just swallowed some chlorine. I am more worried about what Ann-Britt will say to me when she comes here for my lesson today. She might call for the restoration of capital punishment."

Matt had been hoping that he could somehow avoid his teacher, but realised the moment of reckoning couldn't be long avoided.

"You will have to see her too. Better get it over with," Catherine said, reading his thoughts. "Even if you may never be able to father children afterwards. But before she comes, I have something to tell you.

"While I was in London, I spent some time talking on the Ambassadors' network. Many of them have also been threatened with severe cuts. We have been busy exchanging ideas about how to avoid them. Some colleagues are hoping to rely on the old tactic of pretending to comply, and proposing such severe cuts that the administration will take fright. Others have turned to sympathetic members of the Parliamentary Foreign Affairs Committee, asking them to argue their case with the relevant FCO minister over a few glasses of whisky. Some are planning leaks to the media, although in my experience this is not usually a ploy that works very well with the UK press. Most of it is either indifferent, or hostile to the FCO.

"My idea of offering Embassy space-sharing with Iran came as a surprise to all of them, but I think some of them – the more Machiavellian – wished they had thought of something similar. Fortunately, the head of the FCO Department that deals with Iran is an old friend of mine, and is about to retire. He has agreed that I can make an initial, off-the-record approach to the Iranian Ambassador. He even told me that, given recent events, it isn't completely out of the question that I could get some tactical support in London. It might at least put the Treasury in an awkward spot.

"Helena has set up a meeting with the Iranian Ambassador, Mirza Gul, here this morning," Catherine concluded. "I would like you to sit in."

Matt had seen the Ambassador a few times at diplomatic events, but had never spoken to him. He carried around him an atmosphere of serious intent that Matt found rather intimidating. He seemed someone for whom small talk would not only be frivolous, but positively sinful. Catherine, however, had talked to him several times, and found him to be polite, if reserved.

"Everyone has a weakness, and I think I might have spotted his at the Brazilian National Day reception. Let's see."

A little later, Helena shimmered into the office with the Ambassador. He was very neatly dressed as always, with beard and black formal attire. He also appeared slightly flustered as Helena asked him if he wanted a coffee. She was wearing a short skirt that seemed to have been woven from some sort of cling film. As she left the room, the two men found themselves looking at her elegant retreating figure.

"Swedish," said Catherine. "I find that she really helps me to get through the long diplomatic day."

There were a few minutes of discussion about events in Syria before Helena returned with the coffee. She then joined them, adjusted her skirt, which now seemed even shorter, and produced a notebook, something that Matt had never seen her do before at a meeting with another Ambassador.

"Our meeting today is quite informal," said Catherine, "but I find my memory is getting very poor in my old age. So I have asked Helena to take notes. She will be happy to share them with you afterwards if you like."

Gul seemed lost for words. Matt sympathised. Helena had that effect on most men.

Catherine explained the reason for the meeting, and that this was an informal, exploratory conversation. Gul gave a lengthy reply covering all aspects of recent British-Iranian relations. The two diplomats, Matt thought, on the basis of his admittedly shallow experience, operated at different ends of the negotiating spectrum. British diplomats, in the style of many of their football teams, tended to be direct. Two or three passes, and then the long ball straight to the point. Iranian diplomats preferred to model themselves on a more continental style. They enjoyed keeping possession of the conversation to the extent that often there was no end result, which presumably was their intention. For their part, the Americans and Russians seemed to share a common strategy, which involved some initial side-to-side passes, followed by a sudden and full-blooded attack, with or without the ball.

On this occasion, Gul's long exposition ended in an expression of polite but non-committal interest in the idea of becoming co-tenants in the Embassy building. It could be a symbolic expression of a new era. *And it would be a disincentive to burning down the British Embassy in Tehran,* thought Matt cynically, *if that new era proved short-lived.*

"Helena is really our expert on such matters," Catherine said, to Matt's surprise. "She can tell you more, if you wish."

Helena gave Gul an enigmatic smile, which again removed his power of speech. The meeting was over and Helena escorted Gul out of the office.

"I think that went well." Catherine smiled. "I noticed before that he seems to have a weak spot for the ladies. Helena was quite happy to play along. I don't suppose my idea will come to anything, but it may distract London long enough to help us escape the axe."

"Not half as long as Gul will be distracted," Matt replied. "He looked as though he had taken the Vaxholm ferry in the solar plexus."

"Yes, I don't suppose there are many Swedish blondes in Tehran. It's strange," Catherine mused, "how often the simple tactic of exploiting sexual attraction can work. You would think that after centuries of experience, not to mention all the historical dramas, plays and spy stories, you men would have learnt something. But you clearly haven't. Not that I have asked Helena to be a honey trap," she added. "I would never ask her to do that, of course, and she would never agree if I did. It's just to keep him a little off balance, and maybe more interested in coming back here for more talks. Helena thought it would be amusing."

A little while later, Helena returned. "He was happy for me to take him on a short tour of the Embassy," she said. "And he asked for my personal telephone number."

"Did you give it to him?"

"I said it was against Embassy policy, but maybe I could be persuaded next time he came here."

"Excellent," said Matt. "The sturgeon is on the hook. Maybe some caviar will follow."

"I am not sure what sort of trashy novels you are reading these days, Matt," said Catherine, "but perhaps a tacky fishing metaphor is appropriate this time.

"Now for our next task," she continued. "We are going to have some guests. There will be a Labour Party delegation in town later this week. They have been invited by the Social Democrats. It's political party business, so normally we wouldn't be involved. But while I was in London, the Private Office gave me a call. Apparently the Cabinet Secretary is concerned that the party is getting too focused on its domestic disputes and isn't paying enough attention to foreign affairs. He is worried about creeping ignorance in Parliament. He has persuaded the Foreign Secretary to ask Embassies to give Labour MPs some encouragement. So I'm going to give them a dinner at the Residence. I have asked Helena to put together a list of Swedes to invite; mostly Social Democrats and a couple of journalists and political commentators. We should be able to get a good discussion going. I want you to work with her on the list. You can invite your friend Lars if you want."

Helena left, and Catherine asked Matt to stay for a moment.

"There is one other thing. I spoke to a few people in the Office about submarines. They told me that MI6 is totally tied up with terrorism at the moment. Two decades ago they would have been like young children at Christmas at the thought of Russians and mysterious sightings out here. But they don't have the resources to deal with it properly now, so they are content to leave it to the Americans, the Swedes and the Baltic States to sort out. So we won't get any help from them – that is, if we need any help. Do we?"

Matt hesitated. Would this be the right moment to talk about Osipov? He remembered his previous decision to do so, but felt a wave of acute nervousness sweep over him. He still wasn't convinced that he hadn't been dreaming that night out in the Baltic. He shuffled his feet. "No, it seems to be quiet now. Nothing new," he replied.

That afternoon, Matt had to mentally put a newspaper down his trousers in preparation for his lesson with Ann-Britt. He felt a severe caning was imminent. In the event she showed more sorrow than anger, although she did make him feel exceedingly guilty. Matt tried to stress how pleased his audience had been that he had made the effort to speak in Swedish, but he felt that he would never be welcome at an Ann-Britt Midsummer party, except in the form of a stuffed herring. She took some revenge by giving him some very extensive homework, including a list of linguistic false friends.

He did, however, receive some better news later that day. Annika had been invited to a party and asked him to go with her. He felt very encouraged that she wanted him to meet her friends. The party was held in a house in the suburbs of Stockholm. Matt met Annika on the Tunnelbana en route. The party was quite a small one, with a group of Swedes who clearly knew each other very well.

In common with most other foreigners living in Sweden, Matt had found it hard to meet Swedes socially, until he had started seeing Annika. She explained to him that this was not due to xenophobia. Swedes tended to grow up together, beginning at their first nursery school, or *dagis*. They often went to the same primary and secondary schools thereafter. This meant that many of them had a circle of friends from an early age. They had no need to look for new additions to their circle, and so had little incentive to invite foreigners, or even other Swedes, to join it.

As Annika's invitee, Matt was welcomed into the charmed circle on this occasion. Although he tried a few words of Swedish, her friends all spoke perfect English to him and chatted happily about British TV programmes and British football. In the absence of a strong domestic league, most Swedish men tended to follow an English Premier League team, and the more enthusiastic even flew to England to watch them.

On this evening there was a special culinary treat. One of the guests had brought some *surströmming*. To eat it, or at least witness it being eaten, everyone had to go down to the bottom of the garden, as far away from the house as possible. Annika explained to the mystified Matt that it wasn't one of her favourite dishes. *Surströmming* was canned fermented herring. It was a delicacy in the north, and derived from the days when food was so scarce in the winter that people had to preserve and eat almost anything in order to survive. The smell when a can of it was opened was notoriously so strong that it had to be done outdoors. If opened indoors, the house could be uninhabitable for some time.

"It's usually eaten with potatoes and maybe vegetables," whispered Annika. "Someone gave me the best advice for eating it. What you have to do is cook the potatoes and then open the can, best done by someone with a really heavy cold. Then you carefully sprinkle a tiny quantity of *surströmming* on the potatoes. Then you throw it away and eat something edible." With that, she led Matt into the house, before the can was opened outside to some stifled cries.

As they returned to central Stockholm on the Tunnelbana, Matt hoped that Annika might again come back to his flat. That was something he was very keen to develop into an Anglo-Swedish tradition. This time, however, he was to be disappointed. She had another early meeting. But as she left the train, she raised his spirits by telling him that she wanted to stay with him again soon.

"I am sure that you diplomats have lots of interesting stuff in your flats. Secret papers. Codes. Disguises. Once you are asleep, I'm going to search everywhere. You have been warned!"

✦

The next morning, Matt was summoned to a meeting with Catherine and an agitated Philip. "It's the French," Philip said. "This is war now. They are sabotaging us and we need to strike back. London is furious. Thought I had better warn you."

"This is about the French making a bid for the missile guidance system?" Catherine guessed.

"Yes, and what they have done is inexcusable. When I think of all the lunches I have invited that snake to."

"The snake being the French Defence Attaché," Catherine guessed again. Discussions with Philip often involved some interpretation.

"As you know," Philip continued in agitation, "negotiations with the Swedes were going well. We were getting close to a signature. But now the French have passed them some data about our system which suggests that some of the test results weren't quite as good as they seemed."

"And is that true?"

"Of course it's not true." Philip paused. "Maybe some of the results could be interpreted in different ways. But that's always the case with these sorts of tests. There is so much analysis involved. But that's not the real problem." He stopped.

"The real problem being?" Catherine prompted.

"The real problem is with the Moderate Centre Party. You know better than me that the MCP is going through a crisis."

The MCP were one of the smallest parties in the Swedish Parliament, and one of several that supported the Social Democratic Party in their latest shaky governing coalition.

"Yes," Catherine replied. "It's about a disputed expenses claim over a packet of disposable nappies. Their leader failed to disclose that he had bought it with his parliamentary credit card. Said that his wailing baby had clouded his judgement and his memory. If he has to resign, they will have to have a new leadership election. Depending on who wins, the new leader might take the MCP out of the governing coalition. If that happens, there could be a new national election, and who knows what might happen then? The far-right Sweden Democrats could force themselves into government. It's a lot at stake over disposable nappies."

Matt had been trying for a while to understand the Swedish approach to crime and punishment. Some major fraud cases a few decades ago had shocked public opinion, resulting in much stiffer penalties for financial crime. The Swedish press had made investigating fraud a major priority ever since. With every such crime that was discovered, penalties and sentences increased. As a result, someone committing a significant fraud could receive a longer prison sentence than a murderer. The Swedes seemed to accept this. One reason, Matt thought, for the pile of bodies that appeared in every Swedish crime novel. A serial fraudster would be too horrible for a Swede to write about.

Swedish politics were even more complicated, he thought, than the plot of the most fiendish novel. Their system of proportional representation meant that it had become difficult in recent years for one party to win a general election with a clear majority. The long era of dominance by the Social Democratic Party had been followed by a succession of uneasy coalitions. The two largest parties, the SDP and the right-wing Moderates, were the two suns in the small Swedish universe. A number of smaller parties, some little more than interest groups, circulated around them like tiny stars, being pulled one way or the other by political gravity. These stars could implode at any moment, disintegrate and then reform.

The political forces that ruled this universe were often as inscrutable to the foreign observer as any rogue particle in the Large Hadron Collider. Its physics had been thrown into confusion by the recent emergence of the Sweden Democrats, whose whole existence ought to be impossible under the law of Swedish political correctness. But this new sun, or dark star, not only existed, but was growing larger rapidly, perhaps followed by those who wanted to live in a different universe.

Matt was wrenched back from this galactic analogy into reality. Philip was continuing his account of French perfidy.

"They know that the SDP will be desperate to keep the support of the MCP if there is a new leader. The French have privately told the deputy MCP leader, Hans Wallstrom, that they could build a new cheese processing plant in his constituency. It would create some much-needed jobs there. Wallstrom thinks that winning that contract would give him enough prestige to make him the next MCP leader. The French proposal, although they are too clever to make it explicitly, is that the MCP would then make their support for the SDP-led coalition conditional on SDP support for the French bid for the new missile guidance system."

"Ingenious, and classically French," said Catherine admiringly.

"The MOD has called a council of war in London," Philip added. "I am sure they will be asking for our advice. Any thoughts?"

Catherine reflected for a while. "I know Erika Johansson, the MCP spokesperson on the environment. James knows her even better; they go to Pilates together. She has never got on with Wallstrom ever since he didn't support her in her own leadership bid a few years ago. I'll invite her for a drink. Maybe we can encourage her to sponsor a counter-bid for the MCP leadership."

She turned to Matt. "We can't be seen to interfere with Swedish domestic politics. But it wouldn't hurt if we could find some evidence that cheese processing plants can be harmful to the environment. That can be a game-changer here. Maybe there is something we can discover that I could pass on to Erika?"

She looked again at Philip. "The Swedes are always suspicious about any country that is close to Russia. No one could accuse the UK of that, but the French can look vulnerable on that score. I'll speak to the Foreign Minister. Sow a few seeds of doubt about buying a missile guidance system from a country who might later sell the same system to the Russians."

Philip seemed reassured by having a plan of action to follow.

"Anything new on the submarine saga?" Catherine asked.

"The Swedes are absolutely sure that the Russian sub is still out there," Philip replied. "They think they will be able to provide some proof very soon. I am getting daily briefings. Might even go out there myself to take a look."

"Well, be careful if you do," Catherine replied with a laugh. "If your boat has another engine breakdown, the MOD won't be selling any naval kit to the Swedes for a while. It won't be the best advert."

Seeing that Philip was about to launch into a long description of his latest attempt to fix his engine, Catherine quickly brought the meeting to a halt.

"We are all going to the US Independence Day event tomorrow, aren't we? Let's see if we can find out anything more about submarines while we are there."

Matt asked Anke to do some research on the environmental menace of cheese processing. He was more interested in thinking about his next meeting with Annika. He was engaged in a particularly pleasant fantasy when his boss came into his office.

"I'm going to have to carry out this happiness test this week," said Catherine, whose own happiness was clearly at an Eeyore level. "Any thoughts? Who's happy, who's not?"

Matt thought for a moment. "I think it depends on when you ask people," he replied. "Consular and visa staff are usually quite low in the mornings. But they perk up in the afternoon, especially when it gets close to opening time at the Embassy bar, and the visa section have finished their interviews for the day. Chancery staff are the opposite. They always seem to arrive full of enthusiasm, but then some bureaucratic request from London will arrive and burst their bubble. At least, that's what usually happens to me. As for the commercial staff, I think it depends on whether they have helped seal a contract."

"And management?" Catherine asked.

"It's all about cake with them. Talk to them just after *fika*. They'll all be happy." Matt thought for a moment. "Of course, if you want an extreme rating, you can always ask Lotta. She will either be radiant or in despair."

"Yes," Catherine agreed. "She's wasted in Sweden. She should be an actress in a Brazilian soap opera."

"Do you have to include Philip's team as well?" Matt asked.

"I suppose so," said Catherine. "Yes, I'd better wait until I have a good snippet of military gossip for Philip that he can pass back to the MOD. That always makes him happy, whether it's true or not."

Catherine now looked happier herself. While still far from being a Tigger, she was no longer an Eeyore.

NINE

As he sat at his desk the next afternoon, Matt could hear the distant sound of brass band music. The 4th July celebrations had already begun at their big neighbour's brutalist fortress. The US National Day event was the biggest in Stockholm, although an invitation to the Japanese National Day was the most sought after because of the quality of the food. The US provided more basic fare, involving burgers and hot dogs, but they laid on marching bands and cheerleaders. More importantly, all the senior Swedish politicians and VIPs came along, so there were unmatched opportunities for networking. Catherine and Philip had already gone across, together with their spouses. As always, security was tight; getting into the American Embassy was as difficult as getting into a newly washed pair of jeans after a large curry. Matt finally made it past the last row of unsmiling marines and into the large compound where the party was taking place.

The courtyard was packed under a blue summer sky. The brass band played in one corner, while cheerleaders dressed in red, white and blue tossed their batons and ponytails against a pervasive aroma of barbecuing burgers. It was, Matt thought, a quintessentially American scene, except that the performers were all from Swedish high schools. In the middle of the courtyard, Matt could see the distinctively towering figure of the US Ambassador, talking animatedly to the Swedish Foreign Minister, David Bertilson. Other Ambassadors milled around them like minor movie stars waiting to take an inclusive selfie.

Matt was looking around for any familiar faces when he had a shock that made him involuntarily clutch the back of his neck. Either he was hallucinating, or his submarine encounter had actually happened. For, at the edge of the crowd, gazing transfixed at the cheerleaders, was a figure that looked very much like Osipov. He was wearing white trousers, a blue blazer, a crimson-and-gold neck scarf and a yachting cap. Taking a deep breath, and wondering whether a hallucination might be preferable, Matt made his way towards him through the crowd. At close quarters there was no doubt. Matt did his best to steady himself.

"Comrade Osipov," he said. "Or should I say Captain Osipov? This is an unexpected pleasure."

Osipov seemed completely unsurprised to see Matt and gave him an unexpected smile in response. "I was told there would be dancing girls here today. So I had to come. There are only so many days you can spend at the bottom of the Baltic Sea, even in your own underwater palace. Good to see you again. And wearing clothes this time. You almost look like a diplomat." He laughed and took a swig of what Matt suspected was not lemonade. "I don't mind telling you that I'm getting really fed up with this charade. I gave Oleg the slip to come here today, although he has followed me here. He is around here somewhere."

Osipov sighed loudly. "Maybe you can help me? Oleg tells me that the Master still wants me to stay in the Piranha and play games. The Americans are still trying to find the Latvian submarine, if that is what it is, because they still think it's one of ours. As long as they do so, they will be distracted. And if they annoy the Master by putting pressure on him over Ukraine, maybe he can embarrass them by revealing the truth about the Latvian submarine. That would be very hard for NATO to explain. I can understand that. But I am getting very bored here. I have heard that there are beautiful women in Antigua and my wife has gone shopping in Dubai for a month. I just have to escape."

"But how can I help you?" asked Matt, still feeling he might be dreaming.

"Tell your people about my Piranha. Once they know about me, there won't be any point in my staying in the Baltic. The Master will have to let me leave."

"I have thought about it," said Matt. "But I am not sure anyone would believe me. I will have to have some proof."

"How much proof do you need? You are a diplomat, aren't you? So they will believe you."

"Yes, normally, but the more I think about how we met, how you picked me up in your Piranha, the more unbelievable it seems. I need to have something more solid to give them." Matt paused. "My Ambassador is here somewhere. If you tell her what you have told me, that might be enough."

Osipov was about to reply, but then he suddenly tensed. "I have to go now. Oleg has seen us. We'll talk later." He turned and disappeared into the crowd.

Matt saw a large, stocky figure moving purposefully towards him. He didn't look friendly. *Relax*, he told himself. *I have done nothing wrong. And I am in the American Embassy. What could happen to me?*

The man approached with a sort of gunslinger's walk and stopped in front of him. He gave Matt a long stare, followed by an unconvincing smile. "Do you know that man you were just talking to?" he asked in a strong Slavic accent. "I am sure I have met him somewhere."

"We were just talking about the cheerleaders," Matt replied. "He seemed to be a big fan. Maybe he is a film director or something? Perhaps he wants to hire them?"

Oleg said nothing.

"Anyhow," said Matt after a long pause, "I need to get a drink. Nice to meet you."

"I think you know exactly who he is," Oleg replied softly. "And I will soon know exactly who you are."

With a further stare, he moved slightly to one side, leaving Matt just enough room to squeeze past him. He seemed unnecessarily muscular. Matt headed for the bar. He now genuinely needed that drink. *Maybe it's me that should be in a film*, he thought, as he reflected on his first contact with an officer of the Russian Security Service, the FSB.

As he queued for a beer, thinking once again that his life was becoming more surreal by the day, he heard a familiar voice behind him. "It's my favourite diplomat!" For once, Matt was pleased to see Marcella. This was an encounter he felt better suited to survive.

Marcella was dressed in red, white and blue, because, she explained, they were Panama's national colours. Any similarity to the US was just coincidence. "But I think I might be a bit low-cut today, what do you think?" she asked, doing a little flaunting.

"Looks just perfect to me," said a passing elderly Swede. "Makes me glad I bothered to come here today."

Matt had to admit she was looking particularly voluptuous. She took his arm and led him away.

"So what have you been doing and where have you been?" she asked. "Have you been avoiding me?"

Matt was just about to deny this, when he heard a southern drawl behind him.

"Everyone's been looking for Matt," said Mason Hunter, the Deputy American Ambassador. "And now I'm going to take him away from you. My apologies." Hunter took Matt's arm and led him rapidly away from the protesting Marcella.

He took Matt out of the courtyard and into one of the adjoining office buildings. There was sudden silence and solitude as they left the hubbub behind. "So," said Hunter reflectively. "You know some Russians here. Some of the bad guys. Can I ask what they want with you? You seem to have done something to annoy them."

Not wishing to reveal that he knew either of them, Matt tried to explain that his encounter with Osipov had happened by chance, and that with Oleg had been a misunderstanding.

Hunter clearly didn't believe him. "You know there is a submarine out there, don't you?" he said with a hint of menace. "Believe me; you don't know what you're getting involved in. Just drop it, will you? If you don't, you might find that Russian FSB agent you were talking to will make life seriously unpleasant for you. And don't think that we will protect you, because we won't. You'll be on your own." He paused. "Look," he said in a more conciliatory tone, "we're on the same side. But you guys here don't know everything that's going on. I can't tell you more. Just trust me. Leave well alone. And if those Russians contact you again, let me know.

"When you have been in the diplomatic game for longer, you will learn that there are two types of submarines: the bad type and the good type. Never confuse one with the other. Outside Stockholm just now there are both. Until you know which is which, I suggest you say and do nothing."

Having delivered this message, Hunter smiled, clapped Matt on the back and left.

Back in the courtyard the band was still in full swing, as was the party. Philip spotted him and made his way past some blonde ponytails.

"Just been speaking to Admiral Larsson, Swedish Navy. He believes that there are two submarines in the archipelago, and one of them may be American. They originally thought there was just one vessel, a Russian one. But they have now been picking up some traces from another submarine, which seems to indicate that it is American. He has just spoken to the American DA, who has denied it. Larsson doesn't believe him. He thinks the Americans are playing a game, but he can't prove it. Not just now, anyhow."

"So what do you think?" asked Matt.

"I don't know. It wouldn't be the first time the Americans have been less than truthful about their deployments around here. And I guess that the American Navy have something to gain by trying to show there is a Russian threat here. The bigger the threat, the more kit they can get. We would do the same, of course, not that I would ever admit it publicly."

Matt was impressed by this sudden burst of clarity from Philip. His reasoning sounded plausible. "So have they now found the Piranha you have been talking about?"

"No. The Swedes seem to have changed their minds. They now think the other submarine is an older Russian model, and they admit that they might not be able to trace a Piranha even if there was one. I wonder whether the Russians have sent an older, more easily traceable submarine here to rattle the Swedes. And the Balts."

"I don't understand," said Matt, genuinely confused. "If there is a Russian submarine out there, why would the Americans send one as well? If the American Navy wanted a scare story for their own purposes, then the Russians are already doing it for them."

"I'm not sure," Philip replied. "Maybe they deployed it, assuming they have done, before they knew the Russians were doing the same. Maybe they just want more conclusive proof. Maybe they are hunting Piranhas. I'm going to speak to the American DA myself. But I'm not sure, to be honest, that he will be any franker with me than he has been with Larsson. The special relationship only goes so far."

Matt looked across the courtyard and saw Catherine in close conversation with Erika Johansson of the Moderate Centre Party. Johansson was gesticulating in an animated way, clearly quite worked up. It looked as though Catherine had found an ally. There was a swish of red, white and blue and Marcella emerged from a cluster of cheerleaders, now busily chomping burgers. She was heading towards him, leaving a wake behind her like a Baltic ferry, but before she could dock, Matt found himself once again being grabbed by the arm. This time it was Osipov.

"Sorry, my dear," he said to a thwarted Marcella, "but I got to him first. You will have to wait a moment." He drew Matt to one side. "Why were you talking to that man, that American?"

Matt had to think for a moment before he realised Osipov must be talking about Hunter. "He's the Deputy American Ambassador, why shouldn't I speak to him?"

"I know who he is," said Osipov irritably, "and he is dangerous. Look who he is with now." He pointed towards the far corner of the courtyard, where Matt could see Hunter talking intently to Oleg. "I don't know what they are doing. Maybe talking about my Piranha. I don't like it."

Matt once again felt thoroughly confused. Everyone seemed to have an agenda, except him. "Well, if he knows about the Piranha, that will give you what you want, won't it? The Americans will go public and you can go to Antigua."

"No. Not this guy," Osipov replied. "He's State Department, isn't he? Or maybe CIA? They are weak now in Washington, unlike the Defence Department. They won't want to stir things up in the Baltic unless there is a tweet. Perhaps he's talking to Oleg about that."

Matt sighed. "So you are saying that the State Department have their own agenda, which may not be the same as the Defence Department's?"

Osipov looked at him indulgently. "It's charming how naive you young Western diplomats can be. Not like us. We are born cynical. Yes, that's exactly what I mean. So they are our enemies, you and me, and we have to outwit them."

"They aren't my enemies," Matt replied.

"I thought we were friends, you and I," said Osipov, pretending to be hurt. "Anyhow, when we first met, I didn't want you to tell anyone about my Piranha, and now I do. And I suspect that those two would rather you said nothing. So let's work together like good English public schoolboys."

Before Matt could explain that he had gone to his local state school, Osipov disappeared again into the throng.

Marcella had been waiting for a moment to intervene, and now swept forward. "Matt—" she began, but was impeded for a vital second by her erstwhile elderly Swedish admirer, who suddenly appeared in front of her with a bow, offering a plate full of hot dogs.

Just as suddenly, Matt found his arm being grabbed yet again. *I'm going to start charging for the use of this arm*, he thought angrily. He turned and found himself looking into the steely grey eyes of Vanda, the Latvian Deputy Ambassador and, as Matt had gathered from previous chats with her, arch-hater of all things Russian.

"Hello, Matt. I think you and I should have a little chat, don't you?"

She looked over his shoulder to Marcella, who was politely refusing a hot dog. "Hello, Marcella. I just need to talk to Matt for a few minutes about Latvian affairs. Then you can have him." Without waiting for a reply, and ignoring Marcella's furious glare, she led Matt to a quiet corner.

"If you are going to talk to me about submarines you will have to make an appointment," he joked. "It seems that I am the world's leading expert."

Vanda gave him an intense look. "Yes. Submarines are exactly what I want to talk to you about. I am serious."

Matt sighed. Vanda was always serious.

She also wasn't given to the indirect approach. "I want to know what you know," she demanded.

"I can start with my childhood, if you like." Matt was getting fed up by now. A flirtatious conversation with Marcella was becoming more appealing by the minute.

"I saw you talking to those Russians. We Latvians may not know as much about the world as you British do, but we are experts in Russians. We have had to live with them all our lives. We have had to study them to survive. I know when they are up to something. And those two Russians are up to something. Which means you are too. Tell me."

Matt wasn't sure how to reply. Latvia was an ally, and he sympathised with her. But he was still trying to make sense of the other messages that had been given to him that afternoon, not to mention the warnings. He decided to play safe. "We believe that there is a Russian submarine in the archipelago. But we are still trying to get some proof."

Vanda hesitated for a moment. "And what if I were to give you this proof that you want? What would you do with it?"

"I would pass it to London."

"And what would they do with it?"

Matt thought for a moment. He felt strangely compelled to be frank with Vanda. Her intensity gave her a vulnerable appeal, despite being simultaneously irritating. "I guess they would have to take some action with NATO allies. I am not sure what."

"I can tell you what would happen. You would talk first to the Americans. Then there would be a fight in Washington, and who knows what the result of that would be? One day the Russians are their friends, the next their enemies. This is too important to us to take a chance. Our national survival is at stake. The Russians want to get the Baltic States back, and unless we, we Balts, do something, they will get them."

She looked genuinely upset. Matt didn't know what to say.

She continued. "So I have a deal for you. If I give you the proof, you must promise to give it to your media. Not your government. Your media don't like this Russian government and they won't keep quiet. They will publish the proof, there will be some anger, and then your government will have to do something."

"But why me?" asked Matt. "Why can't your government go public with this proof? Or you could give it to the Swedes."

"There is a good reason why we can't go public. I can't tell you now, but you will understand later. And the

Swedes think that there is an American submarine as well, so they are unsure about what to do. They are being very cautious."

Matt recalled Osipov's claim that there was also a Latvian submarine masquerading as a Russian one. He decided to take a chance. "And what about the Latvian submarine? What's that all about?"

Vanda looked shocked, but then recovered. She gave a mirthless smile. "So I was right. You were up to something with those Russians. Is that what they told you?"

Matt decided to reveal more, and told her what Osipov had said about the Latvians hiring an old Soviet submarine from the Ukrainians. She listened intently.

"That is a classic Russian tactic. Fake news. Of course, you can't believe them. How could we, a small nation, have a submarine? They are just trying to confuse you and distract attention from their own actions. That is why it is so important that you see the truth with your own eyes. Isn't it about time that your Embassy got involved here, instead of just watching? I am giving you a chance to do something important. We are the underdogs here, and you British are supposed to support the underdogs. Think about it."

Having delivered the third ultimatum that had been made to Matt that afternoon, Vanda paused for a moment. She seemed uncertain. "So why are Panama interested in submarines?" she asked. "Marcella has been following you around all afternoon. Do they have one to sell, or what? Is it something about the canal? I don't understand."

For a moment, Matt had a vision of Marcella handing the keys of a Panamanian submarine to him. "No," he replied. "It's nothing like that."

"So what does she want from you?"

Matt sighed. Vanda might be alarmingly bright and focused, but knowledge of human nature wasn't her strong point. "We are all human, Vanda," he replied, hoping that she might work out what that meant.

"Anyhow, she has just left," said Vanda, still looking uncertain. "She was being followed by an old Swedish guy who was offering her hot dogs. Maybe she was trying to escape?"

"I couldn't blame her," said Matt. "I didn't like the look of those hot dogs either." With that, he walked away. He had a lot to think about.

What he needed now, he thought, apart from another drink, was a relaxing chat with someone who didn't want to talk to him about submarines. The band had stopped playing, and guests were beginning to leave. Catherine had cornered the Swedish Foreign Minister. Osipov and Oleg seemed to have left. Hunter, standing near the exit, caught Matt's eye and raised his glass in a mock salute. Philip was still chatting to a group of fellow defence attachés, all dressed in ceremonial military uniform, like a chorus from a Gilbert and Sullivan musical. Their wives were gossiping nearby in their best summer frocks. It was a classic diplomatic occasion. *Looks innocent enough on the surface*, thought Matt, *but it's actually full of predators*.

Catherine's husband, James, wandered up to him. "Another routine day at the office?" he joked.

Matt suddenly had a strong desire to tell him what his day had actually involved. He resisted that temptation, but decided instead to go and see Annika. He felt he could tell her, and they could try to make sense of it together.

TEN

RIGA

Without Vanda to lead them, the two men had given up
on the idea of running thirty kilometres in the forest, and
were sitting in a quiet cafe.

"Have you heard from her?"

"She has spoken to the British diplomat. He was
uncertain and doesn't seem to understand the big picture,
but she thinks he will agree to help, if only because he
might be too polite to refuse."

"I thought British diplomats were supposed to be
clever."

"Not all of them, it seems."

"So she won't have to seduce him?"

"Not necessary. Anyhow, the British are not good
subjects for seduction. I think it's because of the damp
climate."

"Her great-aunt, who is some sort of Swedish baroness,
also spoke to him at a big dinner and asked him to help."

"Well, let's hope they can persuade him. The future of
an independent Latvia depends upon it."

They chomped thoughtfully on their pastries.

MOSCOW

The admiral walked slowly around the gigantic gold hot tub in the Moscow Ideal Dacha Exhibition. "Don't tell me," he said to his wife; "this is the latest must-have?"

"I don't know if you have noticed, Sergei, but Russian oligarchs are not getting any smaller. So the hot tubs have to get bigger. And gold can cover many sins. At least, that's what Madame Osipova has told me."

"Mmm." The admiral began wondering again why he had not heard from the slimy Osipov recently. Not a word. What was he up to? Oleg was diligent, but probably didn't have a devious enough mind to monitor him thoroughly. Vitaly Alexandrovich had called again that morning and was clearly impatient for results. The admiral had heard the drumming in the background. "How is Vitaly doing?"

"The wives have heard that he is trying to become head of Gazprom. They are betting he won't succeed. And if he doesn't, he will be caviar."

"Keep me informed, my *dushenka*. Do what you can to turn him into caviar. And keep talking to Madame Osipova. I want to keep maximum pressure on him."

Washington

It was another sleepless, although thankfully tweetless, night. The Undersecretary again stared out into the quiet street. She reflected on Mason Hunter's latest message. The man was building a discreet alliance in Stockholm that he thought could result in the removal of their submarine from the archipelago. The Swedes were getting increasingly jumpy, and it seemed the Brits were being helpful, whether knowingly or not. It was too early to act in Washington, but the Undersecretary had begun to prepare the way. It was a constant struggle for her and her colleagues in the other departments to keep the wilder hawks at bay. Moving the submarine would be one more small victory.

STOCKHOLM

There was a languid air in the SÄPO offices, but some were awake.

"Mmm."

"Delicious."

"This is what we are fighting for. Without people like us, there will be no saffron *bullar* in Sweden in a few years' time. Only baklava."

"Finally, they are going to put the next stage of their plan into action."

"At last! When will we know if it is going to work?"

"In a few days. Our Latvian friend is already persuading her chosen agent. She thinks it will not take long."

"No one has found the submarine yet?"

"It seems not. But our Defence Ministry think that there is now an American submarine outside Stockholm as well."

"They are going to need an underwater congestion charge at this rate."

"But it's a good thing, if it's true. It means that it is even more likely that the US will be forced to respond."

"We are close. Our team is ready. They can deploy at any time."

"Are there any more *bullar*?"

"Mmm."

Luckily, Annika was free that evening. She suggested meeting at Gondolen, an unusual restaurant perched on the top of a giant elevator in the middle of Stockholm. The building looked like an inverted 'L' and wasn't the most beautiful adornment to the Stockholm skyline. But the views from the bar were stunning, so it was always a popular spot. She was already there when Matt arrived and had found a table looking out over one of Stockholm's many islands.

"I know I am biased, being Swedish," she said contentedly, "but there can't be many better places to be in this world than in Stockholm in the summer."

Matt agreed and ordered a seafood salad as an appetiser. He hadn't been given the chance to eat anything at the American Embassy. Over the salad and a glass of wine, he told Annika about the events of the afternoon. She looked as confused as he felt.

"So what you are telling me is that one Russian wants you to tell the world about his submarine, but one doesn't. There are also some Americans who want to tell the world about what they think is a Russian submarine, but is probably actually Latvian, and others who want you to say nothing. Then there is a Latvian who wants you to tell the world that 'their' submarine is actually Russian. Finally, we have the Swedes, who think there is both an American and a Russian submarine and who don't know what to do about it."

"Yes, that just about sums it up," Matt agreed.

Annika thought a little more as she helped herself to Matt's salad. "And you, poor Matt, have really got yourself right in the middle of all this mess, haven't you? Pressure, threats and demands from all sides." She looked upset. "I blame myself. If I hadn't encouraged you to go and talk to that man on his bicycle, none of this would have happened."

"We don't know that," said Matt, touched by her concern. "Anyhow, I need to think about what to do next. I feel that I should go and tell Catherine everything before I get into even more trouble."

"Are you sure?" asked Annika. "It sounds to me that if you start talking now, your FCO will think that you have been less than truthful with them. In my world that would mean the end of my job. Wouldn't it be better to wait a little longer? These threats might just be intended to scare you."

"Well, they do scare me," Matt replied, "and I am out of my depth now. I need someone to help me. I will think about what you said, but I think I have to make a clean breast of everything to Catherine tomorrow."

The arrival of their main courses of venison with blueberries and poached salmon with dill provided a distraction, and the conversation moved on to lighter issues. Annika's presence was a tonic in itself. After the meal, she took his arm, and without either saying anything, they drifted back to his apartment, idling on the way by the still-shimmering sea and the moored, gently stirring boats. Later, as they lay close together, she whispered to him, "Don't forget, Mr Diplomat, I'm going to search everywhere while you sleep, and then blackmail you."

"Please do," he murmured, "but don't take my Zlatan autograph."

As he cycled to work the next morning, Matt felt elated after the night with Annika, but also nervous about coming clean to Catherine. He had woken up several times in the night to find himself thinking about whether he should do it. He still hadn't made up his mind as he parked his bike and walked into the Embassy, but common sense told him that the longer the silence, the more painful the consequences. Lotta gave him a muted smile as he passed reception. *Ah! She's probably just met someone new and she's not sure how it's going to go*, he thought. *We'll all know by the end of the week.*

When he opened the Chancery door, he saw Philip marching into Catherine's office.

"Just in time," Philip said. "SMS council of war."

Matt followed him. Catherine was sitting in one of the armchairs around a glass table covered in pieces of paper.

"Come in, gentlemen. These are some of the technical documents on our missile guidance system that Philip has kindly given me. I can't say that I understand most of them. Matt, do you have any information on cheese processing plants yet?"

Matt went back into the corridor to look for Anke, whom he found in the small office kitchen surrounded by an enticing aroma. It was her turn to provide *fika* that week and she had clearly been baking that morning. She put her saffron *bullar* to one side and gave Matt a quick summary of her research, which he then repeated to Catherine back in her office.

"Well, that's not going to be a killer fact," said Catherine, "but it will give me some ammunition to use with Johansson. It's to our advantage that the Swedes will usually choose the greener option if there is any doubt." She paused. "I must admit I am surprised that they process cheese in Barbados. But it's good news for us that their plant had to be closed down for environmental reasons."

Catherine then gave a quick debrief on her conversations at the US Embassy. "Johansson is still a sworn enemy of Wallstrom and makes no secret of it. She doesn't want to stand for the leadership again if there is a contest, but she will do anything to stop him winning. She's going to encourage one of her male protégés to stand. If he does, we should think about how we could support him. He will need some publicity."

Catherine's conversation with the Swedish Foreign Minister had also gone quite well. "Pierre had got to him first, of course," she said, referring to the French Ambassador. "He made some proposal of talks in Carcassonne next month, a new joint initiative on peacekeeping research. Clever. There is a film festival there at the same time. He knows that the Foreign Minister is a film buff. So I had to think quickly. I offered him the chance to speak next week at a conference in Scotland on 'international futures'. It's taking place in a hotel with some of the best salmon fishing in the country."

"Don't tell me," said Matt, "the minister likes salmon fishing too."

"Crazy about it. And I think I might have hooked him. Fortunately, I know the conference organiser. It's very short notice, but he can probably arrange a speaking slot for the minister. If he does, I will go too. That will give me two days with him. It might be enough to get him on our side."

"Better make sure he catches some salmon," said Philip. "Tricky creatures, I believe. So, do you want me to explain all this?" he asked, waving at the technical papers.

"I tell you what," Catherine replied, "why don't you boil it down to around three pages that I might have some chance of understanding?"

Philip gathered up the documents and marched purposefully out of the room.

"Could I have a quick word?" asked Matt.

"Not now. No time. I have to set up this visit to Scotland, and I am still working on the Labour Party dinner. I have lunch today with Johansson and her protégé, and the Iranian Ambassador has asked for another meeting here to discuss the shared Embassy. I have lined up Helena to give him an extensive tour. So let's talk later."

With that, Matt was dismissed without a chance to tell Catherine about Osipov and company. He felt instantly both relieved and anxious in equal part.

Matt had to go to the Foreign Ministry the next morning for a routine briefing. As he was about to take his seat, Vanda tapped him on the shoulder.

"Hi, Matt," she said. "Can we have a word afterwards?"

He nodded his agreement, wondering what she had in store for him.

After the meeting the Political Director, Svenson, took Matt to one side. He seemed to be in a much more conciliatory mood than at their last meeting.

"You know, of course, that we are worried about submarines off our coast. Our Defence Ministries are talking together, and we appreciate your advice. I have to admit that we don't know all that is happening out there, and we are no longer quite sure who our friends are. It's difficult to know who to trust. So let's keep in touch. We might ask for your help quite soon."

Matt was surprised and nervous that Svenson was now confiding in him. He still had no idea what was being expected of him. As Matt left the building, he saw Vanda waiting patiently outside.

"Come and walk with me a little," she said.

She set off down towards the Old Town, which stood on its own island nearby. It was a picturesque, charming area, but one that Matt, like most Stockholm residents, tended to avoid in the summer afternoons, when it became packed with tourists from visiting cruise ships. Vanda didn't walk far. She stopped in a quiet side street just around the corner.

"We talked about proof, didn't we? We are ready to give you some. Do you know someone with a boat?"

"My Defence Attaché has a boat."

"No, this has to be very unofficial."

Matt thought for a while. "Well, I can probably find someone, if I really need to."

"Yes, you really need to," said Vanda, giving him her intense stare. She was standing very close to him. "This is very important. You may not understand now how important it is, but you will do. We have a friend within the Russian Navy. He has been helping us to track their submarine. He knows its standard movements and routine drills, and when and where it comes to the surface. We are confident that we can get you to a place where you can take photos. It will be up to you to decide what to do with them. But I don't think you can refuse, can you? You might have a lot to gain, but nothing to lose." She hurried on. "So get a boat and meet me at midday on Sunday at the Vaxholm motor boat petrol station. I will tell you more then. You can bring someone to help you if you want, but only someone you trust. No one official.

"Please don't contact me directly if you need to leave a message. It is not safe. The Russians have bugs all over the building. Leave a note for me at my gym on Sveagården. I go there every day." With that she marched off, giving Matt no time to reply.

As he cycled back to the Embassy along his familiar, but always beautiful path beside the Baltic, ignoring the pants and grunts of passing cyclists, he had plenty to think about. He wasn't sure if he should take up Vanda's invitation. He knew that Annika had a standing offer from a friend to use his boat whenever she wanted. She would love to go out in search of a submarine. Matt would too, he had to admit. But would it be a sensible thing for him to do?

He also thought again about Svenson's change of tone. The Swedes were concerned about the Americans as well as the Russians, he concluded. They were worried that they were being played by both sides. *And they probably are*, he thought, remembering his various discussions at the US National Day party. He once again had a strong desire to talk to Catherine. But when he returned to the Embassy, Helena wasn't able to help him.

"She's busy all day," she said, "and she is out of town tomorrow with a visiting group of UK agronomists. She is going to spend the weekend with James in Malmö. But you will be able to catch her at the Labour Party dinner on Monday. She wants you to come."

Matt had a restless evening in his flat trying to decide what to do. He had a strong feeling that going submarine hunting would involve all sorts of hidden pitfalls. He felt completely unsure whether he would be taken to see a genuine Russian submarine, or a Latvian submarine pretending to be Russian. The latter scenario seemed more likely. But to do nothing would mean that he would lose any chance to become a player in this Baltic game, rather than just a pawn. In Catherine's absence he felt there was no one to talk to. He could tell Philip, but he thought it only too likely that the DA would overreact with a series of instant actions that might spiral out of control. Finally he called Annika and arranged to meet her for lunch the next day.

Over a traditional Swedish Thursday meal of pea soup and pancakes, he told her about Vanda's proposal. As he had expected, Annika was instantly enthusiastic.

"I will call my friend Bjorn straight away," she said, "but I don't think there will be a problem. I think he is still abroad. He has a lovely boat; a real flyer. You will enjoy the trip, even if we don't see this submarine. Let's take a picnic."

After lunch, Matt wrote a message for Vanda. As he did so, he wondered if she had become paranoid about security, but then remembered some of the stories told to him by old Moscow hands, and recent revelations in the UK press about Russian computer hacking, and did as she asked. He simply said that he accepted her invitation.

Late that Sunday morning, Matt made his way down to the jetty on Strandvägen, the same place where Lars moored his boat. Annika was due to pick him up there. He felt excited and intrigued, his earlier doubts temporarily dispelled by his decision to join the game of submarines. It was again a beautiful day, with only a gentle breeze disturbing the Baltic carpet. Exactly on time, he saw Annika at the wheel of a sleek-looking speedboat which she drove expertly up to the jetty. She looked enticing in a blue-and-white striped top and tight white shorts.

"You look as though you are going to a fashion shoot," he said.

"Well, if I am going to appear on the front cover of *Submarine Weekly*, I want to look my best," she joked.

Matt sat next to her as she drove slowly along the narrow canal that led to the open sea, doing her best to avoid numerous strings of ducklings paddling obediently behind their mothers. Once out of the canal, she accelerated. The boat leapt forward like a bull released into an arena. Matt held on to his seat as he felt its power.

The tiny town of Vaxholm lay on one of only a handful of entrances into the inner archipelago from the Baltic Sea. All were narrow and easily defended. This geological quirk had been a major factor in the development of Stockholm as Sweden's capital. The route that Annika was taking was a sort of marine motorway, since most of the boats travelling to the northern half of the outer archipelago chose to pass through the narrow channel at Vaxholm. Swedish motor boat drivers behaved like Swedish cyclists; the faster the better. Annika was no different, so they had a bumpy ride as she overtook as many boats as she could, cutting across wakes and laughing as their boat bounced and weaved. Matt just clung on.

After thirty rapid minutes they arrived at Vaxholm. Matt could see a cluster of restaurants and souvenir shops, and a castle which was perfectly positioned to defend Stockholm. It stood on a small island, guarding two small channels on either side that led into the outer sea. Not quite Scylla and Charybdis, he thought, although the pretty cafes along the waterfront were doing their best to exert a siren appeal. He had taken a tour of the castle once and had been struck by how much of Vaxholm's history had been dominated by Swedish fears of a Russian attack through those narrow channels. Those fears had existed ever since Sweden's defeat by Russia in the Battle of Poltava in 1709. They had become acute during the Cold War, and Vaxholm had its own long series of Russian submarine scares.

Annika navigated her way through a crowd of speedboats and ferries jostling in the exit channel before heading to a floating platform lined with petrol pumps. This was the last service station on the marine motorway before it branched out into the many routes around the outer islands. As she drew near, Matt spotted Vanda sitting on a bench speaking animatedly into a mobile phone. Annika docked the boat to fill up with petrol. Remembering his last attempt at mooring, Matt left that task to her. He hadn't mastered the art of gracefully springing to shore, being mainly focused on not falling in, so clambered inelegantly onto the platform and made his way over to Vanda.

"Who did you come with?" she asked immediately.

Matt explained.

"You can trust her?"

Matt nodded.

"Then we are ready. Follow me. The submarine will be about two hours away. I know where and when it will surface. Stay close to me and out of sight. Take as many photos as you can. You won't have more than a few minutes. Then you can go back to Stockholm. We can talk early next week when you have decided what to do with the photos."

With those brisk words, Vanda marched over to where her boat was moored, leaving Matt no chance to ask her where they were headed. He rejoined Annika and said to her simply, "Follow that boat." Vanda pulled away from the platform, Matt clumsily clambered aboard, and Annika set off in pursuit.

Vanda's boat didn't seem quite as powerful as Annika's, so she had no problem following it as Vanda drove first though a couple of inner lakes, then some narrower channels, and finally into more open water. Annika had GPS so she was able to tell Matt the names of the many islands they passed during the next couple of hours. They drove to the north of the large island of Möja, famous, according to Annika, for nude saunas. She chatted at intervals, having to concentrate because of the number of rocks and the shallow waters. Any inattention could result in a broken propeller, or worse.

After a while the islands became smaller and more spread out. There were fewer and fewer houses and other boats as they pushed on towards the wilder edges of the archipelago. After another thirty minutes Matt guessed that they had left the last real islands behind. Now there were just scattered small, rocky islets. Vanda's boat began to slow and then came to a halt behind some rocks. Annika followed. She was getting pink and excited.

"Get the camera out, Matt. I can't believe this. I am actually going to see a submarine!"

"But remember you can't tell anyone," Matt cautioned. "At least not yet."

"I remember, but it will make a great story when I can talk about it. I can see myself already on the evening news."

Vanda turned to indicate something to them, presumably to get ready. They waited alone in the sea, bobbing gently behind the rocks. There weren't even any seabirds that far out. Time passed slowly and Matt began to wonder if Vanda had invited them out on a fool's errand. Her still figure in the boat ahead showed no signs of impatience or anxiety. Annika was stifling yawns and shifting restlessly. Just as she was about to speak, Matt thought he could hear a change in the sound of the ocean and there was a bubbling noise ahead.

A dark grey object rose slowly from the waters. Matt had seen enough movies to recognise it as a submarine turret. It continued upwards, followed by the rest of the boat. It looked enormous. Matt hadn't realised until then how large a submarine could be. Osipov's Piranha was very modest in comparison. The wash created by its emergence made their boat dance. Matt half-stood, trying to remain as invisible as possible, and began to take as many photos as he could, while trying to hang on. The giant submarine stopped for a moment, and then began to descend, churning up the waters yet again. Matt took some final photos, hoping that they wouldn't be blurred due to the rocking. Within a couple of minutes the sea was calm and they were once again alone. Vanda had already turned her boat around and motioned them to go back to Stockholm. She either wanted to make her own way back, or had other unfinished business to deal with. Matt waved to show he had understood and they began their return.

The journey back seemed much longer now that the excitement was over. As they approached the island of Möja, Annika suggested they stop for their picnic.

"You're not taking me to a nude sauna, are you?" asked Matt a little nervously, his inbred British prudishness coming to the fore.

"Not unless you want me to. I thought we could find a quiet spot to moor and have the picnic. We could do some nude swimming just by ourselves."

That sounded fine to Matt, and after Annika had stopped the boat in a peaceful and deserted cove, he looked through the photos he had taken. Some were blurry, but there were enough clear shots of the submarine.

"My Defence Attaché will know what kind of model that is, or he can find out."

"So, what are you going to do with them?" Annika asked.

"I don't know yet. I think I will wait until I next meet Vanda and listen to what she has to say. I still don't know whether to believe her or not. And I want to talk to Catherine when I get the chance."

"It's very exciting," said Annika, who was enjoying the day immensely. "Can we do it again next weekend?" With that, she took off her blue-and-white shirt and white shorts, and even a matching thong, and dived into the water.

Matt arrived at the Embassy early the next morning, hoping he would have a chance to catch Catherine. Once again he was frustrated. Helena told him that Catherine had stayed an extra night in Malmö and would be returning to Stockholm in time for the Labour Party dinner that evening. She showed Matt the list of participants. There were four visiting MPs, and a young party member who was described on Google entries as an up-and-coming activist. Matt was delighted to see that Arwel Williams was one of the MPs. Although he foresaw some potential embarrassment ahead, since he felt sure Williams would want to reminisce about their Cuba visit, he had liked the roguish MP, who had been the only one to thank Matt for his efforts. He was equally pleased that Lars Eriksson would be coming. Lars would be joined by some MPs from the governing Social Democrats, one from the Left Party, and one of Sweden's leading political commentators, whom Catherine often invited to this sort of occasion. Apart from Catherine, it was an all-male affair in the privately preferred tradition of British left-wing politics.

Matt arrived at the Residence shortly before 7pm. His hope of a quick chat with Catherine was dashed immediately. He could hear raised voices from the kitchen, and made the rookie diplomat's mistake of going to investigate. He found James and Birgitta standing eyeball to eyeball in the middle of the kitchen, separated only by a large plate of cold herring.

"Matt. Just the person!" said James in a low but intense voice. "Haven't you heard me say that I never want herring to be served in this house again? Never. Ever. But look at this. Perhaps I need to learn Swedish? I thought everyone here could understand English, but clearly I was wrong."

Birgitta was in no mood to yield. "I happen to know Gunnar from the Left Party very well, and he told me that the British visitors had asked for herring this evening."

"So you work for the Left Party now?"

"I work for the good of this house."

Both turned to Matt. In a few seconds he had turned from an innocent bystander into the referee of a heavyweight boxing match. They stared at him in furious silence. Luckily for him, he was saved by the bell. The first of the Swedish guests had arrived. Matt fled the kitchen, opened the front door, showed them where they could leave their bicycles and led them into the living room.

Catherine, who as an experienced diplomat and wife had sensibly stayed upstairs out of harm's way during the kitchen fracas, came down and welcomed her guests. A few minutes later the British visitors arrived.

"Well, well," said Arwel Williams, who was pleased to see Matt. "This is the young man who led me astray in Havana and caused a diplomatic incident. Good to see you. I will have a chat with you later. I have been wondering where the nightlife is in Stockholm, and now I have found just the man to tell me."

Matt was happy to see Lars coming towards him. He was delighted to have been invited, and was looking forward to a long chat with Gunnar, a friend from long-gone protest marches.

"Anything new on submarines?" asked Lars.

Before Matt could reply, Catherine took his arm and led him into the dining room. "We have a problem. The sort of problem that we diplomats are supposed to be able to solve. So we better had."

"Yes," said Matt, "but I am sure James and Birgitta will speak to each other again eventually."

"No, not that problem. I am not sure even the UN Secretary General would want to take that on. It's the Labour Party group. Apparently they come from two wings of the party who can't stand each other. They have been spoiling for a fight ever since they got to Stockholm, and I don't want battle to begin at my dinner table. You know that the Swedes have their own divisions too, ever since the SDP began to take a tougher stance on immigration. I am sure that Gunnar will want to have a go at them."

"So what can we do?" Matt asked.

"I will try to keep the conversation on safe subjects, like the Sweden Democrats."

"The common enemy?" said Matt, thinking about that party's far-right policies.

"No, the opposition. The enemy lies within."

Catherine led her guests into the simple, but elegant dining room. Matt sat at the bottom of the table and watched as she skilfully directed the conversation. All went well for a while, as the guests united in their condemnation of the far right, and moved on to an excoriation of the centre right.

"It gives me joy," said Lars, "to see a true socialist party again in the UK."

"If only," said the Labour Party activist. "But we have a long way to go."

"Same in Sweden," said Gunnar.

There was a hubbub as everyone spoke at once. Voices were raised, cutlery flourished, herring impaled and wine spilt. It looked as though blood might follow suit. Catherine looked at Matt, who felt equally helpless.

They were rescued by an unlikely saviour. Arwel Williams had seen their despairing glances, and rose to his feet. "Gentlemen and our Ambassador. A toast." Having got everyone's attention, he gave an exaggerated and embellished account of that evening with Matt in the Havana cabaret, in which he portrayed himself as a serious, well-intentioned politician led into a sort of public honey trap by two diplomats, who were either scheming, lustful, or both. He ended with a toast to "diplomacy, good and bad". He said it all with enough of a twinkle as to leave the Swedes uncertain whether to view Matt as someone to avoid, or invite to an evening out.

"I wish more of our diplomats were like that," said one of them, only half-jokingly. "Ours are far too serious."

After Williams's intervention, tempers cooled and the rest of the evening passed fairly smoothly. As the guests left, Matt thanked Williams.

"I have probably been a politician for too long," he said. "There was a time when I would have relished that sort of shouting match, but I actually prefer a quiet debate now. Anyhow, I owed you one for that evening in Havana. It's like I said at the time. In the Labour Party everything that goes around, comes around. That photo has done no end of good for my image with the left. I might even get a Shadow Cabinet job. So maybe I should thank you."

"Well, that could have been a lot worse," said Catherine when the last Swedes had put on their bicycle clips and wobbled unsteadily into the night. "Thank you for your help. Now I have to start my own peacekeeping mission. With no UN support." She sighed and walked slowly up the stairs. Once again, Matt had missed the chance to talk to her.

ELEVEN

When he got back to his apartment, he found a note under his door. It was from Vanda, who wanted to meet him the next day at 1pm in the NK cafe. Matt wondered how whoever left the note had got into his building, since the front door had a coded lock. But he supposed that it would be easy for anyone with espionage training to do such a thing. *Useful if you are the type to lock yourself out*, he thought.

NK was the largest and most celebrated department store in Stockholm. The cafe was a favourite meeting place for smorgasbord-eating ladies. Matt guessed that Vanda had chosen it because it would be too crowded and noisy for anyone to pay any attention to them. He strolled down Strandvägen, and then into Birger Jarlsgatan, one of the city's main shopping streets. He made his way through the store and up to the cafe. Vanda was already there, sipping at a glass of water.

"You had better order something," she suggested. "It will make us look inconspicuous."

"What about you?"

"I never eat in places like this. I have my own food at home, from the Latvian countryside. Much better for you."

Matt reluctantly ordered a sandwich from a menu designed for the very affluent.

"Did you take some good photos?" she asked.

"They are good enough. I am sure an expert could recognise what sort of submarine it is."

"I can tell you. It is a Romeo. Very old now, but easily recognisable as a Russian model. I could never have found it out there myself. We don't know much about submarines in Latvia. We are better on skis than under water. But we had help from our friend in the Russian Navy and some others."

"Which others?"

"I can't tell you that just now. You will understand that we have some friends in this neighbourhood. We may be small, but we are not alone." She took a sip of water. "So have you decided what to do with your photos?"

Matt hesitated. "No, not yet. I need more time to think. You may be used to this sort of thing, but I am not."

Vanda gave him a long look. "I will let you think about it," she said. "But don't think too long. If you don't want to help us, we will find someone who does. Be brave, Matt, and support the underdog. One day, I will take you to my country and then you will understand us." She hesitated for a moment. "I was born in the Soviet Union. As a child I spent a lot of time with my grandparents, who talked all the time about Latvia's period of freedom between the wars. As a young teenager, I used to dream of leading an uprising to get that freedom back. I wanted to be a heroine, to make them proud. But all I could do was write anti-Russian graffiti in the school lavatory. When Yeltsin took over and we got our country back, I was still too young to help. But now I can do something. And I will. The Russians like to think they are the most cunning, that they are the masters of trickery. But we are going to trick and surprise them."

With that, she took a final sip of water and left just as Matt's expensive sandwich arrived. He munched it slowly amid the chattering horde, thinking about his options, and wishing he had never got involved.

Catherine had been working in her office at the Residence that morning, and when Matt returned to the Embassy, his hopes of a meeting were dashed by Helena, who told him that she had already gone to the airport. The Swedish Foreign Minister had decided to go to the Scottish conference, and Catherine was going to accompany him.

"She would like you to represent the Embassy at the French National Day party this week," said Helena. "So you will have to put up with all that delicious food. And so will I."

Matt was pleased, although surprised, to hear that Catherine wanted Helena to accompany him. Invitations to Embassy parties were usually only given to diplomats.

"Do you know why Catherine wants me to go to the French party?" asked Helena with a mischievous smile. "She wants me to charm the Iranian Ambassador."

"I think you have done that already," said Matt, not without envy.

"Yes, but I have to charm him a little more. So that he genuinely supports the idea of sharing the Embassy and tells that to his Ministry. Then Catherine will have some real ammunition to use in London."

"And you don't mind?"

"No. He is harmless enough. And I never usually get the chance to go to these sorts of parties. I am curious." Helena's private life was a mystery which she took pains not to unveil. Nobody knew if she was single, although many had tried to find out. She floated serenely above it all.

When Matt checked his emails, he saw there was one from Annika. *Our friend has requested a meeting this evening. Usual place and time.* Matt guessed that the 'friend' was Gunilla from SÄPO. It seemed that Annika had become infected by Vanda's love of secrecy. *She will be arranging dead-letter drops next*, he thought, recalling spy novels he had read. *OK*, he emailed back. *Will be there. Wearing an M&S tie.*

Annika was waiting on their traditional bench when he arrived in the small park that evening.

"Did she say what she wanted?" he asked.

"Only that she wanted to know if we had any information for her."

Matt reflected. There was a lot he could tell Gunilla, but he wasn't sure how much he should say.

"Let's be open with her," Annika suggested. "You want to talk to someone who might help, and Catherine isn't around."

A moment later Gunilla appeared in her usual unobtrusive way and sat down. "Let me tell you something first," she said, "and then you can decide what to tell me." She went on to tell them the same information that Admiral Larsson had passed to Philip. The Swedes now believed there were two submarines in the archipelago. One was Russian, the other American, although the Americans were not admitting it. "The government doesn't know what to do," she concluded.

Matt looked at Annika. He trusted Gunilla, and had an overwhelming urge to confide in someone. He took a deep breath and told her the latest developments, including his conversations at the American Embassy on Independence Day, and his second submarine sighting with Vanda. Gunilla listened in intent silence, a slight smile on her lips.

"You have been busy," she said, when Matt had finally finished. "It's remarkable how much you have discovered, or at least how much people have been willing to tell you. You must have a face people want to trust. Perhaps you should have been a priest. On second thoughts, these days maybe that's not a good suggestion. Perhaps a barber. Anyhow, a lot of what you have said makes sense. I have seen the divisions in SÄPO. There are many there that want our government to confront the Russians. They want the Americans to get more involved. I can understand, although I think myself that any confrontation would be too risky and the consequences would be unpredictable.

"But I am afraid that some in SÄPO have a wider and more dangerous objective. They think that the government has been much too soft on immigration. They believe that all the asylum seekers and migrants that we have let into the country in recent years will give them a security problem in the future that will be impossible to deal with. So Sweden will be threatened externally by a dominant Russia, and internally by extremism unless the government acts firmly and quickly."

"But that sounds like the agenda of the Sweden Democrats," said Annika, sounding very alarmed. "Does SÄPO support them now? Is this the beginning of a coup?"

"It's true that these views are similar to theirs. I don't believe that this faction in SÄPO support the Sweden Democrats. They are motivated only by worries about security. But the situation is dangerous, and who knows where it might lead unless they are stopped? My faction, if you can call them that, are worried that there will be a repeat of what happened in the 1970s and '80s when a group within SÄK tried to subvert democracy, to destabilise the government for their own purposes. We can't allow that."

"So what about the submarine we saw?" asked Matt, who was wondering where that fitted in.

"I believe that your friend Osipov was actually telling the truth," Gunilla said, "and that the submarine is being used by the Latvians. It fits in with everything else we know."

"Vanda said that they had help from their neighbours," Matt continued, "but didn't want to tell me from whom."

"Interesting point," said Gunilla thoughtfully. "Yes, it's very possible that this faction in SÄPO has been helping them. They would know how to pass on information about which routes to take within the archipelago, and how to remain undetected. Especially if they had some help from someone in naval intelligence here. That is more believable than Vanda's claim that someone inside the Russian Navy is assisting them."

Annika had been getting redder and redder and now couldn't contain herself. "Do you think that these Latvians want to change our government?" she almost yelled.

"I doubt that," Gunilla replied calmly. "They will be focusing only on the Russian angle. And I can see why they want a third party like you to reveal the existence of this 'Russian' submarine, rather than for it to come from a Swedish or Latvian source. They want to keep some distance and make it more plausible."

There was a long pause as they each took some time to think. Several crocodiles of kindergarten children filed past them in the usual obedient Swedish way.

"So what do we do now?" asked the fuming Annika.

"I would like you to do nothing, for now," said Gunilla. "I need to talk to my allies. It will be better for us if all of this plotting comes to an end, and if all those submarines go back to where they came from. Maybe we will talk to Mr Hunter. There are some in the US that could be our allies over this; those who don't want an artificial crisis in the Baltic. And we will talk to our colleagues in Riga too. I am wondering whether the Latvian government knows about this submarine, or whether they have their own secret group with an agenda. We shall have to prepare carefully for a meeting with the top people in SÄPO. To be honest, I don't know where their sympathies lie. The faction that we are opposing has some powerful friends."

Annika looked ready to explode, but somehow managed to contain herself. "OK. I won't say anything to anyone just now. But I can't promise to stay silent unless you can solve this. It's too important."

Matt also agreed to wait for Gunilla to talk to her colleagues. But he was privately determined to tell all to Catherine when he got the chance. "I will be going to the French National Day tomorrow," he said. "I might pick up some more information there."

They agreed to meet soon, and Gunilla left as unobtrusively as she had arrived. Annika spent some time venting her feelings about what they had heard, which she clearly viewed as a betrayal of Swedish democracy, but she eventually calmed down and left to go to a meeting. Matt sat for a while to enjoy the peace of the park. Stockholm was not turning out to be the sort of posting he had expected.

The French National Day party was the last major diplomatic event of the summer season. The streets were quiet as Helena drove Matt to the nearby French Embassy. She looked even more stunning than usual in a polka-dotted cream summer dress. Philip had also already left by car. Defence attachés didn't cycle, presumably because it was below the dignity of their office, although Matt had to admit that cycling while dressed as a Ruritanian admiral would look more than a little ridiculous.

The French, of course, regarded the 14th July as the diplomatic high point of the year. Although it couldn't quite match the US for VIP appeal, or the Japanese for food, it was in top place for self-regard. The party was held in the Embassy gardens, a large, leafy space with plenty of room for small marquees offering exquisitely presented food and drink. Well-dressed French couples circulated politely and there was a soporific late-summer atmosphere.

As Matt and Helena walked into the garden, plenty of heads turned in their direction. They were mostly male, although quite a few of the women were also staring at Helena.

"I never have this effect when I arrive at a national day," Matt said. "Be careful. You might have already made a few female French enemies."

Helena just smiled. She was used to such reactions. Matt had to admit that she dealt with her beauty in a mature way. She was very aware of it, but didn't seem to let it dominate her life. Today, however, she intended to use it.

"So where is my Iranian lamb?" she said with an intent look.

Matt looked around. Gul was usually quite easy to spot because of his distinctive dress. *It must be difficult, by contrast, if you are in Tehran*, he thought. *So many men with beards wearing the same clothes.* He finally saw him near one of the marquees, inspecting the food on offer.

"The lamb is over there," he said. "Innocently grazing."

"I don't think he is so innocent," Helena replied. "I am going to start stalking. See you later." She flicked back her hair and strolled slowly in Gul's direction.

Now alone, Matt looked around for potential pitfalls. To his relief, he could see neither Osipov nor Oleg. Nor was there any sign of Vanda. He was pleased to see Marcella in the distance, dressed in another combination of red, white and blue. She might provide him with a refuge if he wanted to escape unwanted attention. For a while, he was left undisturbed to browse the food stalls and sip some wine. But such peace couldn't last for long. Mason Hunter had spotted him, left a small group of fellow diplomats and strolled up.

"So, how is the hunt for Red October?" he asked, with his usual knowing smile.

"I should be asking you the same question."

"Fair enough." Hunter looked steadily at him. "How much do you trust your Defence Attaché? I mean, do you guys talk to each other? Go for beers, that sort of thing?"

"We get on all right," said Matt, surprised by the question. "We don't often go out drinking together. He has a lot of military functions to go to. But our relations are good. Why do you want to know?"

"Because I don't trust my DA, and he doesn't trust me. If he offered me a drink, I would send it for testing. And that's fine. We have different interests. The reason I asked you that question is that our interests in this case are the same, and your DA's should be too. I don't think I need to spell it out too much. We do have a submarine in the Baltic. I never wanted it here, I always thought that it would cause trouble for us. But the Defence Department insisted. They thought that we needed to have a presence, to show the Russians we hadn't abandoned the Baltic. And they wanted to try to find a Piranha. But they decided not to tell the Swedes. They say it's for reasons of operational security; Sweden not being a member of NATO. But I have it on good authority that it is really because of some stupid, macho argument our Defence Secretary had a few months ago with the Swedish Defence Minister. About how to hunt deer, of all things! That was bound to lead to problems, but again they didn't listen to us."

"Who are 'us'?" Matt interrupted.

"State, CIA, it's not important. We both have the same interests here. Personally, I don't trust the Russians. Never have, and I have never concealed it. I trust them even less than Defence. And in this case, Defence can't see the bigger picture. The action isn't here. It's in the Middle East and Ukraine. This is not the time to get into a fight with the Russians in the Baltic."

"So why are you telling me all this?" asked Matt.

"Because you can help. Or rather, your DA can help. We want Defence to move their submarine away from this region and out of harm's way. Our guys may be on bad terms with the Swedes, at least at the top, but they sometimes listen to you. If you start telling them that keeping our submarine here, now that the Swedes have found it, is counterproductive then they might pay attention."

"But your submarine isn't the only one in the archipelago, is it? There is another one. What do you know about that one?"

"We aren't sure," Hunter admitted. "There is something very strange about its movements. From the little information we have, it seems to spend a lot of time resting on the bottom of the Baltic. But we are assuming it is Russian. What else could it be?"

"All right," said Matt. "I can't promise anything, but I will speak to our Defence Attaché."

"Good," said Hunter. "And if you do, we might put in a good word for you with the Swedes about your missile guidance system."

Matt was again surprised by Hunter's knowledge of confidential UK business, but felt a little more reassured by the rest of their conversation. At least he wasn't being threatened this time, and what Hunter said chimed with Philip's own analysis. With that thought, he looked for his Defence Attaché and saw him, as usual, chatting with his fellow attachés and their wives. Matt remembered Catherine saying some months before that she always felt more comfortable when she saw a group of attachés together: "If they leave the herd and start talking to other people, they can get all sorts of strange ideas. They can't do much harm when they stick to their own."

Matt headed across the lawn. Philip was in full flow, but his wife Jane saw Matt coming, understood and firmly induced him to bring his story to a quick conclusion.

"Just telling the chaps something that happened to a pal of mine in Iraq," he told Matt as he took him to one side. "So, what can I do for you?"

Matt gave Philip a quick summary of what Hunter had said to him.

"Makes sense," said Philip. "I know that the Swedes are getting very annoyed with the Americans about their submarine, which they still deny is theirs, by the way. They want the Americans to come clean, and they want them to move it. I will have to check with London, but I think that we would be willing to talk to the Americans as a third party; encourage them to redeploy the submarine where it can be more useful. That will put us in the Swedes' good books, which might help us with the SMS contract. And if the State Department put in a word for us as well, so much the better. I can't tell you how pleased I would be to get one over on the French Defence Attaché. He has been acting like God Almighty today, and his wife isn't any better. She told Jane how impressed she is that Jane recycles her dresses so economically. That really got under her skin."

They separated. Matt was feeling pleased with himself. Perhaps he could be an effective diplomat, after all? It was probably Philip's reference to God Almighty that conjured up the elegant presence of Pierre de Longeville, French Ambassador to the Kingdom of Sweden, at Matt's elbow. De Longeville had never previously acknowledged Matt's existence, and indeed Matt was surprised that he knew of his existence, as a humble Second Secretary.

"*Bonjour,*" he said, in his habitually grand manner. "Catherine is away, I understand. In Scotland with the Swedish Foreign Minister. I am sure it is very agreeable there, and that they will solve many of the world's problems while fishing together. But I would like you to pass a message to her when she returns. She should know that I have it on good authority that the crucial decision about, let's say, missile guidance systems will not be taken by the Foreign Minister, but by the Defence Minister.

"That makes much more sense, don't you think? The Defence Minister, who is a fine fellow, will be going next month to look at our system. He knows very little about wine, but firmly believes that he is an expert. As it happens, one of our missile plants is near Bordeaux. I think Catherine will find that wine will always beat salmon. I am telling you this because I like her, and I don't want her to get too disappointed." With that, de Longeville strolled away, looking very pleased with himself.

Matt was reflecting on de Longeville's arrogance in casually passing on that information to a rival, when an excited figure in red, white and blue sped towards him.

"Matt, you have to help me," said a slightly breathless Marcella. "I can't get rid of him. I have tried everything. And he is much faster than he looks."

"What are you talking about?"

"That Swede. You remember, from the US National Day? It was very difficult to escape from him that time, too. He used to be a senior Ambassador. And he seems to think, well, I don't know what. That I am interested in him or something. Which I am not. Why should I be? He must be seventy years old. Oh God! He's found me again. Do something, please."

Matt turned to see the elderly Swede he had last seen offering hot dogs to Marcella. He was approaching with a very determined expression.

"Kiss me!" said Marcella, and before Matt had a chance to react, she proceeded to put her request into action. It was a long and, Matt had to admit, perfectly pleasant kiss. When she finally finished, there was some applause from those around them. "Sorry," she whispered, "but I had to make it look convincing."

"Bravo, Matt," said a French diplomat, who was standing nearby. "Perhaps it's not true what they say about you British."

Marcella's ardent pursuer opened his arms in a gesture of surrender. "I yield to the younger man," he said.

One of Marcella's Latina colleagues came over to them. "Oh, Marcella," she said. "At last! I am so happy for you."

Matt took Marcella's arm, politely but firmly, and led

her away. It was time he told her about Annika. But he didn't get the chance.

"Thank you, Matt, you saved me! My hero. But I will go now. People are talking. See you very soon." She left in a flurry of scent and colour before he could speak.

As he was watching her leave, the urbane figure of Mikhail Rogozhin of the Russian Embassy approached him, glass in hand. "Well, well. You are once again the centre of attention. First, His Excellency talking to a mere Second Secretary. And then passion on the lawns of the French Embassy. Very appropriate."

Matt felt deeply embarrassed, but Rogozhin wasn't intending to be difficult. "You and I have a lot in common, I think. We are the ones who have to sort out the mess that other people make. Just now, we have a problem in the Baltic that affects both of us. A Ukrainian submarine, or is it now Latvian? Who would have thought it?! We really don't want that when we need to work together in other parts of the world." He looked expectantly at Matt. "I know you British pride yourselves on your pragmatism. So you will know that sending such a submarine here can only cause unnecessary trouble."

"What do you think I could do about such a submarine, if it exists?" asked Matt.

"I think you could persuade the Latvians to remove it. Give it back to the Ukrainians. Take it somewhere where it won't cause any misunderstandings. I think if you do that, the Swedes will be grateful. Probably the Americans too, or at least some of them."

"And what makes you think that we have a special influence with the Latvians?" asked Matt.

"Let's say it seems that you have somehow got yourself into a position from which you can influence them, whether you realise that or not. And if you do, we might be able to help you with your missile systems bid."

Naively, Matt hadn't previously realised that other countries would know quite so much about the UK bid, but he was beginning to understand that acquiring such knowledge was normal diplomatic business.

"The French guidance system is better than yours," Rogozhin continued, "so it wouldn't suit us for the Swedes to choose it. Who knows what may happen in the future? We don't mind your system. As it happens, the French are quite interested in selling theirs to us. They wouldn't admit it, of course. But we could discreetly let the Swedes find that out. If we were to do that, they would be angry and would definitely choose your system. So everyone would be happy. You and the French would both have a sale and we would end up with the better system. So I suggest you speak to your Latvian colleague. She is a bit headstrong, but she might listen to you."

"Why do people think I have any influence? I am only a junior diplomat. I don't really understand," said Matt.

Rogozhin thought for a moment. "You British used to be a major player. Not just here, but in many other places too. No longer. Now it's just us, the Americans and the French. Yes, the Chinese get powerfully involved whenever they want to, and regional powers will always want to join the game in their neighbourhood. But you are mostly a spectator now. Look at you here. Two British diplomats in your Embassy, and a Defence Attaché. How can you expect to do anything significant? You joined our game here by accident. I guess because you are young and harmless, you have been trusted to be a messenger, a go-between. And it seems you have done a good job, even though you may not have known what you were doing or why. That's why your Latvian friend might listen to you. She knows you don't have an agenda and you don't have any power. Perhaps that will be the British role in diplomacy in the future. To hold coats and deliver messages."

He strolled away, looking as though he had been chatting about the food, rather than high – or was it low? – politics. Matt felt it was a good moment to leave so that he could think about the messages he had received. It was time for another talk with Annika. First, however, he wanted to check on Helena. He couldn't see her, so he wandered around the marquees for a little while, nibbling small French delicacies and stopping for brief chats with his fellow diplomats. It seemed they had all seen, or heard about, the kiss, so Matt received a lot of teasing, mostly good-humoured.

"So, next posting Panama?" said one. "I hear they have a canal. Good for immensely long, romantic walks, perhaps?"

Matt took it in good part, and continued his search for Helena. He finally found her in a quiet corner of the garden, listening to Gul, who had exchanged his usual politely remote demeanour for something much more human. Helena smiled slightly as she saw Matt. Gul gave him a scowl.

"I am so sorry, Ambassador," she murmured. "My colleague has come to take me away. I will remember everything you told me. I am looking forward so much to your next visit to our Embassy." She gave Gul one long departing look and joined Matt.

"So how did it go? Is the lamb tender?"

"Oh, yes. If he was any more tender he would start to fall apart."

"What was he saying to you?"

"Oh, the usual promises. It seems his wife is in Tehran – she doesn't like Swedish food – and he is lonely here. He writes poetry and wants someone to recite it to. I don't believe him for a moment, but he does have a sort of intense charm."

"So, are we all lambs to you?" asked Matt, feeling an irrational stab of jealousy.

"Only when I am bored," Helena said. "I like to practise sometimes, in case some real prey comes along. I think he is ready now to talk seriously to Catherine about this Embassy-sharing idea. Although I am glad that she has promised me that it will never happen. I would have to leave if it did. Or become a vegetarian. You can only have so much lamb."

TWELVE

When Matt got back to the Embassy, he sent an email to Annika, suggesting a meeting 'in the usual place'. This had become their code for a rendezvous with Gunilla. She replied with alacrity and an evening meeting was quickly arranged.

Gunilla had always looked the epitome of calm during their previous encounters in the park, but today she looked tired and anxious. Matt told her and Annika about his conversations at the French Embassy.

"You get all the fun," Annika complained. "All this cloak-and-dagger stuff. I feel jealous."

"There isn't much fun involved," Matt replied. "It's more like being a bar of chocolate at a slimming convention. You know you are going to be bitten, but you don't know when."

"There is a big battle going on within SÄPO now, and I fear my side are losing," said Gunilla grimly. "The other faction has prepared well, and has good cover stories. They are telling the bosses that the report about the Latvian submarine is a Russian decoy, fake news, designed to distract us from the truth. The bosses are inclined to believe them. They are concerned that while we are confused and uncertain, the Russians will begin a series of destabilising actions aimed at the Baltic States."

"But what about the Latvians?" said Annika. "Surely they will be able to tell you the truth?"

"The Latvian Security Service tell us that they know nothing about a submarine. So I can only assume that Vanda is involved in a clandestine operation. Of course, our opposing faction in SÄPO denies any knowledge of it, even though we are convinced that they are involved."

"Have you spoken to the Americans?" asked Matt.

"Yes, but they are telling us nothing. I think they might have their own internal differences."

"Maybe I should speak to Vanda?" Matt suggested.

"You could try," Gunilla replied, "but I doubt very much whether she would want to compromise or stop what she has been doing now. I guess that they will be planning to expose their 'Russian' submarine at any moment, since you haven't done it. They must be waiting for something that will give them maximum publicity, while making it difficult for the Russians to disprove it. Anyway, Vanda isn't here now. She has gone back to Riga. To talk to her group, I suppose."

"So what next?" asked Annika.

"I am not quite sure," Gunilla replied, looking a little despondent. "We will continue to fight within SÄPO. We haven't lost quite yet. But we need more proof. If we lose and people believe there is a Russian submarine in our archipelago, there will be a big increase in tension in our area. Sweden and then NATO will start a diplomatic battle with Russia. Who knows where that might lead? I also worry about the possible implications for Sweden if that causes us to have another election. The nationalist faction in SÄPO might get what they want. Voters often turn to the right if they feel threatened. We need to make sure they know the truth before they decide."

She left, walking without her usual brisk stride. Annika also looked despondent.

"We have to stop this, somehow," she muttered.

"I will go to see Vanda as soon as she gets back, although I don't hold much hope of persuading her to change what she and her colleagues are planning. But I don't want to do anything else until I have had a chance to talk to Catherine."

They parted in low spirits.

Matt's mood wasn't improved by the sight of a teary Lotta when he went into the Embassy the next morning.

"I gave up on men," she sniffed, as Matt found a tissue for her. "And then I met Sonia at a bar last week. She seemed so nice and she listened to me. So I thought I might try with a woman, just to see if that might be better for me. But last night in her apartment, just when things were going really well, she told me that she was a man. He was so pleased that I hadn't realised. He was only interested in me because he thought I could give him advice on how to behave like a woman. It was terrible. I feel I can't trust anyone now. So I guess it's back to men. Real men. Do you know any?" she added with a note of hope.

Matt promised her that he would give it some serious thought and left her busily reapplying her make-up. Just in case.

It was Matt's turn to provide cakes for *fika* that week, and as usual he had forgotten.

"We are looking forward to something special today, Matt," said Anke when he met her in the kitchen. "I can't see any cakes yet."

"Ah," said Matt.

"You have forgotten again, haven't you?"

That was a major sin, but Matt had to confess to it. His penance was to cycle to the nearest bakery on Valhallavägen and buy the most expensive cakes he could find. The good weather had broken temporarily and it was drizzling as he cycled back. He was greeted by the sight of Tom standing proudly in reception by a large new machine, just inside the Embassy doors.

"Our new security detector," he explained. "Just arrived. We asked London and they gave us some money straight away. No argument. It shows how important security is these days. And security officers, of course. I found this one online. It's Chinese. Very good value. Can't afford an expensive one. Now if you would just put that package you are carrying through the machine. It will be the first thing through it."

"But it's only cakes," said Matt. "For *fika*. Look." He opened the bag, but Tom was adamant.

"It's the rules, he said. "I don't make them. Nothing can be allowed into the Embassy unless it goes through the machine."

Matt capitulated. He put the package on the small conveyor belt. As it entered the machine there was a loud noise like a siren and lights flashed.

"Ah!" said Tom. "That means your package has been identified as a security threat. I am obliged to destroy it."

"But they are only cakes," repeated the irritated Matt. "You can eat one if you like, just to prove it."

"I am sorry," Tom replied implacably, "but those are the rules. I am going to have to put them in the incinerator. Interesting, though. It must be a very sensitive machine." He retired to his nearby office, gingerly carrying the offending cakes.

With a resigned sigh, Matt cycled back to the bakery through the increasingly heavy rain. Fortunately, Tom was still busy with the incinerator when he got back and he was able to smuggle the new bag of cakes upstairs without him noticing.

By *fika* time, the story of the burnt cakes had circulated around the Embassy and Matt had been christened 'Alfred' by the Chancery team.

"Of course, Alfred fought against us, the Vikings," said Tina, while munching a Danish pastry.

"And won," added Philip.

"It's true that he kept us Vikings out of London and southern England," Anke agreed, "but look at us now. There are Swedes everywhere in the City, making money. So we got there in the end. And I hear that you had a battle with Vikings last weekend, Philip, and lost."

Philip reluctantly described his latest nautical mishap, which took place at the island of Birka, near Stockholm, where a Viking village had been excavated some years previously. There was small museum there and the island was sometimes used for Viking re-enactments. Boat engines, as is well known, always tend to break down in the most inconvenient places. Naturally, Philip's did so as he was approaching Birka at the same time as a Viking longboat, drunkenly crewed by Swedes on a corporate away day, dressed in their best medieval clothes. The collision was quite dramatic, and several 'Vikings' had an early dip, still clutching their oars.

The 'Vikings' then invaded Philip's boat, declared it to be theirs by conquest, and happily downed his gin while waiting for him to repair the engine. He finally managed to coax some life into it and tow the longboat to the jetty. The story hadn't made the press, to Philip's relief, but had somehow leaked out to the military community, and he had come in for a great deal of teasing. *Glad we aren't trying to sell any naval kit to the Swedes*, thought Matt, yet again.

Catherine returned to the Embassy on Friday morning and Matt felt very nervous going into work that day, as he built up his courage to tell her everything. When he entered the building, he saw a disconsolate Tom once again studying a battered instruction manual.

"The security scanner didn't like Catherine's handbag this morning," he explained. "But she took it into the building anyhow. She was very rude about the machine and told me to get rid of it. So now I will have to report a security breach to London."

Matt left him to it and went upstairs.

Helena was gliding down the corridor with a tray of coffee in hand. "She wants to see you and Philip straight away. And then the two of us," she murmured.

Matt followed her into Catherine's office. To his relief, the incident with the machine didn't provoke a Luddite rant from his boss. On the contrary, Catherine seemed in good spirits. When Philip arrived she told them about her Scottish trip, which had gone very well. The conference itself had been a fairly tedious affair, but the Swedish Foreign Minister, David Bertilson, had enjoyed the networking and the evening discussions about the state of the world, fuelled by high-quality whisky. More importantly, he had managed to catch a salmon, with the aid of an experienced ghillie, which had put him in an exceptionally good mood, making him very responsive to a sales pitch about the virtues of the British missile guidance system and the total unreliability of the French.

"By the end of the conference he had agreed to recommend to the Swedish Cabinet that they should buy our system." Catherine looked at Philip. "To be honest, he still wasn't entirely convinced that our system was the best on the market, but he did believe that we would never sell it to the Russians."

Philip then told her about his discussions at the French National Day.

"I haven't spoken to my chaps back at the MOD yet. As far as I am aware, the Americans haven't told them about their submarine either. The MOD will probably be quite annoyed when they find out, and I think they will have no objection to suggesting to the Americans that they remove it. I have been waiting for you to get back before doing anything because this is a diplomatic matter as much as a military one."

"Good," said Catherine. "I will speak to Bertilson, since I am now his best friend, and tell him what we plan to do. Then we can both speak to our departments back home to suggest they talk to the Americans on both channels and encourage them to remove their submarine. That should give us some extra credit with the Swedes."

"Any news on the Moderate Centre Party?" asked Matt.

"I am talking to Johansson every day. They are beginning to get cold feet about provoking a national election, because the more pragmatic amongst them realise that they might do badly in the current climate. The majority are now hoping that their leader will escape from Nappygate with nothing worse than a nasty stain on his character. If he does have to resign, it looks as though the same majority will support any candidate who wants to stay within the governing coalition. So, either way, it's looking better for us. But we can't be complacent. You know what these small parties are like. One big row at a party meeting, one glass of schnapps too many, and it could all go tits up."

Matt then told them about de Longeville's message.

"That makes sense, I don't expect the French to give up easily," said Catherine. "That's why I did something else at this conference. As chance would have it, the Deputy Permanent Secretary at the MOD was also there and we had a long chat. I persuaded him that it would be a good time for the Defence Secretary, Stephen Glover, to visit Stockholm. He could make a pitch for the missile system deal and at the same time give the Swedes some reassurance that we haven't forgotten about the Baltic, even if we can't offer much practical support. He promised to try to sell this idea to his minister when he got back to London. He was optimistic because there is an unexpected gap in the minister's programme. We should know in the next couple of days if he is going to come. But it looks as though you and your team are going to be busy, Philip."

A delighted Philip left to begin preparing his signal to London, a lengthy and laborious task. Catherine then asked Helena to join her and Matt.

"I am telling you both this in confidence," she began. "I don't want to alarm the rest of the Embassy staff yet. As you know, I called in at the Office on my way back here. It's not looking good. The Europe Director, Giles Featherstone, told me that a new round of cuts is inevitable. He wasn't sure yet what the implications might be for us, but we have to be prepared for anything. We might even have to set up a Nordic Embassy, with Consulates in the other capitals. If that were to happen, there would be a big fight between us and Copenhagen as to where the Embassy would be. Oslo and Helsinki would compete too, but we would be the two favourites. There would be no guarantee that we would win. If we were to lose, we would have to reduce the size of our operation here quite dramatically. We would be obliged to move into a smaller building somewhere and would lose a lot of staff.

"None of this is certain, of course, but we need to plan ahead. In the meantime, my idea of Embassy-sharing with Iran to save costs is the sort of radical idea that might convince London that we are more cutting-edge than Copenhagen, so deserve to be the new hub. If it gets some political backing, it doesn't matter if it then gets rejected on security grounds. We will have got some attention back home, which we don't have at the moment. It should assist us too if we help British Aerospace to win this contract with SMS. So, Helena, how is His Excellency, Mr Gul?"

"Mr Gul is being very responsive," said Helena, with a mischievous smile. "Maybe too responsive. I am running out of excuses not to give him my telephone number and not to come and listen to his poetry. He has told me that the Foreign Ministry in Tehran are interested in the idea of an Embassy share, but more because it could help them with some internal power struggles than because it might actually happen."

"A bit like us, then," said Matt.

"Yes, quite similar. For them it's not a question of resources, but of politics. The reformers at the Ministry would use the proposal as a bargaining tool to get concessions on other things. He didn't want to go into detail, but perhaps he didn't need to."

Matt was, as always, impressed by Helena's perception, and wondered, not for the first time, why she had chosen to be a PA, and in a medium-sized Embassy, rather than for the CEO of a large company. He had asked her before, but she had only given an enigmatic smile and said that she liked the hours.

"Excellent," said Catherine. "I think it's time to get him here for another chat. Can you do that?"

"Oh, yes!" Helena replied. "But I might need an escort if I give him another tour of the Embassy. For my sake. And it had better not be Matt. I don't think Mr Gul likes him very much since he took me away from him at the French Embassy. Maybe Anke could do it."

"Agreed," Catherine said, to Matt's relief. The job of an unwelcome chaperone was rarely a popular one.

Helena left to begin planning for her next session of lamb-fattening. Matt stayed behind, shut the door, said a silent prayer, and told Catherine about his meetings with Osipov, Gunilla and Vanda, his encounters with the two submarines, and all the attendant discussions. The only detail he omitted was Annika's involvement. Catherine listened intently and took some time to think before she spoke. When she did so, she surprised Matt by apologising to him.

"I shouldn't have left you on your own to deal with all this during the last fortnight. You are still learning your job, and my job is to guide and mentor you. I am not going to blame you for not knowing what to do, although I don't think London are likely to be so forgiving with either of us. Still, it's happened, so let's think about how we can make the best of it."

Matt let out a long, silent breath and unclenched his fingers.

Catherine gave him a half-smile as she noticed his reaction. "I did talk to Giles in London about those earlier reports of a Russian submarine. He told me something similar to what Mason Hunter has been saying. London also views the Baltic as a sideshow at the moment. They are focused on the Middle East just like the Americans, and they also don't want any distractions elsewhere. So the message I got was that we should keep our heads down and encourage others in the region to do the same. That gives us our context.

"Maybe we should take each submarine in turn," she continued. "The American one is easy. We have already decided what to do about that, and we should get some credit from London for finding out about it. The Latvian one is more difficult. Are you absolutely sure about it? It sounds so improbable."

Matt again confirmed that he had seen a submarine, and reiterated Gunilla's assessment.

"We will have to tell London about it soon, but this news will be as welcome as an American lion hunter at a WWF party. And it might be the messenger that gets shot. So I will have a quiet chat first with the Latvian Ambassador here, and will ask our Riga Embassy to ask some discreet questions. Please don't tell Philip about this; the FCO might want to keep this information within a very small circle. By all means try to persuade Vanda that going public about the submarine would be counterproductive, whether or not people believe it to be Russian. And keep in touch with your contact in SÄPO. She sounds very sensible. I share her worries, by the way, about the potential implications for Sweden if public anxiety about immigration were to be coupled with new fears about Russia. It could be very toxic.

"I also need some time to think about your Russian friend and his Piranha. We will have to tell London about that too, but you could get into a lot of trouble if we tell them the whole story without some careful preparation. I am coming to the end of my career, but you are at the start of yours and I don't want you to find yourself being transferred to some other department to count laptops. In any event, that news will be no more welcome than the news about the Latvian submarine.

"If I tell Giles about the submarines just after he has asked me to make sure nothing unusual happens in the Baltic, he will think that I have lost my grip completely. So, I'm not going to do anything just yet. I might wait until after the Defence Secretary's visit. After all, from what you say, the Russians aren't planning to go public about the Latvian submarine, and no one else except us knows it's there."

"I am not sure how much Mason Hunter knows," said Matt. "I saw him talking to Osipov's FSB minder at the American Embassy."

"Well, it's not in the State Department's interest to cause any trouble with the Russians here either. So I don't think they are going to do anything."

"Osipov would like his submarine to be found, so he can escape from the Baltic," said Matt, "but I didn't get the impression that he would have the guts to do anything to annoy that Oleg. And I don't blame him."

"So let's say nothing for now," Catherine agreed. "Again, say nothing to Philip. And I guess we will just have to hope that any upheavals within SÄPO stay within SÄPO. I will think of a way of telling London about it when the time is right without getting you into hot water. Just a very warm sauna, if you are lucky."

Matt left his office feeling relieved and grateful. If Catherine had been more ambitious and not at the end of her career, he had no doubt that he would already be on his way to Arlanda Airport in deep disgrace.

THiRTEEN

Two days later, Philip received confirmation of the Defence Secretary's visit, and his part of the Chancery corridor went immediately into a state of intense activity: almost as intense as Swedes on the first day of summer, when they would rush to bask outside in a tropical eighteen degrees. Philip was in perpetual motion, while his long-suffering and quietly efficient PA, Karen, did all the real work.

The Swedish Defence Minister, Arne Lundqvist, was a farmer by background, and still kept a farm down in the rural heart of southern Sweden. He was a large, boisterous man, with a love of hunting, fishing and drinking. Since one of the SMS assembly sites was in the Swedish region of Dalarna, a few hours' drive north of Stockholm, he had invited Stephen Glover, the British Defence Secretary, to visit it and to spend an evening in the countryside nearby. Outdoor pursuits would definitely be on the agenda. Both Catherine and Philip were nervous about what the notoriously pedantic and aesthetic Glover would make of that. It was well known that he had not wanted the defence job, and had his eyes set on being Foreign Secretary; a glass of claret and a discussion about the hill towns of Umbria being his idea of post-meeting entertainment.

Nonetheless, it was clearly impossible to refuse the invitation, so they had to hope for the best.

"His private secretary is a sensible fellow," said Philip. "I will get him to prepare the minister as best he can. An evening of drinking schnapps is a small sacrifice for winning the contract."

"You and Matt will have to help with Lundqvist," Catherine added. "I won't join you in a sauna, for obvious reasons. If he starts toasting, you will have to sacrifice your livers for a higher cause. I suppose the taxes that British Aerospace pay help to fund the NHS after all."

Since he was the Embassy press officer, Matt was also involved in the visit and would travel with the minister and his party. On a visit of this kind, his job was not so much to promote good headlines, but avoid or mitigate bad ones. Since the trip involved the Swedish military and Swedish weapons, Matt was expecting their media to ignore it in their normal fashion. The Swedish self-image of virtue was easier to maintain if they could pretend they never sold weapons to the outside world. The British media wouldn't take an interest unless there was a sex scandal to report, and the Defence Secretary wasn't taking his own press secretary with him. It should be a low-key visit, thought Matt hopefully.

Before Glover's arrival, Catherine was preparing for her next meeting with Gul, who wanted to have a lengthy inspection of the Embassy. Catherine's proposal was that the Iranians, who were few in number, would have the sole use of the first-floor corridor, would share the reception and main conference room, and would share the services of the British management team for a fee. They would arrange their own security. She told Matt to keep out of sight and let Helena look after Gul, with Anke acting as chaperone. On the day of the visit, the two women were dressed for action. Anke, uncharacteristically, was wearing a very modest, full length dress. Helena, by contrast, was wearing a dress that managed to be both technically modest, but interestingly revealing at the same time.

Matt duly kept to his room once Gul's arrival had been announced, and despite his curiosity, managed to begin a report on the latest bout of squabbling in the governing coalition in Sweden while waiting for Gul to leave. Eventually, Catherine wandered into his room and shut the door.

"Well, that didn't go too badly, but there were a few surprises."

Gul had seemed very happy that Helena had once again been his Embassy tour guide, especially as Anke had dutifully and silently followed a few steps behind them throughout.

"He told me that he thought my proposal as to how we could share the building could work, but he had a few unusual requests. He has a couple of female staff, but they are not allowed to enter the building along with the male staff. So they will have to use the emergency stairs outside at the back of the building. A bit chilly in winter. They have to have separate kitchens and prayer rooms as well, so we will have to allow some building work in their corridor."

"Isn't that a bit extreme?" asked Matt.

"Yes, it's not normal, but apparently Gul has strong personal views on the dangers of temptation. The Embassy bar will be out of bounds for their staff, but Gul wants to have sole use of one of the basements. He wouldn't say what for; he just said that all Iranian Embassies have to have a secure and soundproof basement. I gather the Saudis are much the same. And he also had a personal request, which he made to me privately while Helena was making some coffee. He wants her to be his PA, not mine. As a special concession, she would even be allowed to use the main entrance. The old devil!"

"What did you say to that?"

"I told him that it isn't up to me; it would be up to Helena. I don't think there is much risk that she will accept. You men, you are all the same, aren't you?! So predictable. Even Ambassador Gul, under that black suit."

"And what do you think London will make of his other suggestions?"

"I don't know. Personally, I hate his ideas about gender separation, and I can't see any Swedish staff accepting them, but then I read that it is already happening at events in some British universities. At the very least it will provoke a lively debate in the Foreign Office and outside it, and it may help us to keep this Embassy intact. If they reject our idea, they may not feel able to abolish us as well. I gather from Gul's own remarks that he thinks that the reactionaries in Tehran will be opposed to any cross-cultural contamination from the depraved West, so there will be a battle there too. So it probably won't happen this time, but I wouldn't rule it out for the future."

Matt met Helena in the kitchen later that morning.

"So you will have heard that I have had the offer of a lifetime," she said. "Same sort of job, except more poetry, long evening hours, and better pay. It's enough to turn a girl's head."

Matt wasn't entirely sure if she was joking.

"But I don't think a chador would suit me. So I will have to stick to the boring British Embassy. As you know, I like the hours."

Matt still wasn't sure. You never were with Helena.

The days leading up to Glover's arrival were very busy, but Matt did find the time to spend a few evenings with Annika. They liked to go to the bar on the jetty near his apartment, where they would drink rosé and eat fresh seafood. Matt was no longer filled with feelings of jealousy or regret when he saw other couples also talking happily over their wine. Now, he was one of them. This was a life he could envisage stretching into the distant future. He hoped Annika was beginning to think the same, and started to wonder whether he might leave the FCO at the end of his posting and find another job in Stockholm.

Of course, he thought, Annika might want to come to London, and perhaps they could find joint postings abroad in future; her working for an NGO. It might not be too difficult. But he still wasn't sure where he stood with her, and whether she fully shared his feelings. It was all too easy to get lost in these thoughts, and he would have probably stopped doing any useful work at all if it wasn't for the urgency imposed by the Defence Secretary's visit.

RIGA

The conspirators were meeting under cover of a Latvian food fair.

"I met Vanda last week," one of them whispered while struggling with a large plate of cabbage and gherkins. "The operation is about to go ahead. A perfect opportunity has arisen. She has decided we can't wait for this British diplomat to make up his mind. As it happens, it seems that the British are going to help us anyhow, even though it may be unwittingly."

"I can't wait. This will be a great moment for Latvia."

"Yes. Can you help me with these gherkins?"

MOSCOW

The admiral sighed deeply. Under pressure, he had bought the twelve-bedroom dacha near Sevastopol. He tried to console himself with the thought that he had carried out his patriotic duty. His wife wasn't happy, but was now devoting all her waking moments to sabotaging the disgusting Vitaly Alexandrovich. To do this she had entered an alliance with Madame Osipova, who wanted to use their Piranha to host a very exclusive party near Cannes. Reluctantly, he might have to let the slimy Osipov escape from the Baltic. But if so, it would be a price worth paying.

STOCKHOLM

Fika was in full swing. There were cinnamon *bullar* and the conversation was focused on last night's edition of

'*Will the Farmer Find A Spouse?*' The consensus was that he wouldn't. The conspirators happily joined in. There was no more need for planning. Everyone was ready to go.

The day before Glover's arrival, Catherine held a meeting to run through the arrangements. Glover would be accompanied by a senior representative of British Aerospace. He was due to go by car straight to the Swedish Missile Systems production plant. Catherine would accompany him, followed by the rest of the party. Lundqvist would meet him at the plant, they would have a joint tour, and then he would take Glover to a cottage on a nearby lake where they would spend the night. Glover would then be taken back to Stockholm, where there would be a more formal round of talks at the Defence Ministry. Catherine would host a late lunch at the Residence afterwards.

This was mostly very straightforward; the only wild card was the evening at the cottage. "Do we know what Lundqvist has in mind?" Catherine asked.

"Not really," Philip replied, "and neither do his staff, but I guess there may be some fishing, possibly swimming, and almost certainly a sauna at some stage. Glover's assistant private secretary, who will be coming with him, knows about this and should have warned his minister what to expect. We have just had one piece of bad news. Glover's special adviser, Nicola Roberts, is coming with him."

"And why is that bad news?"

"She has a reputation for being very ambitious and much more interested in promoting herself than anything else. She has made no secret of her wish to be an MP soon, and is looking around for a suitable constituency. She has some good contacts in the media and has been very ready to blame the civil service for any failings." Philip paused. "What else? She has been very hawkish towards Russia and is constantly urging Glover to take a tougher stance. He reportedly doesn't like her very much, but puts up with her because she is also very well connected within her party. So she could complicate things."

Matt, who had been looking heavenwards with a look of profound reproach since hearing this news, chipped in. "I came across her a couple of years ago on a trip to Cuba. She was very difficult. Seemed to have some sort of agenda against the FCO. And me."

"Sounds as though we could really do without her coming," Catherine agreed, "but we shall just have to manage it. Hopefully the assistant secretary will help us with that. Matt, you had better be ready to handle any negative comments she might decide to leak."

"There is some better news," Philip added. "The MOD has agreed to approach the Americans quietly and encourage them to remove their submarine. Glover can tell Lundqvist that we are supporting him."

"Good," Catherine replied. "I have had a similar message from the FCO. I am feeling optimistic about this contract now, unless there is some unexpected last-minute disaster."

Matt felt a superstitious twinge. *If there is a disaster, please let it not be my fault*, he thought.

The next day, Matt joined Philip to go to Arlanda Airport. Philip was driving his own car, a Land Rover Discovery of the type beloved by all British defence attachés. Catherine was being driven there by her driver, a retired British traffic warden called Frank, in the one remaining Embassy car, a rather ancient Rover. They arrived absurdly early. Philip was in full fig, a vision in braid and gold epaulettes. Matt was reminded of Osipov in his underwater palace of bling, and wondered where he was now. Still skulking somewhere beneath the Baltic, he assumed. There had been no sign of Vanda either during the last week or so. Perhaps she was being grilled in Riga about her role in the submarine saga. *Just as long as nothing surfaces until Glover leaves for London*, he thought.

After a long wait, during which Philip paced around like a football manager during a penalty shoot-out, the British Airways plane touched down. Shortly afterwards, Philip and Matt joined Catherine in the VIP lounge to greet the ministerial party. Glover, a familiar, rather gaunt figure, seemed quite relaxed: more so than the short, anxious man alongside him, who Matt guessed must be from British Aerospace. They were followed by the equally relaxed thirty-something assistant secretary, who immediately introduced himself to Matt.

"Hi, I'm Chris," he said. "I gather you will be looking after us, together with your Defence Attaché. Should be fun. My first time in Sweden. I'm looking forward to it. I think the minister is as well, although I can never tell with him. Keeps his thoughts to himself. And I don't know about Nicola either. I am not sure why she decided to join us at the last minute. She might be up to something. She usually is."

He nodded in the direction of Nicola Roberts, who was talking at great speed into her mobile phone. She paused briefly to acknowledge Catherine when they were introduced, ignored Matt completely, and then continued her conversation all the way out of the VIP lounge. The three-car convoy set off for Dalarna. Chris joined Matt in Philip's car. It was going to be a slow journey. It was a toss-up between Frank and Philip as to who was the world's most cautious driver.

Matt and Chris chatted easily enough as the small convoy left Stockholm and headed north through the rocky, fir-lined landscape of central Sweden. There was little traffic once they had left the city well behind, and Matt happily responded to Chris's many questions, first about the SMS contract, and then about life in Sweden. After a while, they fell silent and looked out at the unwavering wall of trees, only occasionally interrupted by small settlements in the distance, or lone red-painted houses. Matt was reminded of how large Sweden was, how empty much of it was, and how antisocial some of its inhabitants must be to want to live so far from their nearest neighbour.

He had never been to Dalarna and was looking forward to seeing it. It was often described as the Swedish heartland, an area of rolling hills and deep blue lakes, where every house looked as though it had come straight from the Swedish equivalent of *Homes & Gardens*. It was a popular area for Stockholmers to visit in the summer, and lakeside cottages were much sought after. There were plenty of cultural events, and even an outdoor opera theatre. The centre of the region was Lake Siljan, where they were due to spend the night in one of those sought-after cottages. The convoy skirted the edge of the lake, drove through the tourist town of Rättvik, and then turned into the hills for the final part of the journey.

Matt had never seen a weapon manufacturing plant except in movies, so wasn't quite sure what to expect. The reality was rather dull: a couple of large hangars with a few smaller buildings alongside, all nestled discreetly in a small valley. Philip, however, was very animated and started to reel out a series of technical details about the missiles produced there. As a result of the Swedish practice of omertà about their arms industry, Matt hadn't even known that the country made missiles until he learnt about the SMS contract. According to Philip, Sweden had a successful programme and exported several types of missiles. The kind made in this plant were air-to-ship missiles, which Philip explained would be an important part of Sweden's defence in the Baltic if they were to find themselves in conflict with, for example, their large, restless Eastern neighbour. That also made them a popular buy for any countries with a coastline and a history of regional spats.

The convoy passed quickly through some casual security and drove to the main reception area. Matt could see the burly figure of Lundqvist, who strode up to Glover as he emerged from the wheezing Rover, and gave him a handshake which made Matt wince even at a safe distance away. The visitors were swept inside and, in typical Swedish fashion, began their tour immediately, without wasting any time on formalities.

Matt lagged behind as they were marched around one of the large hangars, which was empty except for a few long metal cylinders, which he realised were the missiles. They managed to look both harmless and sinister at the same time. Their tour guide was the plant's technical director, an earnest-looking man who did his best to explain the new specifications of the missiles, while being constantly interrupted by the energetic Lundqvist. Glover, who seemed well briefed, intervened with a few detailed questions. The man from BAe chipped in with some mini sales pitches. Catherine and Chris hovered nearby, while the still-excited Philip talked enthusiastically to a couple of bluff Swedish military men. Nicola Roberts was once again on her mobile and paid little attention to the boys and their toys, although Matt noticed that she was never more than a couple of steps away from her minister.

After the tour of the hangar, the group went to a small office block where the technical director gave a short presentation and showed a film of missiles being launched, and then of missiles landing. Dummy targets in the sea were all satisfactorily destroyed. The man from BAe then gave his presentation, which also ended with a film of targets being obliterated. There was a general air of contentment in the room and the technical director proposed lunch.

Lunch was a simple affair of meatballs in the communal canteen. Swedish Missile Systems obviously didn't attach much importance to frivolous ostentation. Osipov wouldn't approve, Matt thought. He sat at the end of one of the wooden tables, next to one of the production managers at the plant, who gave him a long description of his work. Matt understood about twenty per cent of it, but in the best diplomatic tradition tried to follow it and ask the occasional intelligent question. After a while, the manager took pity on him and reverted to the familiar Swedish fallback topics of *Midsomer Murders* and the English Premier League.

It was already mid afternoon when lunch was finished, and the two ministerial convoys joined forces to return to Lake Siljan. The lakeside 'cottage' where the ministers were due to spend the night turned out to be a very grand house, although it was indeed next to the lake. It had its own jetty, with a powerful-looking boat bobbing gently next to it, and an extensive, well-manicured garden. Matt had wondered how a cottage could accommodate a large group, but he needn't have worried. The house could have accommodated a Brazilian carnival procession. He had been allocated a room on one of the upper floors, along with the other minor players. Glover, Lundqvist, Catherine and the man from BAe had the grander rooms overlooking the lake. Nicola Roberts had somehow managed to get herself upgraded to a room close to Glover. She clearly didn't intend to let him stray far out of her sight.

After he had inspected his room, Matt ventured outside to take a look around. Lundqvist and Catherine were already down by the jetty. Matt went across to join them. Lundqvist was extolling the joys of lake fishing and wanted to take Glover to try his luck at his favourite spot.

Catherine, at first politely, and then more directly, was trying to dissuade him.

"I'll be honest, Arne, the minister is not an outdoor type. I doubt that he has ever been fishing in his life, and if he caught a fish, he wouldn't know what to do with it. Why don't you take him for a ride in your speedboat instead? It's a beauty. You can show him the lake and tell him about Dalarna. A bit of history and culture. Just the two of you. He would enjoy that. I checked, he doesn't get seasick."

Reluctantly, Lundqvist agreed, with several grumbles about the feebleness of city types and the degeneration of the British as a maritime people.

Glover then appeared, followed by Chris and Nicola, who had changed into a short skirt and low-cut top. It seemed she wanted to have all her weapons to hand. Catherine intercepted him and quickly told them about the deal she had just negotiated.

"Thank you, Ambassador," Glover said. "I have had an intense dislike of fish ever since I had to support a colleague at a local election in Hull. I was attacked by a lunatic with a halibut. A boat trip sounds a much better option, and as you say, it will give me the chance to have a private chat with Lundqvist. There are some messages I want to give him."

Glover then joined the Swedish minister and the two men walked over to the boat. Nicola followed close behind, and as Lundqvist was extolling the vigour of the engine, she coolly stepped aboard and made herself comfortable. Glover saw her, his face tightened, and for a moment they stared at each other like two shoppers about to seize the last fur coat in the Harrods sale. Glover then gave a resigned shake of his head, and muttered something to himself. Lundqvist hadn't noticed this exchange, but gave a big grin when he saw Nicola sitting unabashed near the driver's seat.

"It's always good to have a pretty woman on a boat," he said. Before climbing on board, he nodded towards a huge, wolf-like dog that was sleeping next to the jetty. "That's Boris, my Swedish elkhound. I normally take him with me, but I won't this time. He gets very bad-tempered if he is woken up." He climbed in and, with a couple of practised moves, started the engine, and cast off. The boat roared off into the lake with Glover hanging on to his seat like a poorly prepared rodeo rider.

"Nicola isn't going to let him out of her sight," said Chris, "whatever the minister says to her. I think it must be something to do with Russia. She wants us to adopt a much tougher policy, and she thinks that Glover intends to ask Lundqvist to back off from any possible conflicts with Russia in the Baltic. I guess she wants to stop Glover from doing that, or at least give Lundqvist a contrary view if he does."

"But surely Glover can do and say what he wants? He is the minister," said Matt.

"You would think so, but there is a lot going on in party politics just now. Glover's position is not very secure and there is a reshuffle imminent. He's been told by the Prime Minister to be a dove, but the party tends to eat doves, usually after shooting and roasting them."

Chris and Matt went for a stroll around the grounds. Catherine went to check on her emails. In the distance they could see Philip and the two military types chatting energetically.

"Say what you like about the military," said Chris, "but they all seem to love their jobs. It's a passion for them, not just work combined with intellectual curiosity as it often is for us."

After an hour, they heard a roaring noise and the powerful boat came into view, heading at high speed towards the jetty.

"He's going to crash!" said an alarmed Catherine, who had just rejoined them.

Just as it seemed the jetty was going to be demolished, Lundqvist executed a dramatic last-second turn that sent spray flying in all directions and woke the elkhound. The giant animal was clearly very displeased and began noisily looking for the culprit. It fell to Philip to try to quieten it while Lundqvist leapt ashore laughing, followed by a pale Glover and a damp Nicola.

"Your Admiral Nelson would have liked that turn," said Lundqvist. "Now you must be hungry. Let's go to the barbecue. Normally I would have hunted something for us to eat, but my cook has done it for us this time." He strode off.

"The man's a lunatic," said Glover to Catherine. "I have been on more peaceful fairground rides. We had better get this contract after all this."

Although clearly annoyed by her unwanted hair wash, Nicola stayed silent and renewed her umbilical contact with her mobile. Behind her, Philip had lost his battle to calm Boris and was retreating in less than good order to the house. His best dress trousers had already been partially captured by the enemy.

The Swedish party were at the back of the house, standing around an already lit barbecue. The carcass of a large animal hung nearby and a bearded man in a chef's hat was expertly cutting slices from it. A nearby trestle table was covered by piles of various types of meat and sausages. The only other food was a gigantic pot of potatoes.

"This is my cook, Sven," said Lundqvist, "and this is the deer he killed for us. He is a good hunter, better than me, I don't have his patience. It's simple food, but natural, in the Swedish way. Enjoy!"

Matt could see that Glover was no more accustomed to nature raw in hoof and antler than he was to an uninvited halibut, but the minister gamely went over to inspect the slowly burning offerings.

Nicola Roberts swore under her breath. "Didn't you tell them that I am a vegetarian?" she muttered angrily.

"There are lots of potatoes, Nicola," Chris replied, trying unsuccessfully to hide a smile. "A real feast of them."

She gave him an evil look in reply and turned to her mobile.

When the first pieces of meat were ready, everyone started to eat. The food was delicious, enhanced by the outdoor setting. Lundqvist held court with stories of his hunting exploits and eulogies to the Swedish countryside. There was plenty of schnapps and beer, and even Glover began to enjoy himself, coming up with a few quotes from the Roman poet Grattius about the art of hunting. After the meal, Lundqvist announced that the next course of a classic Swedish evening was to be the sauna. Matt had noticed earlier that there was a wooden hut at the end of a rickety gangplank that protruded into the lake. He had idly wondered what it might be, and now he was about to find out. Catherine made her excuses and went into the house to relax.

"Let's go, gentlemen," said Lundqvist, as he marched off towards the lake. "My staff will bring the schnapps. The evening is only just beginning."

"If this is going to go the way I think it's going to go, I am going to rely on you to rescue me," Glover said quietly to Philip. "There is no way I'm going to drink all night and then help negotiate a contract tomorrow."

"I think it will go that way, and yes, Minister, Matt and I will do the drinking on your behalf. You just need to come up with some excuse to leave."

"Thank you."

"And you should have a chance to have a quiet word with Lundqvist in between the toasts," added Matt, who was aware of the tension between Glover and his special adviser. "You don't wear more than a towel in saunas here, if that, so this will probably be men only." The men followed Lundqvist down to the hut, Nicola in tow, but again on her mobile.

As they approached the hut, Boris reappeared and loudly greeted the sight of his old adversary. He made a rapid advance, eyes fixed on the remaining part of Philip's trousers. Showing both speed of thought and tactical appreciation of the ground in the face of a better armed force, Philip used the Swedish military as a shield, before sprinting to the hut, passing a surprised Lundqvist en route. This cunning manoeuvre foiled the elkhound, who clearly didn't think much of the state of the gangplank. He settled down instead to await their next encounter.

The rest of the men walked the plank and disappeared into the hut. Matt was next to last and could hear behind him the beginnings of a major argument between one of the two Swedish officers and Nicola, who was demanding to be allowed in. The Swede was politely but firmly telling her that the sauna was male only. As Matt entered the hut, the rest of the group were already undressing and hanging up their clothes in the small changing room next to the sauna. The sauna itself was large enough to accommodate them all in comfort, and was already getting very warm.

"No towels in the sauna," said an already naked Lundqvist, who seemed even bulkier unclothed. "That is my rule and there are no exceptions. Let's talk, drink, and when we get hot, we just take a little dip in the lake."

Glover, who seemed even skinnier unclothed, and Chris looked at each other and resignedly dropped their towels. Everyone sat down.

As Lundqvist started to pour glasses of schnapps for his guests, there was a commotion at the door and Nicola thrust herself into the room. "I will stay with my minister," she declared, with a set expression. "That's my job, and no one will stop me from doing it."

Glover looked embarrassed, but Lundqvist was unperturbed.

"You are welcome, of course. No one is trying to separate you from your minister. I wish my staff had the same loyalty. But there is a condition, of course. My rule. You have to be as nature intended, like the rest of us."

Nicola looked undeterred. Without a word, she swiftly stripped and sat down next to Glover. After a surprised pause, the other Swedish officer made the first toast of the evening, and the drinking began.

As he looked around, Matt noticed that the Swedes were much more relaxed than their British counterparts in the face of Nicola's naked presence. He realised that they were quite used to mixed saunas. They started to tease her about a tattoo of a dragon entwined with the Chinese flag she had on one thigh, the result, she finally admitted, of a drunken evening during a gap-year visit to Hong Kong. She had never had the courage to bear the pain of getting it removed. The British men couldn't comment. They were too busy trying not to look at her.

As the heat increased, the men began to go outside for a cold but refreshing splash in the lake. As the consumption of schnapps increased, the splashes got louder and longer. Eventually, Nicola could take no more and abandoned Glover for a moment to take a dip herself. Without a word, Chris went over to his clothes, retrieved a small camera and went outside. There was a scream and a loud splash, and then he returned.

"It's not what you might think," he said quietly to Matt. "She fights dirty, and so do I. I have to protect my minister too. I don't think she would want these photos to be made public; not at the angle I took them from. And not with that tattoo. I don't think many constituency selection committees would be impressed by that. It's just an insurance policy." He calmly returned the camera to its hiding place.

Glover then got to his feet and apologised to Lundqvist. "I had some emails just before we ate. I am afraid that there are some matters that I absolutely have to deal with tonight. I'm very sorry. But our Defence Attaché and the others will stay and continue the party."

Lundqvist protested, but he could see that Glover's mind was made up. The minister quickly dressed and left. He had escaped.

Just after he did so, Nicola stormed in. "Which of you did that?" she demanded. "I saw a flash. I know someone took a photo." She looked accusingly along the row of red faces and sweating torsos. But before giving anyone a chance to reply, she noticed that Glover had left, swiftly grabbed her clothes and ran out of the hut.

"Some woman," said Lundqvist admiringly. "She could almost be Swedish. I hope you have good medical insurance," he added, turning to Chris. "You are going to need it if she finds out it was you. More schnapps?"

FOURTEEN

Matt awoke with a throbbing head and a painfully cricked neck. He was lying across one of the wooden benches in the sauna. Philip and Chris were also stirring. There was no sign of the others. He looked at his watch. It was 4am and the sun was already shining brightly outside. Some memories of the previous night began to flicker through his mind. There had been many toasts and glasses of schnapps. So many toasts. There had been singing. He remembered the man from BAe slipping away early.

"Where are the Swedes?" he blearily asked Philip, who was slowly struggling into his clothes.

"Lundqvist wanted to go fishing. So the two officers went with him."

Matt started to shake his head in wonder at the minister's energy, but quickly changed his mind. Any bodily movement had to be negotiated as carefully as a meeting with North Koreans. He gingerly unravelled himself from the bench and immediately felt worse.

"Better go back to the house and get a bit more sleep," said Philip. "Long day today." He left the hut, and there were a few seconds of complete silence, followed by violent barking, sounds of a skirmish and the rapid return of a panting Defence Attaché. "Blasted dog!" he said. "It was lying in wait for me." He looked down at his now even shorter trousers.

"I'll deal with it," Chris muttered as he slowly got dressed. "Give me your trousers."

"What?!"

"Come on, you are a military man, not a politician, and I know that no military man would go anywhere without a spare pair of trousers in his suitcase. First rule of Alexander the Great. Besides, this pair are no use to you now."

Philip didn't have the energy to argue and tamely surrendered his trousers to Chris, who staggered out of the hut carrying them. There was another flurry of barking. Matt and a boxer-clad Philip walked to the entrance to see Chris carry the trousers just out of reach of the very purposeful elkhound and then throw them behind a bush. Boris rushed to claim his prize, there was an outburst of growling, and Chris beckoned to them to go back to the house. Philip had made the penultimate sacrifice, but was now safe.

After what seemed an indecently short time, Matt was woken by his alarm clock and struggled downstairs to the dining room. Lundqvist was in the midst of demolishing a mound of fish and potatoes. He looked indecently fresh. The rest of the party were just starting their breakfast.

"*Hej, hej*, Matt," said Lundqvist. "Have some fish. I caught some this morning while you were sleeping. Delicious."

He was right. They were. Glover looked revived, Nicola looked sulky, and Catherine looked pleased by signs of some growing rapport between the two ministers. Lundqvist was an admirer of the painter George Stubbs, particularly of his portraits of bulls, and Glover was always happy to talk about art. Matt sat silently, drank strong coffee in the Swedish style and began to feel better.

After their early breakfast, the whole party set off for Stockholm. As they left the entrance hall, they all had to step over Boris, who was lying sprawled out in front of the door, peacefully chewing the remains of Philip's trousers. As Philip reached the door, their eyes met for a moment, and then Boris continued his chewing. There was no need for any further words between them. The cars rolled up, and at the very last moment, Glover deftly stepped into Lundqvist's car, which drove off with a rattle of gravel. Nicola was left standing, looking furious, mobile in hand.

No one had the energy to talk during the return journey, and Matt turned his mobile to silent and dozed in the back of the car. He woke as they were driving through the Stockholm suburbs, which gave him just enough time to recover his senses and some degree of energy before they got to the Defence Ministry. Lundqvist had already escorted Glover inside, and the rest of the party followed. For once, Nicola showed no interest in catching up with her minister. Any damage had already been done.

The meeting that followed was, Matt assumed, a standard one of its kind. There was a more detailed presentation by the man from BAe, followed by a lengthy question-and-answer session about missile guidance technology, and after coffee, a second session on financing.

As far as Matt could work out, it was going well, although he was still too sleepy to concentrate with any success. After a while, his only objective was to keep his head from falling onto the table in front of him. Looking around, he could see that Chris and Philip were struggling too. The Swedes were, irritatingly, still as lively as elk in the rutting season. The meeting concluded with smiles and handshakes.

"Almost in the bag," the man from BAe confided to Matt as they left. "It looks as though Lundqvist is going to make a positive recommendation to the Cabinet. We just need to give him one final push. We will still have to keep a close eye on the French, of course, but it's looking good. Bringing in the Chinese as a silent partner was our master stroke. It will cut the costs considerably."

"The Chinese?" asked Matt, to whom this was news.

"Oh yes. You can't sign a big contract these days without the Chinese being involved. That's not always made public, but it's standard practice now. We couldn't get on without them. We will have to clear this with them in Beijing, but I don't think there will be a problem."

The discussions had been concluded, and it was time for lunch at the Residence. Matt finally felt awake as Philip drove him there. He wondered what they would be eating. Helena had told him that a late-night negotiation chaired by Catherine a few days previously had reached the promised deal on a herring quota. In line with the best deals, neither party was satisfied, but both had reluctantly agreed to it. Birgitta would no longer serve herring for breakfast when guests were staying at the Residence, although she remained adamant that it was the best way to start the day. James would have to put up with herring at buffets, and there would be an annual limit on the amount that could be served at other times. Someone from the management section would carry out independent monitoring and verification. Catherine had made her own concessions: a trip to the opera in Verona for James, and a nomination for Swedish Fish Cook of the Year for Birgitta. She had achieved peace in her time, but no one was sure for how long.

As the cars reached the Residence, Matt was surprised not to see Tom. In the lead-up to the visit, Tom had made some elaborate security plans, all of which had been vetoed by Catherine on the grounds that no one would actually be allowed into the building. Frustrated, Tom had to revert to normal procedures, but had still been anxiously running through drills before the party went up to Dalarna. Now he was nowhere to be seen. There was one Swedish security guard, hired for the day, lounging outside the gates, who waved them through in normal, casual Swedish style.

As Matt got out of the car, James, who had come out to welcome Glover, beckoned him over. "You'd better get over to the Embassy. There's some kind of problem. Tom's gone over there to sort it out, which is why there is almost no security here."

Matt set off immediately. As he walked briskly along the park towards the Embassy, he wondered what sort of emergency would cause Tom to abandon his post. It must be something serious. But, in that case, why hadn't he called? Various possibilities flashed through his mind. Perhaps something had happened to him and he couldn't call? Had there been an attack on the Embassy? Feeling increasingly nervous, Matt arrived at the Embassy gates and went inside.

Lotta was sitting in her reception office, staring at one of the CCTV cameras. "Oh, Matt. Thank goodness you have come. I think Tom has gone crazy. You must go and talk to him. He is outside the Embassy bar."

Matt hurried back outside and round the corner to the bar entrance. Tom and John from Consular were standing there, arguing furiously, while the other hired security guard looked on impassively.

"Matt, thank God!" said John. "Please talk some sense into this maniac."

"Matt, I am glad you are here," said Tom stiffly. "We have a security emergency here and we need immediate action."

"OK," said Matt, "could one of you explain what has happened?"

Both men spoke at once and it took a few minutes before Matt could understand the situation. The facts became clear; it was the solution that was being disputed. The previous evening, John had met a few fellow Brits in a pub in Stockholm and had invited them back to the Embassy bar. It had turned into a long evening, and when John had finally left he had accidentally locked two of the Brits in the bar.

"I thought they had gone. They must have fallen asleep in a corner," he explained sheepishly.

Lotta had seen them that morning on the CCTV and called Tom, who had told them they were trespassing on diplomatic premises, that they were committing a very serious offence, and then threatened them with the full majesty of the law. In response, they had locked themselves in the bar, had refused to come out, and were now working their way through a bottle of single malt.

"I have been talking to them," said John. "They have said they will only come out if Tom lets them go. But he keeps on threatening them. I don't blame them for staying there. They have booze, TV, a pool table, frozen pizzas and a microwave. What more could a man want? They could stay there for weeks. Months, even."

"I have spoken to my contacts in the police," said Tom. "They are ready to send an armed response team here. I recommend we ask them to go ahead. This is the thin end of the wedge. If we let this sort of thing go unpunished, we might as well all go back to the UK. Everyone will know that the British Embassy is a soft target."

"If you want to see your girlfriend turn up in uniform and fire a gun, you can do that at home," John replied. "No need to involve us."

"The last thing we want is the police coming here, said Matt. "The press are bound to find out about it. We don't want any comedy news stories when the Secretary of Defence is here. Tom, you need to be at the Residence providing security there. John, just sort this out. I don't care how you do it as long as the two guys aren't here when I get back later today."

He marched away, taking the still-expostulating Tom with him.

As they left the Embassy, a woman crossed the road to them. "*Hej, hej.* Are you from the British Embassy? I am a journalist and I just got a call to say that there is a siege going on there."

"Take a look," said Matt, pointing at the peaceful scene. "Does it look as though there is a siege? Nothing interesting ever happens to Embassies and diplomats around here. This is Stockholm, not Baghdad." He walked away.

As they neared the Residence, Matt was surprised to see Annika cycling rapidly towards them. "*Hej*, Matt," she said breathlessly. "I am so glad I found you. Gunilla called me. She thinks there is some kind of plot against your minister. She has been trying to call you, but she got no answer so I said I would come and find you. She has alerted SÄPO, but she said the situation was complicated. I don't know what she meant."

"Come on," said Matt, "we have to warn everyone." He looked across to the Residence, where he could see Glover and Nicola standing outside the front door. It looked as though they were arguing about something. There was no sign of the security guard.

Before they could cross the road, a white van sped up and came to a crunching halt by the gates. Four men in balaclavas leapt out, sprinted across to the startled Glover and Nicola, and bundled them into the van. It drove off towards the city. The whole action was over in seconds.

Annika was the first to react. "Quick, follow them!" she cried and set off on her bicycle.

The security guard had left his bike outside the gate and Matt rushed across, grabbed it and set off in hot pursuit, leaving a stunned Tom behind. Cycling for once like a Swede, he hurtled along the quiet road. He saw

Annika take a left ahead and followed her past the small Nobel Park. The van had turned onto Strandvägen and then suddenly braked. Two figures were bundled out by the men in balaclavas and were pushed down onto the long wooden jetty where Lars usually moored his boat. Annika, who was close behind, dropped her bicycle and ran after them.

Matt followed a few moments later. Looking towards the end of the jetty, he could see the four men pushing their captives onto a black speedboat. Annika had stopped and was urgently talking to someone. He kept running past the rows of elegant boats until, panting and breathless, he reached her.

"Quick, get in!" said Annika, who was already removing the mooring ropes from a familiar boat.

"Hello, Matt," said Lars calmly. "I only came here to replace an old rope, but I understand we are now going to save your minister. It's a pity that he is from the wrong party, but never mind. Sit down now and hold on. Let's go!"

He started the engine and set off after the other boat. It was heading towards the canal that led to the sea. Ignoring the five-miles-per-hour speed limit, the first boat sped into the canal, sending a huge wake onto the grassy banks alongside. Lars followed, cursing. Matt could see a line of other boats ahead, crawling along in disciplined Swedish obedience to the speed limit. There was barely room for two boats to pass in the narrow canal, but the boat ahead didn't slacken its speed as it shot past them towards the sea. Lars had no choice but to follow it, although by doing so he was committing a huge crime against Swedish maritime culture. As he rushed past, the other boats were thrown against the banks of the canal. Picnic food and glasses of wine were tossed everywhere. Matt could hear screams and some choice Swedish swear words. They hurtled under one of the picturesque small bridges on which a group of Asian tourists stood staring at them, selfies temporarily forgotten. He fumbled for his mobile. He had to turn it on with one hand, holding on with the other, as the boat rocked around the curves of the canal. He got a signal and called Tom. The line was busy. He tried Catherine with the same result and left a jerky voicemail explaining what had happened. *This can't last too long, surely*, he thought. *Catherine or Tom must have already called the police.*

He leant forward and yelled to Annika as their boat flew under the final bridge and shot into the sea. "What is Gunilla going to do?"

But Annika couldn't hear him over the noise of the engine and the turbulence of the wake caused by the boat ahead. Their boat was bouncing on the waves like a small child on a garden trampoline. He mouthed the words to her, but she still couldn't understand him. He gave up and concentrated on protecting himself as they powered onwards. The black boat was now about three hundred yards ahead. It was heading towards Vaxholm, on the same route that he and Annika had taken a couple of weeks previously. *The Swedes will be able to cut it off at Vaxholm*, Matt thought. He tried his mobile again, and was half-thrown across the deck in doing so. He landed painfully against the edge of the seat and was still unable to get through. Annika gestured to him to sit down and hold on. She pointed ahead and mouthed the word 'Vaxholm'. She was thinking the same as him. The Swedish police would intercept them there.

Matt held on to his seat as tightly as a Finn to a last glass of schnapps and wondered who had seized Glover and why. He couldn't help but think that it must have something to do with submarines. If his previous boat ride to Vaxholm with Annika had seemed lively, this was in a different league altogether. Even though Lars's boat looked considerably more ancient than the one they were pursuing, it had an unexpectedly powerful engine. The same might be said for its owner, who seemed to have the edge in skill. They were slowly gaining as the two boats raced across the long expanse of open water leading to Vaxholm.

A towering ten-storey cruise ship was heading towards them on its way to Stockholm. The leading boat now steered straight towards it. At the last moment, it veered sharply left just in front of the enormous bow. Lars had no choice but to continue straight on, passing along the other side of the ship. They were suddenly faced with a series of five-foot-high wakes left by the ferry. Matt saw the wall of water coming, held on even more tightly and closed his eyes. He felt the boat leap like a Baltic dolphin. There was a moment of silent calm and then a wrenching crash. Water cascaded over his head and he heard Annika yell. *This is it*, he thought. *Drowned in the Baltic. What a way to go!* He opened his eyes, fearing the worst, only to see her laughing jubilantly. Lars was still at the wheel readying the boat for the next wave, which again sent it flying through the air. Annika whooped again and laughed even harder at Matt's terrified expression. Lars was grinning too as he continued to ride the waves. *Swedes!* thought Matt. *It must be the Viking blood.*

Now that he realised he might live after all, he became concerned that the other boat might have eluded them. They reached the end of the giant ship, and to his relief he saw that it was still in sight, although its manoeuvre had gained it a couple of hundred yards. He could see a couple of balaclava-clad figures at the back of the boat, and one at the wheel. He hoped that Glover and Nicola were being held out of sight. The alternative didn't bear thinking about. Lars resumed his skilled and methodical pursuit, and had again begun to close the gap as the leading boat took the left turn between two small islands that led to Vaxholm. After a few more minutes, Matt could see the familiar shape of the castle in the distance.

The boat ahead showed no sign of slackening its pace as it approached a bobbing group of boats waiting to take the channel to the left of the castle that led into the next stretch of open water beyond. Suddenly, Annika pointed excitedly to her left. A coastguard vessel was heading across the course of the black boat, clearly intending to cut the kidnappers off. Matt's spirits rose. The driver of the kidnappers' boat had seen it too, and steered left, heading straight towards the coastguard vessel. A collision looked inevitable, and the coastguard vessel began to turn sideways to meet it front on. Matt could see two men with guns standing in the bow. He guessed it would be difficult for them to shoot at such a rapidly moving target if Glover and Nicola were at risk.

At the last moment, the black speedboat again changed direction and made a dramatic right turn. It shot past the line of waiting boats and headed towards the channel on the right side of the castle, which was usually for incoming vessels. It was heading up the marine motorway on the wrong side of the road. Taken by surprise, it took the coastguard a few moments to respond.

In the meantime, Lars, who had slowed down to watch what was happening, gunned the engine and resumed his pursuit. As their boat entered the narrow channel, Matt saw one of the small ferries that hopped from island to island coming towards them. The leading speedboat flew past it through a very narrow gap between the ferry and the castle wall. The ferry driver, obviously disconcerted, began to stop and make a slow turn. That gap had now disappeared. With impressive reactions, Lars slewed his boat to the right and shot past the other side of the ferry. There was a magisterial hoot behind them. Matt turned to see that the ferry had now drifted into the middle of the channel, temporarily blocking the way ahead for the coastguard. He looked forward again. The pursuit was continuing.

Lars accelerated as the black boat sped across another broad stretch of water. They were now only a couple of hundred yards behind. Lars was again gaining as they approached the next island, which lay across their paths. The black boat veered right towards yet another narrow channel with signs reading *Danger* and *Dead slow* in Swedish. It was lined with picture-perfect houses, each with its little jetty and boat, and beautifully manicured lawns. It looked as though it had been painted by numbers by the Swedish Tourist Board. A man was fishing peacefully and a couple were standing in a small boat, doing something to a rope. Lars yelled something as the black boat rushed though the channel, sending a wave crashing over the nearest lawns. His boat then only added to the carnage. Matt was aware of flailing arms and at least three figures in the water behind them, as they scraped past some rocks, narrowly avoided a wooden channel marker, and shot into the next section of open water.

This should be made into a video game, thought Matt, as the chase resumed. The boats were now about one hundred yards apart. Matt could see three men in balaclavas at the back of the other boat. They were conferring urgently. The leading boat turned right past a string of small islands. Just as they were about to pass them, the boat made yet another of its trademark rapid turns and headed towards a narrow gap between two rocky islands, only a few metres wide. As it began to enter the channel, it suddenly slowed and then stopped in a slew of foaming water. Lars slowed in turn as he followed them. A surreal scene met Matt's eyes. Immediately in front of the kidnappers' boat was another, blocking the way out. It was identical to the boat they had been chasing and was also full of men in balaclavas. Matt wondered for a moment if too much bouncing could induce hallucinations. All three boats had now stopped. It was a Swedish stand-off.

There was a pause as the men in both of the other boats assessed the situation. Then a woman emerged from the back of the boat that was blocking the exit. It was Gunilla. She shouted something urgently to the kidnappers. They replied, and soon a full-scale argument was taking place. Matt could see at least two men on each boat with pointed guns. He could feel the tension and the anger. Lars and Annika were silent as they too felt the volatile atmosphere.

Suddenly there was a splash and a figure appeared in the water beside the kidnappers' boat. It was Glover. He must have taken advantage of the distraction caused by the argument. Everyone stopped shouting for a moment and watched him as he clumsily swam the few metres to the nearest group of rocks. He struggled out of the water and looked around hopefully. But there was only more water and, in the distance, a few more rocks. He looked helplessly back at the boats. Both crews just shrugged and resumed the dispute.

"What is happening?" Matt asked Annika. He spoke quietly even though there was no chance of being heard over the shouting.

"I think they are all SÄPO," she whispered. "I am not sure exactly what is going on, but Gunilla is trying to persuade the men who took your minister to give him back. They are very angry with her, but I guess they are stuck here in this channel, and they don't want to shoot at colleagues."

The shouting continued, but Matt thought he detected a slight lessening of intensity. Guns were lowered. After a few more moments, the tension began to slip away and voices returned to normal volume. Gunilla was beginning to take control and seemed to be proposing something. There was some more discussion, but after a few more minutes some sort of agreement appeared to have been reached, with great reluctance on behalf of the kidnappers. The two boats edged towards each other. Gunilla stepped onto the kidnappers' boat and, a few moments later,

Nicola briefly appeared. Gunilla then beckoned to Lars, who drove his boat forward to join the others.

Gunilla came to the edge of her boat to speak to them. She was very angry. "These men are idiots. Criminals, even," she said in a low but emotional voice. "They are from that group within SÄPO that I told you about. They admitted they have been plotting with similar groups within the Latvian Security Service and military. They took your minister because they wanted him to believe there was a Russian submarine in the archipelago and that his kidnapping was part of a Russian plan to destabilise the region. They have been pretending to be Russians today, speaking in Russian to each other, and your minister probably still believes they are. It was hard to persuade them to abandon that plan, but they now realise that they have lost, for today at least. They would have had to have killed us, and that would have been a step too far even for them. Some of them would have been killed too, and maybe even your minister and his colleague. They have agreed to let them go.

"I don't have time to say any more now. My boss, the head of SÄPO, will come to your Embassy later today to explain everything. Please don't talk to anyone about this until he has done so. It may even be better for you not to say much to your minister just yet. It is still a very complicated situation. But thank you for helping us today." She turned to Lars, gave him a big hug and spoke intensely to him for a couple of minutes. At the end of the conversation he nodded in agreement.

Gunilla looked across to Glover, who was still standing in splendid isolation on the mound of rocks, like a bedraggled Nelson on a very short column. "I don't know why he swam over there. But since he did, someone had better go and get him. Lars has agreed to take him and his colleague back to Stockholm."

"I can't get any closer to the rocks," said Lars. "Someone will have to swim across and bring him back."

Gunilla, Lars and Annika all looked at Matt.

"Yes, OK, me again," he grumbled. "At least this time I am wet already." With a resigned sigh he took off his suit, shirt and shoes. "To hell with it. I am not going to get seaweed in my boxers again." He took them off too and once again dived into the Baltic on a rescue mission, this time naked, in the best Swedish tradition. A few moments later he clambered onto the rocks. He and Glover looked at each other.

"It's over, Minister," he said. "We are going to take you back to Stockholm. You are safe now."

Glover seemed dazed and uncertain, but nodded weakly.

"We have to swim back to that boat. The captain is a friend of mine. Actually, it was him that rescued you. Shall we go?" Matt took the shivering man by the hand and led him into the water. *What a photo this would make for a UK tabloid*, he thought. He swam back to the boat, Glover splashing slowly behind him. Lars had found a blanket and Glover gratefully wrapped it around him.

While Matt had been in the water, Nicola had been escorted to the boat by the very deflated kidnappers. She looked more angry than scared. "Minister, this is totally outrageous!" she began.

Glover just shook his head and then buried it in his blanket.

"I think he needs some time to recover," Annika suggested.

Nicola was still fuming, but decided to save her energy for the moment. Matt had put his boxers on again, and was searching for his mobile.

"You probably won't get a signal out here," said Gunilla. "We have our own communications and one of my colleagues has already informed your Ambassador that you are all safe and are returning to Stockholm. So now you had better go." She climbed back onto the neighbouring boat and Lars started the engine and slowly turned around. Gunilla waved and turned back to talk to her colleagues, some looking crushed, others quietly jubilant.

The return journey was considerably more sedate than the outward one. Lars had reverted to being a careful Swedish driver. Glover still sat with his head in the blanket, deep in thought. Nicola fumed with even greater intensity, having discovered that her mobile had run out of power. Matt and Annika also sat silently, reflecting on what had happened. As they passed, slowly this time, through the now less than picture-perfect channel, Matt could see a group of angry houseowners complaining loudly, presumably about the state of their sea-drenched lawns. Lars kept his head down and managed to slip through without being recognised as one of the culprits. About forty minutes later they reached the Strandvägen jetty and Lars moored his boat. Everyone struggled off, bruised and still in a state of shock.

Matt shook Lars's hand warmly. "Actually, I have to thank you," Lars said. "This afternoon was much more interesting than I expected. And now I have an excuse to spend some days this week retuning my poor engine. It has been through a lot today. Don't worry," he added, "I am not going to tell anyone about what I saw today. I promised Gunilla. I owe her a favour and this will repay her."

Frank and Philip were waiting to drive them back to the Residence. When they arrived, a relieved James and Chris met them at the door. A sheepish Tom lurked in the background. Glover and Nicola went to change into dry clothes. Annika and Matt had a long, damp hug and she walked back to Strandvägen to get her bicycle. Birgitta gave Matt a cup of tea and a dry shirt, and Catherine took him into her study, where Matt described what had happened.

"We were very lucky," Catherine said. "That could have gone very badly. We owe a lot to your friend – or is it girlfriend? – and to your contact in SÄPO. Between you, you have done a very good job. The head of SÄPO will be here in a few minutes. He wants to speak to Glover. In the meantime, drink your tea. You probably need it."

As Matt was changing his shirt, Chris walked in. "Great job, mate," he said. "I don't know exactly what you did, but you brought him back in one piece. It was very confusing here, as you might imagine. We were about to have lunch, Nicola wanted to have a chat with the minister outside, and then the next moment, they had gone. We didn't see or hear anything. We didn't know what had happened, and then the Ambassador got a call from someone and she and Lundqvist had a private council of war. The Swedes rushed off, and Frank took the guy from BAe to the Embassy. Then the Ambassador told me what had happened and called the FCO in London. After that we just had to wait until the Swedes told us that you were safe. Must have been exciting. You must promise to tell me everything over a few beers later."

FiFTEEN

As promised, a large black car drove onto the Residence's drive a few moments later. *It must be serious*, Matt thought, *if he hasn't come by bicycle.* A tall, imposing figure entered the building, accompanied by two aides. Matt had never met Andreas Berg, director of SÄPO. He looked the part. Glover and Nicola came downstairs and everyone went to the living room, sat on the floral-print FCO-issue sofas, and waited. Berg didn't look like someone who was in the habit of apologising, but today he had no choice. After he had briefly done so, he began to explain what had happened.

"What happened today was deeply regrettable and inexcusable. A group within my organisation thought themselves to be above the law. They believed that this country and its friends and allies were ignoring a threat to us and to our region from Russia. They got in touch with a similar group in Latvia and with contacts in the Ukrainian military, and between them they hatched a plot to make it impossible for our allies and us not to act.

"Their plan was first to make us believe that there was a Russian submarine in the archipelago. Then they would do something that would provoke a crisis. It seems they were unsure about what to do, but finally they decided to pretend to kidnap your minister. They were going to take him out into the archipelago. The submarine would surface long enough for him to take a good look at it. Since he is Defence Minister, they thought that he should have been able to identify it as a Russian model, and if not, his experts could have done. Apparently, Matthew Simmonds here already has photos of it. Then they would pretend that there was a problem and that the 'kidnapping' had to be aborted. They would dump him on a nearby island and disappear. There would be a big political storm and the world's attention would be drawn to the Baltic. The Russians would deny it, but would find it hard to disprove that one of their submarines was involved. NATO would react by sending ships and troops to the Baltic. The plotters would then have achieved what they wanted.

"My colleague, Gunilla Sandberg, who was working with your Embassy, knew about this group and about the submarine, but only found out today about the kidnapping plot. It was thanks to her quick actions, and to those of Matthew Simmonds, that this plot was foiled. I have to accept some blame myself. When she first told me about this group I didn't believe her. I had spoken to them and they were very convincing in their denials."

"So what are you intending to do with them?" asked Catherine.

"I think I shall leave the next part of our conversation to our Defence Minister," said Berg, as the familiar figure of Lundqvist appeared at the door.

"Stephen!" he boomed. "What an adventure! I am so jealous." He thumped Glover on the shoulder, and then whispered something to him, probably a more personal word of apology and relief, thought Matt. It seemed that the two men had begun to bond further during their return from Lake Siljan.

"I understand that the director of SÄPO has been explaining to you what his renegades have been up to. Now we have to decide what to do next. As we were discussing in the car, Stephen, on the way back from Dalarna, we have to look at the big picture. It is true that we and our Baltic neighbours are worried about Russia. We don't trust them and we don't know what their intentions are. While I wouldn't condone the actions of those mavericks for a moment, it is no secret that we would welcome a greater NATO presence here. But we also know that the Baltic is not your priority just now.

"So, my suggestion is that we draw a veil over what happened here today, even though it was very distressing to you personally. We have already been talking to the Latvians, who will bring their mavericks into line. That Ukrainian submarine will leave the Baltic. We will quietly ask NATO to upgrade their presence here. I would like you to speak to the Americans on our behalf. That would give us some more reassurance and silence our critics in the media and in the right-wing parties. Publicly, nothing will change and NATO's relationship with the Russians will stay as it is."

"But what about everything that happened today?" asked Catherine. "How will you keep that quiet?"

"We will say that it was a special forces training exercise," said Berg. "All those involved will say nothing. And no one else will know that a British minister was 'kidnapped'. You were asking me earlier what would happen to the renegades. We will have a very thorough internal investigation, and all those who took part, or who knew about it and said nothing, will be disciplined. The worst offenders will be sent up to work in the far north for a few years. Believe me, the punishment they will get from their spouses and partners will be much worse than anything I could do to them. But we shall not make anything public. It would make it impossible to do the deal that Arne has just been talking about. And cleaning our dirty ski boots in public is not the SÄPO way."

"Thank you, Arne, and thank you, Andreas," said Glover. "I will have to think about it, but what you have suggested seems very sensible. I will never forget what happened to me today, I still feel quite shaky. I was very scared, I admit that. But, as you say, we have to look at the bigger picture." He paused. "There is one other thing I might mention. I think you were just about to confirm that you have agreed to buy our missile guidance system. Isn't that correct?"

"Yes, of course," said Lundqvist after a slight pause; "how could I have forgotten? Yes, we shall be happy to buy your excellent system. I am sure I can persuade my Cabinet colleagues to endorse that."

"Well then, I think we have an understanding," Glover said.

"You might, but I don't," said Nicola. She looked very determined. "I don't believe a word of what Mr Berg has been saying to us. I heard those men who kidnapped us speaking Russian and I am sure they were Russian. And I am equally sure that this submarine is theirs also. All this talk of an internal plot is just nonsense designed to distract us from the truth. I do agree with you on one thing, Minister," she added, turning to Lundqvist. "The Russians are a threat in this area, but a much bigger one than you seem to believe. I am not going to stay silent about this and join in your cosy deal. When I get back to London, I am going to tell the media what happened here. Then you will see a proper response to Russia in the Baltic, not just a couple more ships. Force is the only thing that they respect."

"No, Nicola, I don't think you are going to do that," said Chris coolly.

"And what could you possibly do to stop me?" she asked.

"It's all about dirty secrets. If you show them ours, I will show them yours," he replied. He produced his camera and passed it to her. "I don't think your party colleagues, or any future constituency selection committees, are going to think much of these. But the press will love them. And they really aren't very flattering."

Nicola took a quick look and went pale. "You wouldn't!"

"I most certainly would."

There was a pause.

"I won't forget this," said Nicola finally. "People don't cross me without suffering the consequences. I don't think you are going to go much further in your career." She handed him the camera and flounced out of the room.

Lundqvist and Berg departed to deal with their internal clearing-up operations. The official lunch had been cancelled, but the food hadn't, so everyone sat down to eat. Neither Glover nor Matt had much of an appetite after their fairground ride to the archipelago. Matt did notice that there was no herring on offer. It seemed the peace settlement was holding. There was no sign of Nicola, who was presumably sulking. Nobody was in the mood to talk about anything serious, so Catherine led the conversation onto the safe topics of ABBA and Swedish culture.

After lunch, the whole party set out for the airport. Glover warmly thanked Catherine and Philip, and then turned to Matt. "I don't know exactly what you have been up to in the last few weeks, but I owe you and your friends a great deal. If you ever want to visit a British submarine, just let my office know."

"Thank you, Minister," Matt replied, "but I don't think I want to go either on, or under water for a very long time."

Glover nodded, with a shudder.

On the way back from the airport, Catherine had a private chat with Matt. "We wouldn't have planned a day like this, but I think it might not end too badly. It seems we have the contract, and the Swedes seem confident that they can cover everything up, at least for now. There is a good chance that with our help, they can end this game of submarine hide-and-seek. London will be pleased if that happens. I will have to go to the FCO tomorrow to explain everything to Giles Featherstone. I am not sure, to be honest, what the implications might be for you, and for me. If they want a scapegoat, I will offer myself. After today, I wouldn't mind a quiet life in retirement."

That evening, Matt met Annika at a bar well away from the sea, and told her what had happened. "You might think I am crazy," she said, "but I had a great time today. It makes me want to join our own Foreign Service, but I am not so sure that Swedish diplomats have as much fun as you do. But it's back to boring meetings for me tomorrow. We are having our annual planning meeting this week, so I won't be around much. Never mind – you probably need a few quiet days to let your bruises heal."

Matt denied this, but privately felt that a couple of days largely spent on a static, landlocked mattress had their appeal.

He had his wish. Catherine went to London, Philip wrote and rewrote long signals about the visit, and Embassy life was torpid in the dying days of the short Swedish summer. The Swedish press was silent about the visit, other than a couple of small paragraphs registering that it had happened, and a furious letter in one of the Stockholm-based newspapers about inconsiderate motor boat drivers.

Three days later, Catherine returned and gave an account of her meetings to Philip and Matt. She began with a warning. "The FCO and the MOD have decided to keep what happened to the minister here to a very small circle. As we thought, they don't want to stir anything up in this part of the world. So, please don't talk about it to anyone who doesn't already know. It looks as though the Swedes are doing a good job at keeping any stories out of the press here. We have spoken to the State Department, who think the same as us. They have leant hard on their Defence Ministry, who have agreed to remove the US submarine.

"The Latvians have assured us that they are giving their submarine back to the Ukrainians, with a request that it leaves the Baltic. So, overall, I would say that London is happy. They are certainly delighted that BAe have won the contract. Glover has privately told the Foreign Secretary how grateful he is for our help. And his relationship with Lundqvist is going surprisingly well. Apparently, Lundqvist is a big fan of *Downton Abbey* and wants to go on a classic British shooting party. So you had better brush up on your beating skills, Philip."

As they were leaving Matt's office, Catherine asked him to stay behind. "I had a long talk with Giles. The Office is divided on whether we are heroes or villains, at least the few that know what happened. Everyone agrees that we did a very good job in helping rescue Glover and in keeping the story from the press. But some think we should have kept them properly informed, especially about the Piranha. Others think that our security was too lax. They are both right, of course. So the upshot is that they will have a meeting to discuss everything that happened. Giles will call me tomorrow to let me know the outcome. I wouldn't be too alarmed. My guess is that we will get both a pat on the back and a reprimand. Nothing worse."

That evening, as he sat on his apartment's small balcony and looked at the blue Swedish sky, Matt reflected on the events of the previous two months. He had hoped for some excitement when he joined the FCO, but perhaps not this much. For most of the time, he had felt himself to be completely unprepared for what was happening, watching shadows and trying to understand their meaning. He had made some mistakes and had been too trusting of those senior to him. He remembered his lack of confidence as he prepared to speak at the Royal Clubs' dinner. His doubts about whether he could be a top diplomat hadn't completely gone away. But somehow the events of the last few days had given him some confidence. More importantly, he knew that this was the career he wanted. So, suddenly, the verdict from London had become more important. He felt an anxious pang. Surely the FCO wouldn't decide to end his career just when he had really begun to value it? It would be very unfair!

He had a restless night, and couldn't concentrate at work the next day. At lunchtime he had an email from Annika, suggesting a drink at Stureplan after work. The small square was only half full. The beginning of August meant the beginning of autumn, and the evenings would quickly start to get chilly and dark. But there were a few people who wanted to make the most of what little was left of their gold-and-blue summer.

Surprisingly, Annika was already there, sipping at a glass of rosé. She gave Matt a warm smile, but looked tense. As she talked rapidly about her NGO's annual meeting, she kept gripping and re-gripping her glass. Matt began to feel uneasy. The creature that had swum in his stomach during the Royal Clubs' evening made a surprise reappearance. Annika eventually stopped talking and they looked at each other.

"Matt," she began, her eyes suddenly wet, "I have had a job offer. A really good one."

"Well, that's excellent news," lied Matt, as the creature gained speed.

"It's the sort of job I have been waiting for. It will be really good for my career."

Matt said nothing, waiting for the worst.

"But it won't be in Sweden. They want me to be the head of their South-East Asia office, based in Chiang Mai, Thailand. And they want me to start next week." There was a long pause. "I really want to do this job, Matt. It won't be so bad. We can keep in touch. You can come and see me in Thailand. And I will have to come back to Sweden quite often."

She looked at him and Matt knew that she had already made up her mind. There would be no point in arguing.

"I am pleased for you, really," he said finally, and this time half-truthfully. "We can make it work."

Neither of them could think of anything more to say. Annika said she had to return to her meeting, rapidly finished her wine, and they had a long hug before she left. Matt felt desolate. He knew his feelings were stronger than hers.

MOSCOW

The former admiral hummed *Kalinka* as he drummed his fingers on the large desk. It had all gone even better than he had expected. The wives' plotting had been successful. The disgusting Vitaly Alexandrovich had tried to fly too high, and had got burnt and been demoted to Deputy Governor of the Crimea. The former admiral had been promoted to his position. The only downside was that Alexandrovich was now his neighbour just outside Sevastopol. But he had a plan to deal with that. It was amazing what some clever fake news could do. There was no reason why fake news could not be used domestically as well as abroad. And on that subject, it seemed that neither the Swedes nor NATO had managed to find the Piranha, and were unsure if it really existed. He was going to have some fun with them in the coming months. He just needed to bring that creep Osipov back from the Caribbean, an action that would equally please a very irate Mrs. Osipova.

Washington

The Undersecretary had discovered that if she moved the sofa to one side of the living room, she couldn't see the former steelworks. It wasn't her dream, but at least she had done her patriotic duty. The business in the Baltic had worked out well too. The Defence Secretary had been reined in, and there were rumours that a dismissive tweet might be pending. Her ally, Mason Hunter, had emerged with some credit and she might be able to get him moved across the chessboard to Beijing for another part of the game. They also now knew a bit more about Piranhas. But they were still a concern. Who knew where they might turn up next?

RIGA

The team were back in the gherkin-scented cellar. Vanda sat coiled but silent in the corner. The mood was downbeat, but one of the conspirators had a new plan.

"We are not going to involve any unreliable foreigners this time. Latvians are going to do it for themselves." He brandished a home-made honey cake defiantly.

There was a murmur of support.

ABISKO, THE FAR NORTH OF SWEDEN

It was still light. It had been almost as difficult to get used to the ever-present sunlight, as to the ever-present mosquitoes.

"There isn't much to do here."

"Yes, but there are consolations. The cloudberries are delicious and I have a very good oven."

"Plenty of time for baking."

"And it won't be for long. There will be a new government soon. Our time will come again. *Skol.*"

STOCKHOLM

After another restless night, Matt walked slowly to the Embassy the next morning. As he walked into the building, Lotta gave him a tired smile. She looked exhausted. *Has she started seeing that DJ again?* he wondered, recalling her brief period as a nightclub addict.

"I feel great, Matt," she said. "I read that exercise is the key to happiness. Not men. So I went to the gym for two hours this morning. I am going to do it every day now. And the instructor is really cute. Oh!" she added. "I almost forgot. There is a postcard for you."

She handed it over. It featured a very pale man wearing a gold-braided hat and standing between two tanned beauties.

The printed message above them read *Greetings from Antigua*.

"Strange," said Lotta; "there is only the letter 'O' written on the back, in gold. No message."

"Oh yes," said Matt, smiling, "there is a message." He passed Tom's machine, now relegated to a distant corner, and went upstairs.

Catherine was waiting for him. "Sit down, Matt. I have heard back from Giles. As I predicted, we have got both praise and blame from the Office. The good news for the Embassy is that they have decided that Sweden is too important to ignore. They are actually going to give us a new Third Secretary. And we won't have to share our building with the Iranians, although we did get some credit for being inventive."

She got up and walked over to the window. "Some interesting news for me. It seems that I got top marks among FCO senior management for my Happiness Index exercise. So they have asked me to lead a new cross-Whitehall unit on staff morale and how to improve it. Amazing. It's not really my sort of thing, but both James and I want to go back to London, to be closer to our son. He is out of hospital now, but not fully recovered. So I have told them I will do it."

She came back to her seat and looked at Matt. "I have news for you too. I am not sure whether you will think it is good or bad. They have decided that it would be difficult for you to continue working here after all that has happened. There is a question mark over you about that Piranha business. In a way, you have been compromised. So they have been looking for a new posting for you. Your old department has come up with a proposal. The Embassy in Panama urgently needs some support. So you will be going there for a while. Next month. You will be working closely with other departments on drug smuggling and similar stuff. Can even get a bit dangerous. Chasing bad guys in boats. Should suit you fine." She looked at Matt. "So, how do you feel about that?"

Matt was engulfed by a torrent of thoughts, chief among which was that Panama surely had to be a very long way from Thailand. "I don't know what to think," he said, "but I guess I have no choice. Maybe a new start would be good for me."

"You will do well there," said Catherine. "Whatever London might think, you ended up doing a good job this summer. You are a real diplomat now."

That evening he walked home via his normal route, past the tranquil sea, past the silent dog walkers and into Strandvägen. For the first time in two months there was a chill in the air and the outdoor cafes were semi-deserted. In the distance he could see a woman walking towards him. A familiar woman.

"Hello, my favourite diplomat," said Marcella. "I haven't seen you for a while. Where have you been? I am going to meet my friend Violetta from the Nicaraguan Embassy. I am going to tell her my news. Well, I should tell you too. I have been recalled to Panama. It will be a promotion. I am very happy, although I shall be sad to leave Stockholm, and all my friends here, of course," she said, giving Matt a long, meaningful glance.

Oh well, thought Matt, *here I go*. "I have news for you too. I have a new posting as well. I am going to Panama."

Marcella let out a shriek that sent some nearby seagulls into panicky flight. "That's wonderful." She paused, giving him a big smile. "Don't you think, Matt, that we all have a destiny in our lives? That we are ruled by fate, whatever we might think we want?"

Matt flicked ineffectively at a gift on his shoulder deposited by one of the scared seagulls. "Yes," he said.